FORGOTTEN
BONES

FORGOTTEN BONES

A DEAD REMAINING THRILLER

VIVIAN BARZ

THOMAS & MERCER

Published by Thomas & Mercer, Seattle
www.apub.com

Amazon, the Amazon logo, and Thomas & Mercer are trademarks of Amazon.com, Inc., or its affiliates.

ISBN-13: 9781542041638 (hardcover)
ISBN-10: 1542041635 (hardcover)

ISBN-13: 9781542041645 (paperback)
ISBN-10: 1542041643 (paperback)

Cover design by Shasti O'Leary Soudant

Printed in the United States of America

First edition

This is for Austin Williams, whose words of encouragement kept me going during my starving-artist days.
(He also bought lots of burritos, which were just as motivating and appreciated.)

PROLOGUE

"I really don't understand the appeal, do you?" Derek Ritzeman yammered on from the driver's seat. He did not wait for his girlfriend to answer before he continued, just as she hadn't expected him to. Derek always became rhetorical when he was in a snit. "I mean, we've got to deal with noise and pollution and crackheads and tourists, but at least if we get lost in Frisco, some banjo-playing brother-daddy isn't going to go all *Deliverance* on us in a backwoods shed."

"Uh-huh." Derek could have been talking about the moon for all Danica knew. He'd been going at it for a good ten minutes, and she'd ceased listening after about two.

Danica, unlike her ill-tempered travel companion, was *not* in a snit. She gazed over at Derek, hips swiveling against the heated leather seat, and something inside her stirred. She was feeling rather randy, hoping for a little action.

If he'd only shut the hell up.

"I must've taken a wrong turn," Derek said. "Where, I don't know, since half these damn roads don't have signs. How do they even give directions out here?" He cleared his throat, grunted. *"Okay, what y'all cowpokes are gonna wanna do is turn right at the fork in the road by that big old barn with the missin' door. Turn left when you see the rusty trailer with the bullet holes—the one for cookin' meth, not murderin' hitchhikers. If you hit the junkyard with the feral dogs, you done gone too far."* Derek barked out a laugh and smirked at Danica, impressed with his hick impersonation as much as he was with himself.

Danica, not so much. Derek's incessant yapping was dulling the buzz she'd worked so hard to achieve. Plus, she had that burning itch that required scratching. She tugged at the expensive haircut he loved to brag so much about—*yeah, guys, $200, but come on*—and tickled her fingers up the back of his skull. He placed a hand over hers and moved it downward with a kneading motion, so that she would take the hint and massage his neck.

She said, "Hey, babe, maybe you should pull over for a min—"

"I honestly have no idea where we are." He provided her with a scowl, followed up with an irritated sigh. "Do you?"

Danica let out a sigh of her own as she pulled her hand away. "Nope," she said, the dashed line in the middle of the road going squiggly as she shook her head.

"Here, I'll stop at that Starbucks up at the corner and ask for directions."

Danica hiccupped, and the tide of fullness went out inside her belly, leaving behind a fizzy whitewash of midrange chardonnay. Man, she was drunkety-drunk-drunk, realizing now just how little food she'd eaten but just how much wine she'd tossed back. A whole bottle? Two? But she hadn't been hungry earlier, because who the hell has people over for dinner at six p.m.? On a Friday night?

Oh, that's right—boring married people with kids, that's who.

And *thank God* she wasn't one of them.

Danica squinted. "Wha' Starbucks?"

"Exactly." Derek snorted. "I know I should've asked for better directions before we left, but I *literally* would have burst into flames if we'd stayed there even a millisecond longer. It's like they were trying to hold us hostage. You know it's almost ten? Greg said there'd be an actual 'town' area in Perrick with shops and gas stations and whatever to stop and ask for directions in case we got lost, but I haven't seen anything, have you?"

"Nope."

"Gah! I really wish you hadn't forgotten your phone back at the loft."

"And *I* realllllly wish *you* hadn't let *yourrrrrr* battery die." Danica dipped her head forward lazily, her hair falling over her face. They hit a pothole, and she brought it back up with a sharp jerk.

Derek looked away from the road just long enough to eyeball his swaying passenger. "Jesus, Dani, exactly *how* many glasses of wine did you have?"

"Jus' 'nuff to make Shelly and Greg interesting."

Derek chortled. "I know, right? I seriously thought I was going to stab my eyes out with a fork if Greg showed me one more photo of that goddamn creepy kid of theirs with brownie smeared all over his face like he'd been left alone with the litter box—does that kid have a head shaped like an artichoke or what? And when did it become socially acceptable for parents to wave around photos of their brats gorging themselves like that? I mean, is it supposed to be any less disgusting because their heads are smaller? We've sunk *so low* as a society, Dani! People used to get together to discuss freakin' Plato, but now *this* is the standard, kids with noodles and shit on their faces?"

When was the last time you *discussed Plato, my dear scholar?* Danica thought and then bit back a smile.

The rant continued. "Brownie mashed in that artichoke head's hair! How nauseating. What if I did that?"

She shrugged. "Dunno." *Blah . . . blah . . . blah . . .*

"You know what? I think I will do that," Derek said, slapping a hand down hard on the steering wheel. "Next time I tear into a fat, bloody tenderloin, I'm going to text a photo to Greg before I wipe my mouth, and I'm going to do it while *he's* trying to enjoy *his* dinner. See how he likes it. It's like, 'Until I tell you otherwise, how about you just assume that I don't want to see repulsive photos of your kid shoveling food into his piehole.'" He shook his head. "Can you *believe* those two used to be swingers?"

Danica straightened in her seat as much as a person three sheets to the wind is capable of straightening. It was more of a slanty slouch. "Seriously? No!"

"Yep. This was before they had their suburban lobotomies. Long before Artichoke Head," he said, relishing the opportunity to impart a little gossip about his occasional business associate. "They used to do *a ton* of blow—I'm talking a few grams over the course of a couple hours, noses bleeding all over the place—and then go to this sex club down in the city. Greg liked to watch Shelly get it on with other . . . um, what do you think you're doing?"

"What does it look like I'm doing?" Danica purred, fondling the zipper on Derek's slacks.

Derek extracted his girlfriend's hand from his lap. It was on his crotch again before he had a chance to put his own back on the steering wheel, as if her arm were spring loaded. "Babe, *stop*. I need to concentrate."

"Multitask." Danica was using both hands now, and she was being about as gentle as a ravenous river grizzly pawing for salmon.

"You're actually *hurting* me," he said. "Now stop! You're going to make us crash."

"I'll be gentle."

Zip!

"Jesus! You almost took my dick off!"

"It's *mine*! Mine!"

Squeeze-yank-squeeze.

Derek yelped as the Beemer veered into the opposite lane. Luckily, it was late (or what must be late for people living out in the sticks), so he was able to right them quickly and without any complaint from other motorists. He was the only motorist.

Never one to be easily thwarted, Danica unbuckled her seat belt and launched across the center console, burying her face in his lap. Derek could sense her nipping at his skin in a way that was far too close for comfort—*teeth* and *blowjob* are never two words any man wishes to hear in the same breath—and smell her boozy snuffles wafting up. She burrowed her head down deeper between his thighs, and he squirmed against the unyielding leather seat to put distance between his scared, shrinking penis and her vacuuming mouth.

"Gimme," she demanded, pulling at the waistband of his boxers. She managed to force one side halfway down his hips, her drooly mouth making the thin cotton fabric unpleasantly moist. She smacked her lips and pouted up at him drunkenly, an expression she probably thought was seductive.

It wasn't. Derek did not like the wicked gleam in her eyes. Not one bit.

"Gimme!"

The SUV swerved far right this time, kicking up gravel as they careened dangerously close to the guardrail. Derek's eyes automatically flickered to the rearview mirror—funny how a person's first instinct is to check the rearview mirror after fucking up driving, as if California Highway Patrol only catches drivers fucking up from the rear—and he thought, *If there's a cop back there, the only way he won't stop me is if he's blind, lazy, asleep, or just plain dead. I ought to pull myself over now and save him the trouble of turning on the lights.*

Danica brayed uncontrollably, her grip like a vise. "Come on, baby, release the hound! Release the hound!"

Derek groped around near Danica's breasts, a gesture she misinterpreted as a sexual advance. She moaned, tugging him roughly through the hole of his boxer shorts. The car bucked, made an ugly grinding sound underneath the hood. "I can't shift! Move!"

Derek shoved Danica off. *Hard.* She was angry, but he imagined she'd be a lot angrier if he'd let them crash. Slowly, he let out his breath, which had gotten stuck near the pulse thudding high in his throat. Jesus, that was a close one. He'd missed that guardrail by a gnat's ass. "Look, I'm sor—"

"God, you're *so* boring! Why don't you go screw Swinger Shelly, then, if I don't do it for you? Greg'll watch!"

"Okay, Drunkie, go have another bottle of wine. It really is *so classy* you get this drunk. And you're welcome for not killing us."

"You love this stupid car more than me!"

Derek ignored his girlfriend as she started to bawl, though he thought, *Yeah, right now I kind of do.*

"I don't . . ." Danica hiccupped, belched, patted her chest. "I don't . . . feel so . . . good."

"Hey, you'd better not—*oh shit*!"

Derek wrenched the wheel hard to the left. He did it forcefully enough that he tweaked his bum shoulder painfully out of its socket so that it bulged under his shirt at a grotesquely inhuman angle.

Now, he was forced to sit helplessly as his treasured Beemer fishtailed across the opposite lane, down a slight embankment, through a wobbly barbed wire fence, and straight into a telephone pole, where they came to a windshield-shattering halt. It was a jolt so abrupt that it bounced Danica, rag doll–like, against the dashboard, up to the roof, and then back down to her seat. Derek became aware of her vomit splashing down on the expensive leather and across his right arm, hot, smelling sour but at the same time sweet and grapey. He understood that she might be injured, that he should reach down, unhook his seat belt, and check her over. He could hear the hideous swan song of his dying $80,000 vehicle—the first new car he'd ever bought outright— the whoosh of the airbags, the pops and squeals of the crumpled engine, the hiss of the tires as they deflated.

But Derek was not thinking about any of these things.

He was thinking about the little boy he'd just run over.

No words escaped his lips, but inside his head he was screaming. *Oh dear God, please tell me that did not just happen! Even if I'm not drunk, even if it's dark, even if Danica is to blame for distracting me, and even if that kid had no business standing in the middle of the road—where are his goddamn parents?—I was the one driving. I have just murdered a child, and I am probably going to go to prison for it. Life over.*

Derek hugged the steering wheel and joined his passenger in vomiting.

Danica finished before he did. The surge of adrenaline that had coursed through her during the crash had sobered her enormously, almost as if she'd never been drunk at all. She sprang from the car, ran around to Derek's crumpled-gum-wrapper door, and yanked it with superhuman strength, stunned when it gave without too much fight. "Derek! You okay?"

"You're outside." Derek gaped up at her with wide, uncomprehending eyes. "We're in a field."

"Oh my God, you're bleeding! *Have you been hurt?* Answer me!" Blinded by panic, Danica scrambled up to the side of the deserted road, waving her arms. "Somebody help us!"

Nobody came.

She ran back to the car.

Derek's eyes were fixed on the telephone pole opposite the smashed windshield. It was splintered jaggedly, tilted almost ninety degrees. If it looked that bad, what must be the state of the . . .

"I hit a kid."

Danica's head snapped back. "What? When?"

"Before we crashed."

Danica tugged off her cardigan and pressed it to Derek's face, staunching the steady stream of blood that oozed from a gash that started at his hairline and ended just below his eyebrow. "Shhhh. Derek, it's okay."

Derek swatted her away. "It's *not* okay! Did you hear me? *I hit a little boy!* Stop messing with me, and go check on him!"

Danica shook her head slowly. "No, honey, there was no boy."

"What are you talking about—do you think I drove us into a telephone pole for no good reason?" He was shouting, his face all eyes. "You were drunk and all over the place, so you didn't—"

"Drunk but not blind! Look, your head is *gushing*," she said, thrusting the soaked cardigan at him. "You've been hurt bad. I think you're imagining things. If somebody doesn't drive by soon, I'm going to cross the field to that farmhouse over there."

Derek got out of the car. Either Danica was under a severe spell of denial, or his vision had failed him horribly. "No. I *saw* him," he said with firm conviction. "I swear he looked *right at me* before . . . before I went over him. He was just *so small*. He came out of nowhere!" He put his face in his hands and started to sob. "And I killed him. *I k-killed that l-little boy!*"

Danica placed a hand on his shoulder. "I don't think you should be walking around."

"I'm fine!" Derek snapped, which even he knew was untrue. He wasn't going to die, but he'd be surprised if he *didn't* have a concussion.

Danica took his hand. Having been Derek's girlfriend for over two years, she realized that things would move along faster in the long run if she spared a few moments to placate him. Whatever she needed to do to get him to a hospital sooner. "Okay, how about we go look for him together?"

"It's dark as hell out here!"

"We've got a flashlight in the back, remember?" She pointed up. "And look, a full moon."

"Okay. Grab the flashlight."

Derek and Danica walked for a quarter of a mile in each direction. They searched not only the road but also the fields on either side of it. There was no sign of a child, or even signs that one had been there recently: no footprints, no backpack, no toys, no candy wrappers. The only residue they saw of *any* human was the crumpled beer can they found by the side of the road, and even Derek had to agree that few little boys would go creeping out alone into the darkness just to sneak a few illicit swigs of Budweiser.

Danica said, "*Think* about it: Why would a kid be out in the middle of nowhere on his own at this time of night?"

Derek had been asking himself the same thing during their search. "I don't know. Maybe he was running away from home?"

"But you said he was small, right? Like a kindergartner? So how far do you think a kid that small could actually run? Remember what it was like at that age—two blocks felt like two hundred miles. Honestly, given how late it is and also how cold, I just don't think a kid could've been out here." To drive her point home, Danica went over and under the car with the flashlight. "See. Don't you think there'd be blood or, I don't know, a clump of hair or something stuck in the grille if you'd hit a kid?"

"I guess," Derek admitted.

"And did you actually *feel* a bump before we drove off the road? Because I know *I* didn't."

Had he felt a bump? Now he wasn't quite so sure. So what, then? Had he driven them off the road over nothing?

"It's crazy dark out here, and you're tired. We were lost, and . . ." Danica raised her hands and turned her palms toward him. "And okay, I was being a little obnoxious, so you were distracted dealing with me. My guess is that maybe you saw a deer or something at the edge of the field, and your eyes played a trick on you. That can happen sometimes when you're tired, you know. I used to imagine seeing lots of things scurrying across the I-5 when I'd drive up late at night from LA." Danica felt it unnecessary to point out that, despite her exhaustion, *she'd* never smashed her car into a telephone pole.

"You think?" It was plausible, he supposed. A lot more plausible than a kid being out there on his own.

9

"*Yes,*" Danica said, optimistic that she might finally be getting through. "And Greg had been shoving photos of his kid in your face all night. Maybe you fell asleep, even if for only a second, and then you woke back up and saw—what did you call him?—Artichoke Head in the road."

"I think you're right," he agreed at last. "That will be our official story, then, okay? That I fell asleep?" More than anything, Derek wanted this to be true. And given all the evidence, he had to believe that it *was* true.

Still, he couldn't help thinking about how Artichoke Head was an ugly little twerp, yet the kid he'd seen was cute, with little blue overalls that matched his big blue eyes.

CHAPTER 1

After three and a half hours of standing around in a howling wind, Officer Susan Marlan was finally starting to see an end in sight. One of the R&G Electric guys had fired up the backhoe and was keen to start doing his thing (they seemed to enjoy being out there even less than she did), so if he got down to it, she might be home in bed within the next hour, having a filthy cookie-dough threesome with Ben and Jerry while catching up on *Game of Thrones*.

She sighed tiredly and gave the back of her stiff neck a quick rub, bouncing at the knees in a fruitless effort to keep warm. It could have been worse, she supposed. At least nobody had been killed or even hurt beyond a few cuts and a probable concussion, a miracle given the state of the vehicle. The paperwork wouldn't be too much of a headache, either, with it involving just the one driver.

Still, she wouldn't have even needed to be out in that field freezing her ass off if that pretentious idiot hadn't fallen asleep at the wheel and rammed him and his anorexic girlfriend into that telephone pole, upending it in such a way that it was deemed an electrical hazard to the public—though the only "public" who really used the road were farmers and teenagers looking to get drunk or laid (or both).

On the bright side: overtime.

As Susan waited, she ruminated on the details of the wreck. During her years on the job, she'd become adept at sniffing out bullshit. Those two, Derek and Danica, reeked worse than a Texas pasture.

She'd initially suspected a case of the old driver-passenger switch-eroo: that it had been Danica, her intoxicated dragon breath detectable from five counties over, who'd been operating the vehicle during the wreck and not Derek. However, no matter how many different angles Susan looked at the possibility, it just didn't add up. No way that guy would have let his plastered girlfriend behind the wheel of his precious BMW (that he undoubtedly buffed every day with a cloth diaper; he seemed the type) when he was perfectly capable of driving it himself. And as he'd blown a clean BAC, he *was* capable. Also, when Susan inspected the car, she'd found the front seat pushed back from the ped-als at a distance more accommodating to Derek's six-foot-two build than Danica's tiny five-foot-one frame. Rarely, unless they had a few DUIs under their belts (which Danica and Derek didn't, not even one between the two of them), would a couple doing a switcheroo think to adjust the seat for height. It was even less likely that they would if their automobile was smashed up as badly as Derek's Beemer.

Susan thought they'd reacted to her query about the flashlight a little fishily. It was a standard enough question—*What were you using it for?*—one she'd expected they would provide a simple enough answer to: they'd used it to survey the vehicle's damage. Which was exactly what they'd said. But there had been *a look* after. It was the kind of silent exchange couples had when sharing a mutual opinion they did not wish to voice out loud to others. It was guilt or . . . withhold-ing, maybe. Susan had asked them all the appropriate questions, tested Derek's sobriety, and checked the area surrounding the accident, finding nothing suspicious. There was nothing else she could have done other than let them go with the ambulance.

But it niggled her: What were they hiding?

"Okay, we're good to go," the R&G crew leader said to Susan. Was it Gary? Grant? "Sorry it took so long. We had to wait on a power shutoff from central so we wouldn't be—"

"Zzzzzzzz!" Susan buzzed, her hands clawed out in front of her, making the R&G guy laugh. *Gabe.* That was it. Gabe.

"Yep. You got it." Gabe smiled. "Got anything else you need me to sign?"

Inside the cruiser, Susan called in to dispatch. She let them know she'd finished and gave them an update. Still no location on the property's owner, one recently paroled sex offender named Gerald Nichol. She craned her aching neck, peering behind her right shoulder as she started to back up. There were lots of deep potholes out this way, and wouldn't that just be embarrassing if she dropped the cruiser into one of them? At twenty-nine, she was one of the younger officers at the station and had received her fair share of good-natured hazing. No telling what they'd say if—

"Hey!"

Susan nearly jumped out of her skin when Gabe materialized out of nowhere and began pounding on her window. She became more alarmed when she caught sight of his horrified face. She lurched into park and was out of the cruiser in an instant, her hand moving to her gun instinctively. "What's happened?"

Gabe's eyes were Frisbee huge. "There's something over here you need to see."

Susan frowned. "What? A live wire?" She couldn't think what else it could be. "I'll need to call—"

"No, we found a body. A *dead* body!" He was practically shrieking.

Maybe it was the cold, but it took her a second to process what Gabe was saying. It didn't make sense; she'd *checked* the area, wider than she'd needed to, even. "Where?"

"Buried. Right next to the telephone pole!"

"Oh my God."

"We're pretty sure . . ." Gabe swallowed hard. "Maybe you should come with me."

Susan followed him to the broken telephone pole, where the group of R&G workers was clustered together, staring down into a hole. She nudged her way through and understood the reason for their dumbstruck expressions, since she was now wearing one herself. To Gabe she said, "It's a kid."

CHAPTER 2

Eric Evans was schizophrenic.

He was also a great many other things—a professor of geology, a heavy coffee drinker, a reasonably gifted drummer, a John Carpenter film enthusiast, an occasional smoker, and the ex-husband of an abstract artist named Maggie—yet *schizophrenic* was the title he felt defined him most as an adult. Unlike *smoker*, it was a status he could never quit, no matter how painfully he tried.

Eric did not consider himself an unhinged individual, and he was right in this belief. Despite Hollywood's negative fixation on a particular breed of schizophrenic, a large majority of those diagnosed with psychotic illnesses are not dangerous. Eric fell within the pacifist range, which, as he frequently liked to point out, validated the old adage about not believing everything you see on TV.

When people asked about his schizophrenia, Eric, who didn't exactly flaunt his illness but wasn't ashamed of it, either, offered up the comparison of alcoholism. Not every drunk is a single bourbon away from skid row, just like every schizophrenic is not a tatty-haired, crazy-eyed gunman who delights in murdering alien-people from clock towers. There are functioning alcoholics just as there are functioning schizophrenics, individuals who work, maintain homes, and have hobbies, goals, and relationships like every other slob on the planet.

This was not to say that Eric didn't consider himself a card-carrying member of Club Crazy. He did. Doctors classified his schizophrenia as residual, which was a fancy way of saying that he intermittently heard and saw things "normal" folks didn't: flickers of light, whispering, sirens, and, on the rarest of occasions, people. Now that he had a handle on his mental illness, it typically didn't disrupt his everyday life. Still, as there is no cure for the disease, he would never be perfectly right in the head, a fact he'd come to grips with long ago.

It was at the age of nineteen that Eric first began to suspect there was something wrong with his brain. An old woman standing next to him at a bus stop thumped him hard with her cane, curtly informing him, "Earth is an experiment," and then a black hole consumed him. He awakened hours later sprawled in the shower, shivering and alone, soggy jeans pulled down over his sneakers and a videotape resting on his belly. (It was his brother's borrowed copy of *Gremlins*.)

After the old woman came the real fun. Paranoia, delusions of grandeur, panic attacks, puzzling gaps of time: insanity to a lucid person but everyday reality to an ailing schizophrenic. The government had implanted a microchip in his brain when he'd gone in to have his wisdom teeth pulled. His family was plotting to kill him. Murmurs in the vents confirmed what he'd suspected all along, that *he* was the only one who saw the world how it truly was—it was *everyone else* who needed medicating. When loved ones argued against his delusions, Eric reasoned they weren't real, that they *literally did not exist*. They were holograms created by the microchip, obviously. And they were all out to get him.

Eric now took medication each morning, an antipsychotic and an antidepressant: Minoldezine and Raxin. Like snowflakes, no two schizophrenics are alike. Whenever he was at his sickest, he thought of it as being Inside the Curve. It was a nonsensical phrase, but to Eric it made strange, perfect sense. Though there are some sufferers who grapple daily with hallucinations, he could go years without an episode—*if*, that was, he stayed on top of taking his meds. The pills made him a little sleepy, but they also made him a lot less nuts, so he overlooked the mild drowsiness. Besides, there was always espresso.

His friends to the end, the proprietors of those soft, rambling voices inside his skull, had been harder to shake—you're never alone with schizophrenia, hardy-har-har. On the odd occasions that they grew especially rowdy, Eric would whistle to drown them out, his go-to the theme song to *The Andy Griffith Show*. If there was one positive aspect of growing older, for Eric it was that the voices had softened with age. At thirty-six, he hardly noticed them anymore. They'd become nothing more than background noise, like a TV that had been left on in the other room. He suspected that he might even miss them if they were to ever go away completely, the way a city dweller misses the distant rumble of traffic after moving out into the suburbs.

Like most schizophrenics, Eric found that his symptoms were exacerbated during times of extreme anxiety. Times like last year, when he learned about The Affair.

Eric avoided thinking about The Affair unless he absolutely had to.

Maggie had cheated. Eric considered it a triple whammy because Jim, the other man (a term Eric found as ludicrous as *mistress*), was acquainted with him in more ways than one. Jim was Eric's colleague, his best friend, and also (drumroll, please) his older brother. Now, Jim was only one of three, since the whole brother thing couldn't be avoided.

Eric had seen them through the window.

Jim, after a sly glance around the shamefully trendy vegan café they were cozily holed up in, slid a hand up Maggie's sweater and gave her breast a quick squeeze. Maggie playfully swatted Jim on the thigh, and then they pressed their foreheads together, giggling. The two oldest people in the place behaving like teenagers. For over fifteen chilling minutes, Eric stood out in the snowfall while his wife and his brother snuggled. Whispered in each other's ears. Kissed. He watched their betrayal with unblinking eyes, his heart pounding clear up in his ears, hands fisted into tight balls, fingernails slicing tender flesh, suddenly forgetting how to breathe, how to think rational thoughts, very much wishing he was misreading the situation but knowing deep down that he wasn't. Even a blind man could see that he wasn't. And they were doing it *right there*, right out in the open for everyone to witness, almost as if they'd *hoped* to get caught.

Totally oblivious to Eric's spying.

They became less oblivious after he thundered into Moonflower Café and pummeled Jim senseless while Bob Marley crooned messages of peace and love over the loudspeaker. Jim, who had a good 30 pounds and four inches on Eric's five-foot-ten, 185-pound frame, didn't fight back, which only fueled Eric's indignation. Jim didn't even shield his pretty-boy face, giving Eric carte blanche until he decided he'd had enough.

There was lots of screaming, as one would expect, from both Maggie and the Moonflower regulars. The dreadlocked neo-Rastafarian hipsters—far too traumatized to continue consuming their five-dollar mushroom teas, their seventeen-dollar black bean burgers—weren't accustomed to such raw violence.

Eric's own voice hardly rose above a whisper during the attack. "I knew it. Goddamn, I knew it." The only words he uttered, head shaking in absolute dismay, before he raged back out onto the street like a crazed *Night of the Living Dead* extra, his clothes stained with his brother's blood.

Jim and Eric had engaged in their fair share of fights as kids, petty scuffles rooted in harmless sibling rivalry. But the incident at the café, an event Eric would forever recall as the Great Moonflower Ass Kicking of 2018, was the only time in his entire life that he'd truly intended to cause his brother bodily harm. And he did. Jim suffered two cracked ribs, a broken nose, a dislocated jaw, and a cut above his brow that required five stitches. Eric wasn't a bit sorry, and Jim didn't expect him to be. Jim knew he was a bastard. The police were never called, despite Maggie's insistence. Jim swore he wouldn't press charges even if they were.

Jim and Maggie's lack of discretion, while infuriating, wasn't what had galled Eric into beating his brother until his knuckles split like overripe tomatoes. It was the way they had exploited his schizophrenia to their advantage, wielding it to maim a man who was already mentally crippled.

Eric listened to his gut above all else. With a mind as screwy as the one he possessed, he had to in order to survive. He'd had a feeling something was amiss long before fate stepped in and ruptured the waterline that ran underneath Wills Avenue, altering Eric's usual route home from work so that he'd walk past Moonflower Café. The truth, as it so happened, had been a rotten splinter festering beneath the fragile membrane of their marriage. Suppress it as Maggie had tried, it eventually found a way to drive itself out, as the truth inevitably does.

And did it hurt like hell once it surfaced.

There had been small deceptions that Eric had picked up on along the way. Lies that he couldn't *prove* were lies, but lies just the same. Details from one story that contradicted another. Where Maggie had been, whom she'd been with, how long she'd stayed. Fishy, wide-eyed absentmindedness. *Gee, I guess I must have gotten the days mixed up. Well, now, I just can't remember* where *I was Wednesday afternoon!* Sudden and perplexing changes in the manner in which she handled her cell phone: password protection; an urgent need to take it everywhere, even into the bathroom when she showered; calls fielded by voice mail when she and Eric were together. Sneaky, slippery paltering:

Is there something going on that I need to know about, Maggie?
I thought you were happy with me, Eric.
I am, but have you ever cheated on me?
That would be wrong.
Have you?
We've only been married a few years.
I understand that, but have you been with another man?
It sounds like you're trying to start an argument.
Never real answers. Only circles, circles, circles.

Eric had approached Maggie and Jim separately on the subject of their flirting, which had been eyebrow raising in the beginning and downright shameless toward the end. He'd informed them that while they might not "mean anything" by it (their words, not his), it made him uncomfortable. It embarrassed him, he'd said, especially when they did it in public, and it was disrespectful to him and the marriage. Jim and Maggie both accused him of being paranoid, had even gone as far as suggesting that he was imagining things. And he'd had a hard time disputing their claims.

He was, after all, crazy.

Jim and Maggie knew that accusing a schizophrenic of being paranoid was as damaging as telling a man who is morbidly obese that he should really consider laying off the Ho Hos just as he's raring to blaze into 7-Eleven for a midnight snack. They yanked Eric up short, shamed him into submission, made him question his own reasoning. By doing so they threw him off their scent for the better part of a year. Eric and Maggie had only been married for a little over three; it hadn't been lost on him that approximately one-third of their marriage had been a sham.

Eric understood that if he'd wanted a woman no other men looked at, he shouldn't have married Maggie. He may have been plagued with a lot of useless and unpleasant human emotions, but dumb jealousy wasn't one of them. He was also aware that few men are as uneasy as the husband who has landed himself a wife he believes is well out of his league, as Eric had thought of his Maggie.

Still. There was something in Jim and Maggie's interactions that never sat right with Eric, something about the way their eyes would go just a little too soft.

At the start of his marriage, his brother's interest in Maggie had given Eric a perverse sort of pride. Even as kids, Eric and Jim had been opposite in so many ways. As adults, the story was no different. Eric was vintage rock T-shirts, comic books, obscure horror films; Jim was $200 designer jeans, men's fitness magazines, action blockbusters. Thus, it had amused Eric—thrilled him, even, much to his chagrin—when he'd come to realize that he'd captured the heart of a woman so universally appealing, that *his* girl had been branded with his brother's discerning seal of approval.

Maggie was a beautiful woman—blonde, curvy, tall—there was no question about it. Most males with a considerable interest in the opposite sex turned their heads to get a better look whenever she approached, but Maggie also had that special something that was impossible to articulate. Despite his determination to forget her, Eric had had a hell of a time scrubbing his ex-wife from his brain. Her Maggie-grin in particular: slight tip of the head—so slight it was nearly indiscernible unless you were look-ing for it—lips parted halfway over teeth, amused eyes twinkling. Even now that he hated her (now that he was *trying* to hate her, anyway), it was always that grin he saw whenever he pictured her face.

It wasn't just Maggie's pinup looks that had made her desirable to Eric. It was her acceptance of his schizophrenia. She was okay with him being mentally ill when a lot of women weren't. She'd accepted his moments of darkness with a straightforwardness Eric found saintly. There are worse things you can be than crazy, she'd told him. He had equated Maggie's love to winning the marriage lottery, and he'd often pondered why she'd chosen him when she so easily could have had any man she wanted.

Maggie was also intelligent, which had no doubt come in handy during her manipulation of Eric, though her intelligence extended beyond smarts and into the territory of wit. She was funny and could dish it out just as easily as she could take it, a quality Eric found rare in most people. Her voice was alluringly feminine, like auditory perfume, but it was her laugh that did it: deep and dirty, as if she were visualizing performing a filthy sex act in public. It was what made her truly beautiful. It was also what bugged him most whenever Jim came sniffing around.

Jim, who was movie-star handsome and always would be, possessed what Eric considered That Guy humor. He was That Guy at parties who was hilarious without trying, never leaving a dry eye in the house. His witticisms often tap-danced around taboo subjects, yet he still managed not to offend, even when he was being a little mean. When Eric was a teenager, he'd tried to emulate Jim's humor, but he'd always fallen flat. Jim made Maggie laugh a lot harder than he did, which Eric hated, just like he hated the way she would lean into Jim and clap a hand down on his shoulder whenever he'd said something particularly entertaining. Eric would have detected The Affair a lot sooner had he been wary enough to take such things to heart.

Eric's humor was not as universal as Jim's and Maggie's. His IQ of 138 placed him at a near-genius level, which was reflected in most of his anecdotes. His puns, while extremely clever to those smart enough to understand them, typically referenced science, literature, and pop culture. His geniality rested within his awkwardness and self-deprecation; he was a nerd fortunate enough to have been born attractive, his floppy brown hair and the small gap between his two front teeth only adding to his boyish charm. Thus, he was granted the attention of others more often than not.

But never, of course, as much as Jim.

Though Eric had loved teaching geology to undergrads at Warrenton, a small private university in Philadelphia where he and Jim were both employed, he'd voluntarily, albeit bitterly, resigned from his position. Jim, who'd hoarded most of the practical genes in the family, had never once considered stepping down from *his* position as professor of global economics. Of course he hadn't.

Compounding Eric's bitterness was his loss of colleagues (barring Jim; that went without saying), many of whom he considered family. They, in turn, held Eric in high esteem, often trekking clear across campus to chitchat about music or to get his expert opinion on fossils they'd found on vacation. The problem was that not one of them had seemed surprised when they learned about the divorce. He could see it in their eyes; they knew what Jim had been up to with his wife. How they knew, Eric did not know—he didn't *want* to know, though he'd spent many fitful, sheet-soaked nights speculating. A long, lustful look exchanged at the faculty Christmas party, perhaps, or a compromising discovery in Jim's office after Maggie had forgotten to lock the door. Whatever the case, Eric's former coworkers pitied him—that was humiliatingly obvious—and had maybe even grappled with telling him about The Affair on more than a few occasions.

That his wife and brother had shacked up was almost cliché enough to be funny, though Eric hadn't laughed much when he learned of Jim and Maggie's recent engagement. He'd found it even less hilarious when Maggie told him she was pregnant, news that had shocked him to the core, since she'd insisted throughout their marriage that she didn't want children. He was going to be the uncle of his ex-wife's baby. How sweet.

The disgrace of it all was nearly too much for Eric to bear, and for the initial weeks following The Affair, there had been days when keeping a grasp on his sanity had been a task akin to wrestling a greased pig. The colors around him had started to seem just a little too bright, the sounds too loud, the strangers too close. He failed to recall what day it was, sometimes even what month. He'd been sharing a bed with schizophrenia long enough to grasp that he needed to act fast, or else he might just lose control of his senses completely. And so he'd found a new teaching job at a small community college in Northern California, over three thousand miles away from what he would later come to think of as his past life in Philadelphia. It was a massive step down, both in prestige and pay, but Perrick City College had hired him swiftly and was thrilled to have someone with his expertise.

Most important, they knew nothing of the scandal he'd suffered at the hands of Maggie and Jim.

A fresh start.

CHAPTER 3

Susan found Police Chief Ed Bender in the station's break room, hunched over the latest copy of *Perrick Weekly* and slurping black coffee. A traditional man, he'd sooner cut off his own hand than use it to supply a coffeehouse with a few bucks of his hard-earned money for something he could easily make himself for a couple of dimes.

Ed's mug was cracked on the handle, stained with layers of age like the rings of a redwood's ancient interior. He'd been using it back when Susan had volunteered at the station as a teenager—probably had used it even back when *he'd* volunteered at the station some thirty-odd years ago. Ed was a man who strictly abided by the old axiom about fixing things only if they're broken, though Susan suspected he simply didn't like change.

Ed glanced up at Susan as she entered. "You're looking a little worse for wear, kid." He nudged a chair out for her from underneath the table, which she gratefully accepted.

She wasn't offended—she probably *did* look rough. "Long night. Sun'll be up soon," Susan commented as she lifted her chin toward the clock on the wall. Her adrenaline depleted, she was crashing hard, so exhausted that she was practically slurring. "Flynn's on-site now, holding everything down."

Ed nodded at the clock in acknowledgment. Ed and Susan regularly communicated in gestures, unarticulated insinuations. Neither were particularly chatty, though Ed was certainly the quieter of the two, as if he'd used up all his words during his decades on the job and had only silence left until his impending retirement.

Ed sat back and folded his hands atop the paper. "How are you holding up?" He may have been mildly apathetic toward crime fighting as of late, but they could never say he wasn't unfailingly available to his underlings.

Susan offered Ed a half smile. "I've been better. Upright and breathing, though, so I guess I can't complain." She could feel his eyes taking her in. His fatherly concern for her was a double-edged sword that could sometimes blur professional boundaries, providing both comfort and frustration on the job.

"It's always rough when kids're involved."

"Yep. Sure is."

Susan knew what Ed was getting at, but he was too respectful to come right out and say it—unfortunately, the corpse by the telephone pole wasn't the only dead child she'd encountered on the job. Shortly after Susan had joined the force, she'd been sent to a squatter's den—there were surprisingly many in a town as seemingly wholesome as Perrick—on a noise complaint. It was there that she stumbled across baby girl Gaby. The toddler had been dead for nearly two whole days. Gaby's mother, Darla, was so out of her head on whatever cocktail of chemicals she'd injected into her flat veins that she hadn't spotted Gaby mistaking a sandwich bag of prescription downers for candy. Later, sobered by lockup, Darla had gone so hysterical after she learned of her daughter's death that it had taken three officers to get her under control. Darla overdosed on a speedball, provided by her pimp / occasional boyfriend, before the case was brought to trial.

Susan was far too tired to engage in any Dr. Phil–type conversations about the deceased. One of Ed's finer attributes, Susan felt, was that he didn't pry. Some of the more jaded officers at the station suspected this was mainly due to near-retirement apathy, but Susan didn't agree, at least not when it came to *her* job performance. Ed trusted her competency, she knew. Changing the subject, she said, "Still no sign of Gerald Nichol."

Ed sipped his coffee. "No big shock there. This time, they'll lock him up and throw away the key. He knows that."

"They should've done that to begin with," Susan said. "Locked him up and thrown away the key, I mean."

Ed shrugged. *What can you do?* "I'm surprised you even remember the case. I can hardly remember what I ate for breakfast."

"I remember hearing about it on the news back in the day—"

"Oh, it was a massive story."

"I also read through some reports while I was waiting for Flynn. That Gerald Nichol, he's a real peach."

"They never could nail him with any molestation charges, but they got him on plenty else."

"I read all about it," Susan said with a shiver.

In 2012, the Expressions Studio bust in San Francisco was one of the largest child pornography distribution rings California had ever seen. The kicker—for Gerald, anyway—was that the IRS had initially coordinated the investigation after suspecting Expressions Studio owner Hugh Jarvis of tax evasion; it was during a computer audit that the photographer's private folders were unearthed. Before the Department of Homeland Security could say *thirty years in prison with a $250,000 fine*, Jarvis was rolling on his buyers. All fifty-nine of them, including Gerald Nichol.

Though no evidence had been uncovered to suggest that Gerald had ever *physically* harmed his victims—not until recently, that was, with the discovery of the boy's body—there was enough to prosecute him on possession of child pornography. *And* distribution: he'd traded Jarvis's photos online the same way baseball fans swapped cards of their favorite players.

Ed said, "Gerald didn't stand a chance in court. Don't even know why they bothered to have a trial. Everyone's entitled to one, I guess. They got him some public defender straight out of law school—kid was barely tall enough to reach the bench. His contempt for sex offenders was so obvious that he might as well have hired a skywriter on the day of Gerald's sentencing. That's pretty bad, when even your own lawyer can't hide how much they hate you."

"And now he's on the street," Susan said with a scowl. "Gotta love that overcrowding."

California had more inmates than space to keep them. The nonviolent offenders who behaved themselves in lockup sometimes got out early, and the only violence Gerald had encountered in Millstone Penitentiary had been what *other* inmates had delivered to him. If there was anything convicts hated more than snitches and cops, it was a child predator.

"I called Gerald's parole officer, Juno Tomisato."

Ed raised his eyebrows. "I've dealt with him before—cantankerous on a happy day. Bet he was thrilled to hear from you in the middle of the night."

"Beyond. Anyway, Juno wasn't too surprised that Gerald took off. He said that he'd likely commit suicide before going back to prison."

"Good. Save the taxpayers some money."

Juno Tomisato's exact words to Susan were that prison for "kiddie diddlers" was hell. And that was putting it lightly. Gerald's charges had been kept hush-hush, as they always are for creatures of his ilk, but in lockup people talk. Even in protective custody—PC yard, as it's known to Millstone cronies—Gerald's days had been filled with threats of beatings. Rape. Castration. His food was stolen, his cell ransacked, his mattress and sheets doused in assorted fluids from anonymous donors. He'd been violated every way a man *could* be violated, and in ways no well-balanced human being would ever dream of. One needed to look no further than Gerald's face to find proof of the savagery his criminal peers had bestowed: a wobbly half-moon razor blade scar along the jawline, ear to chin. A Millstone insignia he would wear forever. The mark of a chester.

"A man like him can't hide forever," Ed said. "No money and no friends. No real family, either—his mother's up at Emerald Meadows, so you know she's not keeping him. Eventually that creep's going to crawl out from whatever rock he's hiding under, and we'll nab him."

"Speaking of Gerald's mother, if it's okay, I'd like to interview Mary Nichol in the morning."

"Hell, you won't get much out of her. She must be close to a hundred now." Ed tapped his skull. "She's probably gone a little soft."

"She's ninety-six," Susan confirmed. "Do you know her?"

Ed shook his head. "No, but it's hard not to know a little something about everyone in a town as small as this."

Susan rubbed her eyes, blinked the world into focus. Screw the TV marathon; screw the ice cream. It was straight to bed for her. "Oh, well, I'd still like to interview her. Couldn't hurt, right?"

Another shrug. "If you think it'll help. Just don't get your hopes up." Ed made a move to get up. "Why don't you head on home. There's nothing more you can do tonight, anyway. I'm going to pack it in myself, once I hear back from county."

"Oh? They going to assist on this one?"

"Won't know anything until I hear back. Can't imagine what the hell they'd be doing over at the sheriff's office this time of night that'd keep them from returning my call."

"Want me to swing by on my way home, see what the holdup is?"

"Kid, you're one step away from zombie right now—you've got more red in your eyes than blue. They'll get back to me soon enough." He gave the *Perrick Weekly* a shake. "I've got the paper to read until then. Now, go on home and get some sleep."

He didn't need to tell her again. Home she went, and sleep she did.

CHAPTER 4

Eric had heard that losing everything was cathartic. What he was now beginning to suspect was that this was most likely a claim perpetrated by those who *had* lost everything and were only telling themselves what they needed to so that they could keep crawling out of bed each day and feel like dying a little less, a little less.

Losing everything—not just his wife, his home, his brother, his self-esteem, and his prestigious teaching position but also his actual *stuff*—did not make Eric feel liberated in the slightest. It made him feel like a big fat failure. With his milk crates of records and trash bags of clothes, it gave him the sensation of traveling back in time, like he was more of the directionless college student he'd been at twenty and less of the respectable college professor he supposedly was today. Like each morning he was putting his identity on inside out while dressing in the dark.

It embarrassed Eric greatly when his nice landlady met him in the driveway of his new rental in Perrick. When she looked over his Jeep, whistling, and said, "Boy, you sure do travel light." It embarrassed him because what Doris Kirsch was seeing wasn't just what he was traveling with. It was all that was left of his former life.

In fairness to Maggie (not that she deserved any), Eric's forfeiture of possessions had been his doing. He was so beaten down by the end of their separation—just so *over* it—that he'd told her to keep everything he'd left behind. He didn't want to argue, he'd said, and she could throw a match on it all and dance in the light of the flames, for all he gave a shit. He just wanted to move on with his life and forget the whole thing. Forget that he ever knew *her* too.

Maggie, out of guilt (no question about her motive there), had tried talking Eric into taking what was rightfully his. Or at the very least splitting everything up, fifty-fifty, right down the middle. For the sake of civility. He wouldn't hear of it, not only because they were way beyond civility (they'd passed that point in Moonflower Café around the time Eric's fist touched down on Jim's face) but also because the notion of getting together with Maggie to haggle over who should get what appliance or which one of them had chipped in more for the sofa was too awful to conceive.

There was also the intolerable possibility that Maggie might feel less accountable if he were to accept her offer—that she might actually believe that she could atone for her adultery with nonstick cookware and lamps and rugs and books and power tools and bikes and bullshit. Eric couldn't allow it, being treated like a contestant on some demented game show, where the smiley-slick host, who just so happened to look a lot like Jim, got to bed his ex-wife in exchange for *all this slightly used stuff, a job demotion, and a shitty new life in sunny California!* To even *conceive* that Maggie might feel magnanimous for what she perceived as generosity, the act of offering Eric his own property . . . no. Just fucking no.

And if he wanted to split hairs, he could say that most of it *was* his property. Though his teaching salary hadn't made him a rich man in any sense, he'd earned a hell of a lot more than Maggie had as an artist. There were few things inside their quaint (that was the word she always used, *quaint*) two-bedroom starter home that she had purchased. So if anyone should feel magnanimous, it was Eric.

The bright side of having nothing was that he didn't have too many things to unpack. This was especially convenient because his rental had come furnished. The flip side of this was *what* it had come furnished with. The motif in Doris's cottage was particularly bizarre, a style best described as "Victorian whorehouse meets fisherman's oasis meets gringo Tex-Mex": shelves cluttered with snow globes, dried starfish, and wooden lobsters; bronze lighthouse bookends; glittery sombreros tacked to the kitchen walls; gold-fringed lampshades; black lace throw pillows; a purple-sequined toilet seat cover. Looking around the place was like an LSD trip gone terribly, terribly wrong.

Eric spent a good portion of the morning decluttering the place in head-scratching awe. What is it, he wondered, that compels the elderly to fill every square inch of space with knickknacks, as if each bit of junk they amass will add another year to their dwindling lives? By the time he finished clearing, he had six full boxes of useless crap to store out in the garage. He'd have to worry about how he was going to explain the cottage's bareness to Doris later.

Upon returning from the garage, Eric flopped down on the sofa and put his feet up on the armrest. He knew lounging was dangerous because he could already sense depression creeping over him like a vampire's shadow. In the past, he'd found that the best way to combat this feeling was to keep moving, as if misery were a barnacle that couldn't latch on to him if he didn't sit still for too long.

Regardless, he lacked the enthusiasm to move.

Soon Eric was confronted with a silence denser than any he'd ever experienced, quietness so profound that it practically made his ears ring. He'd been so preoccupied with all the tasks that had followed since discovering The Affair—finding a new job and moving cross-country, mainly—that he now understood that it was tedious distractions that had probably kept him from falling off the deep end completely. Now that he was as settled as he was going to be in his brand-new life, for the first time in weeks he was asking himself: *What am I supposed to do now?*

Eric's network of associates back in Philly hadn't been enormous, and it had been lessened significantly by the loss of his two so-called best friends, that charming wife-stealing
(asshole)
brother of his and his delightful cheating
(bitch)
ex-wife.

It wasn't that Eric was antisocial—he *liked* socializing. But sometimes, especially during those uneasy weeks that had immediately followed The Affair, making small talk was draining when he already had invisible friends chattering at him from within his own head.

Eric had also turned inside himself a great deal during his final days in Philly, avoiding contact with friends and colleagues, and part of his reason for this was that he hadn't wanted to face the awful chore of expounding on his separation from Maggie and his abrupt plans to relocate to California. Although those dearest to him were decent enough not to pry into his personal affairs when it was so patently clear that he did not wish to discuss them, Eric found it equally depressing that they should know to avoid the subject altogether. Somehow, it was almost worse that they said nothing.

The funny thing was that now that Eric seemed to be doing all right out West—*all right* in the sense that he'd finally managed to slog through an entire day without breaking into sobs, the voices in his skull quieting back down to their usual unobtrusive murmurs—he had nobody to talk to locally.

Eric shifted his position on the sofa so that he was at least sitting up, though this did nothing to improve his mood, which was swiftly plummeting.

Going into the move, he'd known, of course, that he didn't know a soul in California. But now that he was there, the reality was truly hitting him: He had zero friends in Perrick. Not a *one*. He was not even *acquainted* with a single person in town—his landlady even lived in a different area, Sebastopol, wherever that was. This meant that when he finally did decide to go out, nobody in the neighborhood would recognize his face. No coffee shop barista, no gas station attendant, no checker at the local grocery store, no friendly clerk at the record shop to set aside a piece of vinyl that he might like.

If for some reason he died

(*overdose, hanging, slit wrists, rooftop leap, oven nap, toaster bubble bath, gunshot to the temple*)

his body could lie there for weeks before being discovered.

There had been countless times in Eric's life when he'd suffered such severe loneliness that he'd felt nearly smothered by it, but he imagined now that his current state was a strong contender for the worst. *I would give just about anything to go back to my life three years ago*, he thought with some astonishment. *Yes, I would happily sacrifice five years off my future for just one good year of the past.*

He leaned back on the sofa and allowed his eyes to fall closed.

Eric's mind, as it tended to do when he was idle, drifted to his failed marriage. On the bright side, at least they hadn't gotten a dog. Matt, a colleague of his back in Philly, and *his* ex-wife, Diane, had shared an English bulldog named Daffodil during their matrimony. (No cheating there, only a loss of passion between two high school sweethearts who'd gotten married far too young and had grown to abhor every little thing about each other as the years marched on.) Eric remembered the time a red-eyed Matt had come barging into his office, having just gotten off the phone with Diane. The odd thing was that Eric hadn't even known Matt that well, but hey, sometimes a man has things he needs to get off his chest, and the nearest ear will do.

Matt needed to vent. "I told her," he'd said with a grim smile that was as sad as it was menacing, "you can take the house, you can take the car, you can take the boat; you can even take what pennies I have left in savings. But if you try to take Daffodil, I *will* kill you." Matt had said this like he was joking, but Eric still wondered if there wasn't some truth behind the statement.

In the end, it didn't matter. Shortly after the conversation, Daffodil choked to death on bones from a rotisserie-chicken carcass she'd pilfered from a neighbor's garbage. A couple of weeks after that, Matt's car veered off the road and into a river with Matt strapped behind the wheel. The death was ruled accidental, but whenever Eric thought of his colleague's ghastly smile that day in his office, he wondered if the car might have stayed on the road if Daffodil had stayed out of the trash.

"Okay, no more dwelling on the past," Eric told the room, hands slapping down on his knees resolutely. "Gotta get out there sometime. Might as well be now." He snapped up the grocery list he'd placed on the coffee table and headed toward the garage.

As Eric pulled his car out onto the street, he realized what a nice Saturday it was outside. It would be such a shame, he thought, to waste it fighting crowds. After a quick internet search on his phone, he decided that a day at the beach would be a better use of his time.

CHAPTER 5

Susan let out a long breath and made a face as she parked her cruiser.

Emerald Meadows Assisted Living was about as awful as anyone could envisage for a state-funded nursing home. The building's exterior was a single-story slab of jail-like blandness, a silent reiteration to would-be escapees abandoned by loved ones that there was no use in putting up a fuss. They were going to stay put whether they liked it or not.

Susan gulped down the remainder of the coffee in her hefty metal tumbler, which had gone as chilly as the autumn air outside. It was far too early for such a depressing task. She crammed the last hunk of cranberry scone in her mouth, immediately choking on its sawdusty sweetness, and was regretful that she no longer had coffee left to wash it down. She picked each crumb of pastry off her shirt using a thumb and forefinger, then folded the scone's wrapper into several neat little squares, crumpled it, and tossed it aside. She made a move to exit the vehicle but picked up her phone instead.

Stalling.

Two rings and then a jovial voice: "Medical Examiner Salvador Martinez."

"Hi, Sal, it's Susan Marlan over at Perrick PD."

A chuckle. "If it isn't my favorite ass kicker! How goes it?"

Susan grinned, laughed a little herself. Even on her toughest days, the man always found a way to lift her mood, like conversational Prozac. "It goes."

"Heard about that meth head you chased off the roof."

Susan frowned. "You did? Who told you about that?"

"Take a guess."

"Marcus."

"Ding! Give the girl a prize," Salvador said. "Though I can't believe he held out on me for as long as he did, the blabbermouth. Such a great story."

"That's Marcus. He's chatty, all right, but you gotta love him."

"You do," Sal agreed. "Marcus said that you were *really* pissed off, but not because you'd almost broken your ankle running after the guy."

Susan knew what was coming next. The arrest had been the source of her teasing at the station for the past two weeks.

"He said that you cuffed him, all out of breath, and yelled, 'Thanks, asshole! Now Delany's is closed!' Is that true?"

"Not entirely," Susan corrected. "I think I called him *shitbird*."

Sal laughed as if it were the funniest thing he'd ever heard. "You must really love those Delany's cupcakes."

"Guilty as charged. And I would've gotten a couple double-fudge ones that day, but then that idiot had to go and make me chase him."

"I don't know how you stay so thin, Suze. If I ate the way you do, I'd have a gut the size of Texas. Oh, wait—too late!"

Sal chortled, and Susan joined in. She thought the extra weight—Sal was pushing three hundred on a *thin* day—added to his jovialness, like Santa Claus. If Santa Claus dissected dead bodies for a living.

"Must be all those meth heads you're chasing across roofs, huh?"

"Don't say that too loud. Don't want anyone trying to do me any favors," she joked.

"My lips are sealed. Anyway, what can I do you for?"

"I've got a question about the body I found with the R&G guys last night." Susan couldn't bring herself to say *child* just yet.

"Overalls Boy," Sal said. "That's what we've been calling him over here. We still have no ID. I doubt we ever will, though. No prints or dental records to speak of."

"Okay, Overalls Boy. That body was old, right—I know that's pretty obvious—but I'm wondering if you might have some kind of date of when he was murdered?"

"Based on his clothes and decomp, our approximation is the 1960s."

"Well, that's weird."

"Not really. Gerald would have been a teenager back then, but that's still old enough to kidnap and murder a small child. Some pedophiles start young, as I'm sure you know, doing the work you do."

"How sure are you about that date?"

If Sal was irritated by her questioning his work, he didn't let on. "Well, I can't give you an *exact* date to the day, but I'm confident saying that the boy died *sometime* during the sixties. Why, is there a specific crime you thought he was linked to from a different time?"

"It's not that," Susan said. "I was there when they found him, Sal. He couldn't have been more than two or three feet deep in the ground, *right* next to the telephone pole. I checked: the pole was replaced in 2012 because of rot issues, so that means—"

"The body must have been moved within the last few years, or else they would've found it when the pole was put in."

"Exactly. The body that you're telling me is decades old." Susan paused. "Here's another thing: the R&G guys had disturbed the surrounding soil before they found the body, so they couldn't be positive, but a couple of them *swore* that the dirt near the grave had recently been excavated, and not by the auto accident that had occurred."

Sal went quiet while he thought. "Weird. Though that would make sense, given the state of the body."

"Meaning?"

"The decomp is bad, but not as bad as what you'd expect for a body so old. It's very plausible that he'd been kept someplace else and then moved. Actually, that theory would make the most sense."

"Okay, so if what the R&G guys said is true, isn't it strange that Gerald would dig up the body of a victim and then rebury it on the edge of the property immediately after getting out of prison for an unrelated crime? He must have realized that it would increase his chances of getting caught."

"Maybe he wants to get caught," Sal said. "Maybe it's a cry for help? You know, some 'I can't stop myself, and I don't think I ever will' kind of thing."

"I don't think Gerald's that noble," Susan said dryly. "Also, if he wants to get caught so badly, why has he vanished?"

"Hmm, good point. But I think we can assume the guy isn't playing with a full deck. He's a psycho, but not all psychos are mad geniuses like Ted Bundy."

Susan snorted. "You got that right."

"Maybe he's just a plain old idiot," Sal said. "I've been reading a lot of true-crime books lately—you'd think I'd get enough doom and gloom here at the morgue, but apparently not—and it's *amazing* how stupid some of these guys are. How careless. They'll get away with murder for *years* but then make some dumb mistake that leads to their undoing. Like, they'll park their car in a red zone with a dead body in the trunk, and then the police'll tow it. Or they'll flood half the neighborhood trying to dig a homemade swimming pool in their backyard, and then a plumber sent by the county will find a bunch of skeletons on the property."

"I think I heard about the swimming pool guy. Nashville, right?"

"Close. Memphis," Sal said. "I just read a story last night about a guy named Rick Mott who murdered his mother and then gave his girlfriend his mother's necklace the *very next day*. It was a cheap gold thing with a huge leaf pendant everyone in town knew that the mother wore. There was even a tiny speck of blood found in the clasp from where Rick bashed his mother's head in. I mean, what was he thinking?"

"That *is* pretty stupid," Susan agreed. She'd certainly seen her fair share of moron criminals on the job. Shoplifters who'd attempted to carry electronics out of the store under their sweatshirts, bellies unnaturally squared. A meth manufacturer who'd burned off half his face while smoking a cigarette next to highly explosive chemicals. Then there was the one genius who'd committed a hit-and-run. At a dairy. Drunk as a skunk, he'd driven off the road and through the dairy's gate, where he proceeded to sideswipe a cow. When he fled the scene, he neglected to notice one very critical detail, which was that the license plate had been ripped from his car when he'd rammed the gate. It had been left behind next to tire tracks and one very pissed-off cow.

"I heard something interesting from one of the techs here. He's a little longer in the tooth than the rest of us, so he knows *a lot* of town secrets."

"Oh yeah?" Susan said. "Juicy gossip?"

She didn't make a habit of taking town gossip at face value, particularly since she'd been the target of outrageous speculation herself. Apparently, she was a lesbian. In a place as small as Perrick, unmarried women past the age of thirty were often thought to be. With no current romantic life to speak of but still one year shy of thirty, she didn't *quite* fit the bill, but exceptions were made. It didn't help matters that she was a cop. On the flip side, she'd also heard that she'd once had an illicit affair with a married man. That one happened to be true. It had occurred many years ago, when Susan was still young and naive enough to consume the lies her slick city beau had fed her—that soon he'd end his unhappy marriage and leave his gold-digging wife, who'd never really loved him anyway (they were leading separate lives, he'd said, and were practically already divorced); he just needed a little more time to sort out finances, a little more time. Eventually, Susan wised up, got tired of waiting, and saw through the BS. It was a smart move on her part: it was almost eight years later, and Paul was still married to the same woman.

Sal said, "Word on the street is that Gerald's dad, Wayne, was, you know, *creepy* toward kids."

Susan thought out loud: "I wonder if any police reports were ever filed."

"Small town in the sixties? I wouldn't bet money on it."

"Do you think it's possible that Wayne helped Gerald murder Overalls Boy? Here's a better question: Do you think it was Wayne who got Gerald *started?*"

"I honestly don't know. We can't find any forensic evidence to substantiate or disprove the theory—you aren't the first to bring this up, believe me. But it would make sense, though, wouldn't it, given how Gerald turned out?"

Yes, Susan agreed with a shudder, *it would.*

She picked up her file on Gerald Nichol and studied his photo. He looked like the classic caricature of a pedophile: thick comb-over haircut, Coke-bottle glasses, the squinty eyes of a weasel. She wondered if Wayne looked the same, if dashing predator features ran in the family.

The inside of Emerald Meadows was no better than the outside, dank and reeking of industrial cleaning solvent and peed-in diapers. Bluish fluorescent lighting underscored barren spaces, magnifying cracks on walls and skin, sickly flaws emerging where none had existed previously. Susan felt as if she'd aged fifty years since she'd stepped into the lobby.

She flashed her badge at the bored-looking teenager manning the check-in. The girl blinked at Susan's credentials, slack jawed and disinterested, as if police visits were a regular thing at the nursing home— though, Susan thought, in a place like this, maybe they were.

The girl picked up a yellowed desk phone and punched in a series of numbers, her gaze glued to the muted television overhead. Susan craned over the divider to see what was so interesting, frowning as she saw that it was an infomercial for vinyl siding that played through a wobbly static haze. Susan waited as the girl murmured a quick conversation into the phone and then hung up.

"Gracie will take you back." The girl took her eyes off the television long enough to roll them at Susan. "I mean *Nurse Hoguin*," she corrected with a snort, as if using formal job titles was akin to putting on airs. "You can have a seat, if you want."

Susan eyed the worn plaid sofa behind her, picturing the years of incontinence and God knew what else that had been absorbed within the lumpy cushions. "I'll wait over here," she said, moving toward the edge of a long hallway.

Hunched over now, the girl shrugged and began rooting through the bowels of her desk. She hauled out a compact mirror and went to work popping a sizable whitehead on her chin. After dabbing the pus away with a crumpled fast-food napkin, she smeared a glob of sparkly pink gloss across her lips and returned to the infomercial. Susan focused her attention on a painting of lilies over the sofa that screamed of mass production. *If it comes down to dying alone or winding up in a place like this, I'll take death.*

"Hello? You with me?" A woman standing not three feet in front of Susan waved.

Susan started. "Oh, hi. You must be . . ." All Susan could conjure was *whitehead. Nurse Whitehead.*

"Thought I'd lost you there." The woman smiled warmly. She was middle aged, with dark, puffy hair that had gone gray at the temples. She was motherly, her body shape the type tactful individuals sometimes described as "pleasantly plump." She held out a hand for Susan to shake. "I'm Nurse Hoguin. Some of the residents here call me Nurse Gracie. Whichever you prefer."

"Sorry, I must've zoned out for a second there," Susan said and then thought: *If she'd had a weapon, I'd have been dead before I realized I'd been murdered.* She swallowed, her mouth starchy . . . *And my last meal would've been that shit-awful scone.*

"This place tends to have that effect on people," the woman chirped with forced merriment, eyebrows raised. *I know this place is awful, and you know this place is awful, but let's keep this between the two of us, mkay?*

"Must be the lighting."

"What can I help you with?"

Susan flashed her badge once again and explained that she was there to speak with Mary Nichol.

The nurse folded her arms over her chest protectively. "Mary? What's this about?"

"I'm afraid I really can't say," Susan apologized, hoping the woman wasn't going to force her to get nasty. She hated it when they did that.

"No, I imagine you can't."

"How long have you worked here?" Susan asked as they made their way down the hall.

"Oh, nearly twenty years. 'Bout as long as Mary's been here. She's a nice lady."

They paused at an activity room off to their left so that the nurse could whisper a terse directive to a lazing subordinate. A few residents shambled about, but most were seated in ratty lounge chairs, saggy flesh pooled around them like halos, lumpy oatmeal incarnate. Like the check-in area, a television held center stage, an imposing Sony-god looming over its faithful disciples. On the screen, a cooking show played at a volume rivaling that of a jet engine. The men licked their lips greedily, while the women, most in housecoats, cooed half-heartedly over a shrimp scampi recipe they had absolutely no intention of ever preparing. In the corner of the room sat two pruned characters sharing a cheap plastic chessboard, the sort of thing one would pick up at a five-and-dime for about ninety-nine cents. Neither man seemed particularly interested in the game, as their eyes were trained on the rather large-breasted chef who was leaning over the sink to shake cooked angel-hair pasta dry. The men turned their attention back to the board as the show cut to commercial, and Susan noted that they were using an incomplete chess set, substituting pennies for the missing pieces. She found the grimy pennies the most harrowing detail of all, that two old men with a collective age easily north of 160 should be denied the dignity of a complete game, albeit a cheap one.

A bubble of ache popped sharply in the center of her chest, coating her insides with a foul residue of repulsion. *How can you stand it?* she nearly blurted to the nurse. *Day after day?*

She asked instead, "Do you know Mary well?"

"Sure, she's one of our few long-term residents. Only person been here longer is Jack, and he's a hundred one. Dementia," Nurse Gracie said as they continued their journey down the hall. "And you get used to it," she added primly, as if addressing Susan's silent disdain. "There are homes far worse'n this—believe me. Things happen in those places that'd curl your hair—neglect, theft . . . abuse. But I keep an eye on my staff here, make sure everything's aboveboard. I like to think that I make the residents' lives better by staying. Some of them are just dumped off like dogs at the pound, and I'm talking about by their own *family*."

"How about Mary—she get many visitors?" Susan made a move to pull out her notepad and then reconsidered. Better to keep things friendly, off the cuff. People tended to clam up once they saw that every word they said was being documented. Or worse, they felt the need to go Oscar Wilde with their stories and embellished.

The nurse shook her head. "She doesn't have much family. That good-for-nothing son of hers never bothered to visit—that's for sure. *Before* he went to prison, I'm talking about." Gracie flushed. "Please don't mention to anyone that I said that. I don't like to encourage scandal."

Susan flashed her palms and shook her head. "So how about after?"

The nurse looked at Susan blankly. "After what?"

"Has Gerald come by since he's been out of prison?"

Nurse Gracie frowned. "I didn't even know he'd gotten out. I don't think Mary knows either."

Susan believed her. Shock was one of the harder emotions to fake, and besides, the nurse would have no reason to lie. "He was just released on parole. A little over a week ago."

"They must've released him early, then. Mary said he wasn't due to get out for another seven, eight years." Nurse Gracie's color had faded some, her lips curled down at the edges in marked revulsion; the dropping of Gerald Nichol's name tended to have that effect on people, Susan had found. Like letting out a silent, stinky fart in a packed elevator.

"Is she, uh, coherent?" Susan asked delicately, eschewing Ed's harsher syntax, *gone soft*.

"Mary?" Nurse Gracie said with a low *ha* sound. "She's sharper than a tack. Her *body* is what's in bad shape. The poor thing can hardly move. But she's tough, never complains." The admiration in her voice was unmistakable.

They turned down another long hallway. This one was entirely vacant, with a series of nondescript doors running its entire length. "Resident housing," the nurse said. It made Susan think of that classic horror-film scene where a hapless victim runs from a monster but gets nowhere, the corridor stretching out before him or her like taffy.

"Here we are," Nurse Gracie said. She surprised Susan by rapping a knuckle on Mary's closed door and then immediately entering. They could have walked in on the poor woman half-naked and scrambling to get dressed, for all the warning she was given. Like a complete chess set, personal privacy was apparently something Emerald Meadows did not provide. Guess they figured that the seventy-plus crowd wasn't a part of the nudist set.

They found Mary sitting on the sofa, though she was thankfully clothed, a skeletal figure wrapped in a fleece blanket. She wasn't doing much of anything other than staring off into space, a basket of yarn and knitting needles cast off to her left. As Nurse Gracie explained that Officer Marlan had a few questions, a calm smile spread across Mary's well-worn face, as if she'd been expecting them.

As soon as the nurse left, Mary turned to Susan. "Is he dead?"

CHAPTER 6

Susan was confused by the question. Maybe Nurse Gracie was wrong, and Mary actually wasn't all there. "I'm not following, Mrs. Nichol."

"Call me Mary." Her voice warbled with age, but yes, she seemed to still be very sharp. She motioned for Susan to take a seat, and her expression grew shrewd. "There's only two reasons you could be here: Gerald's escaped, or he's dead."

Straight down to business with this one. Susan quickly clarified, "No, no. He's not dead."

"He's escaped, then."

"So you haven't heard from your son?"

"Wouldn't have asked you if he was dead if I had, now would I?" Mary cracked.

Susan felt the color rise to her cheeks. Good point, though Mary could be faking her obliviousness. She didn't think so, though. "Fair enough. Gerald was released from prison about a week ago. You obviously didn't know."

Mary pursed her lips. "I didn't."

"I take it you two aren't close?"

"And I take it *you* know what he was locked up for."

"I do."

Mary sighed deeply, her body so frail that it seemed as if she'd lost a few pounds along with the air spent from her lungs. "But I suppose he'll always be my son, no matter what he did."

Mary's comment was one that Susan had heard copiously, and it never ceased to get her hackles up. Perhaps if more mothers held their sons accountable instead of blindly standing by their sides the way Mary did, there'd be a hell of a lot fewer wife beaters and rapists out in the world. "You mean violating innocent children."

Mary, of course, had nothing to say about that. "Why are you here, Officer?"

Susan checked herself silently. It wasn't her job to place judgment, at least not vocally. And if she got too snarky, Mary would be of no help. "I'm here about Gerald's charges."

Mary leaned forward, her expression cautious. "Go on."

"First, I'd like to confirm with you: your son owns your farm now—is that correct?"

Mary nodded. "I signed it over to him when my body started going to pot. With the way the system works, the government would've taken everything I owned to pay for my medical bills."

"I understand. Is there a possibility that Gerald could have been . . . operating longer than we've known?" Susan typically wouldn't have been so cryptic, but it felt dirty and wrong, speaking to this ancient woman about a child predator. Despite her standoffishness, Mary Nichol seemed far too sweet to have any affiliation with the monster that was Gerald Nichol. Of course, they always did. People were great at pretending.

"Honey, this'll go a lot faster if you just tell me what this is about," Mary said. "Me, I have all the time in the world—don't get too many visitors these days—but I bet you've got better things to do than sit here yarning with me all day."

True, Susan *was* eager to get the hell out of the creepy place, but she was only working a half day. Her plan after Emerald Meadows was to head home, where she'd remain in her pajamas for the next three and a half days. Maybe, *maybe* catch up on some paperwork. She rarely had so many consecutive days off, so she was going to enjoy them in all her slothful glory.

"We found a body on the edge of your son's property," Susan began. "It's a small boy."

Mary raised her eyebrows. "Oh?" Susan expected her to say more, but she didn't.

"It appears that he died"—*was murdered by your good-for-nothing son*—"many years ago, perhaps around the 1960s. Gerald would've been just a teenager then, but given the nature of the crimes we already know he committed . . ."

Mary's chin quivered. Still, she remained mute.

But what was there for her to say, exactly? Certainly, there was no section in any parenting handbook in existence that instructed mothers on how to cope with police inquiries regarding their pedophile offspring. Susan wondered if Mary would still be so determined to stand by her son's side now that she knew that he, in addition to having a predilection for child pornography, was the murderer of a little boy.

"You're lucky, you know," Mary said at last.

She'd spoken so softly that Susan wondered if she'd actually heard her at all. "Sorry?"

"These days, women have choices. They're *independent*." Mary closed her eyes, thoughtful. "It wasn't always this way."

Susan opened her mouth and then closed it. There was more Mary had to say, and she knew better than to deter her by filling the silence with banalities.

"I married Wayne—Gerald's father—young. I was just shy of seventeen, but that's what we did back then. My family was poor, and Wayne's family had money. You wouldn't believe it now, but I was a very beautiful girl, and . . ." She raised her scrawny shoulders. "It was a way out."

Susan nodded, though her insides were itching with impatience. She couldn't imagine the relevance of Mary's story, but something in her gut told her that it *was* going somewhere, that she should just shut it for once and listen.

"I was never *in love* with Wayne—he was an awful, awful man, truth be told. But he did give me a child, so I guess some part of me loved him for that."

"Your only child," Susan said.

Mary went on as if Susan had never spoken. "I knew what Wayne was doing to Gerald. God help me, I *knew*, but I turned a blind eye to it for so many years. And for that I'll never forgive myself." Mary's words were coming out more quickly now, had taken on a feverish quality, as if she'd been stabbed in the chest by an invisible sword and was blood-letting personal demons. "Wayne, he went . . . *funny* when kids were around. But we didn't talk about that sort of thing back in the sixties; we didn't say things like *child molester*—I doubt the phrase had even been invented yet. Nobody in town ever said anything to me outright, but I think most everyone suspected. They sure never left Wayne alone with their *own* children."

Susan, a product of a small town herself, could picture it all too well: Hushed conversations in the market that abruptly ceased whenever Mary neared. Stealthy glances that were both pitying and judgmental. Mary hemmed in by the same people who probably called themselves her friends, all of them aware of her dirty secret, yet not one of them willing to help, maybe because they didn't care enough to, maybe because they had problems of their own, maybe simply because they *couldn't*.

Mary lowered her eyes to her lap and dropped her head forward, as if the sheer weight of the words that followed were too heavy for her mouth to carry. "Of course, I didn't *always* know what Wayne was doing to Gerald. I had my *suspicions* at first, but over time there was just no denying it. I . . ."

50

Mary slid a hand up her blouse, rooted around in her bra, and pulled out a crumpled tissue. She blew her nose into it, stuffed it back where she'd gotten it, and continued. "But like I said, things were different back then. I was uneducated and had no money other than the paltry allowance that Wayne gave me to buy groceries. I tried to skim from it, but it was never enough. I couldn't just *leave*. Where would I go? The one time I tried reaching out to my parents for help, they told me to go home to my husband. So I . . ."

Mary rubbed her chest as she began to cough. Susan quickly crossed the room to the kitchenette and filled a glass of water for the old woman. She accepted it gratefully and took a few sips. Moments later, she cleared her throat and raised her head, determined to get her story out.

"As silly—*stupid*—as it sounds, I thought that if Gerald could only wait a little longer, if he could just manage to hold it together until he turned eighteen, then he could move out on his own and forget the horrible business of his childhood."

Forget, as if it'd be that easy to put from his mind, Susan scoffed in silence. *Forget years of abuse, as if it were just some dumb, mortifying experience of his youth, like wetting his pants in the schoolyard.* Susan focused hard to keep her head straight. If she hadn't, she would have wildly shaken it, maybe even shouted a little.

"I killed him, you know," Mary said, and Susan went very still.

The two women sat so silently now that the only noise was the dripping faucet on the other side of the room.

"You heard me right," Mary said, sounding utterly drained. "But what are you really going to do? If you arrest me, I'll be dead by the time I'm brought to trial. And any jail you take me to in the meantime will be an upgrade from *this* place."

There was more to the story that Susan wanted to hear. "Mary, I'm not sure what any of this has to do with why I'm here."

Mary ignored her. "Don't you want to know how I did it?" She answered before Susan did. "Mushrooms."

"Mushrooms?"

"I ground them up and put them in his meatloaf. I picked them in the field just behind our house. They were poisonous, of course," Mary said with a coy half smile.

Susan was at a loss about what to do. Never had she heard such a brazen admission of guilt, not even when the perps had been caught red-handed. Should she call in to the station? Get Mary's confession down on paper? She'd dealt with plenty of violent offenders, but this was her first murder. She decided to play it cool for the time being, keep Mary talking.

Mary didn't need any encouragement to continue. "One night at dinner—Gerald was away at football practice, so it was just the two of us—I told Wayne I had cramps, so I wasn't much in the mood to eat. I said that he should go on without me. He did, and I'm sure it was to keep me from discussing my 'lady issues,' as he called them. Wayne was always squeamish when it came to female anatomy."

No surprise there, Susan thought.

"He died that night in the hospital."

"Of accidental poisoning," Susan murmured.

"That's right. I was uneducated and unworldly, as everyone knew, so how was *I* to know that some mushrooms are lethal? People had been treating me like I was dumb my whole life. I figured, Why correct them now?"

"You were never brought up on charges."

"That's right, but I'm guessing you already knew that."

Mary adjusted her blanket, a small task that seemed to take her a great deal of effort. *Hell, if I put her in handcuffs, it'd probably break her wrists*, Susan thought. Mary coughed a little—the struggle with the blanket had disrupted her breath—and then asked Susan a surprising question. "You know *how* I did it, but don't you want to know *why*?"

"I assume it was because of what he was doing to Gerald."

"Yes," Mary said. "And no."

Susan sat even stiller now, her pulse racing.

"I was washing up after breakfast when I decided to murder my husband," Mary said and then swallowed. Speaking was a great effort for her, the pauses between her words increasing in length. Susan hoped she'd get to her conclusion before she passed out completely. "I was at the sink, watching Gerald play out front with the little boy from next door, Lenny Lincoln."

Susan filed the boy's name in her memory. Like with the nurse, she didn't dare write anything down just yet, lest Mary suddenly grow skittish.

"Though Nora and Henry Lincoln—Lenny's parents—were cordial to me, I sensed that they despised us. As a family, I mean. They were frightened of Gerald; a lot of people were—he was a big boy, even back then—but they downright *hated* Wayne. You could see it in their eyes. They weren't the only ones in town who felt this way about my husband, so it was a look I had become familiar with." Mary shook her head at the memory. "Lenny had been forbidden to come to our property—this I knew because I overheard Henry giving Lenny the business one day after he came home with some apples that I'd given him from the tree in our yard. In the country, sound can carry for miles, especially when someone's shouting. And Henry had certainly been shouting at Lenny."

Susan frowned. "But he was on your property again?"

Mary shrugged. "The Lincolns had two boys—Lenny's older brother was the responsible sibling. He came from a different father, who'd been killed in a farming accident some years earlier, so maybe that had something to do with it. Lenny never listened. He was spoiled, all right, but just so precious. But I was worried that he would get into trouble with Henry for coming over, so I was going to tell him to go home as soon as I finished with the washing up. Gerald never had friends over at the house, and they seemed like they were having fun—they were racing caterpillars or some damn thing—so I didn't see the harm in letting them be for a few minutes . . ."

Mary toyed with the basket of yarn and needles at her side. "But then I saw something that didn't sit right with me," said the old woman, looking every one of her ninety-six years. "It was the way Gerald was *looking* at Lenny."

Susan suddenly felt cold all over. "Looking?"

Mary met Susan's eyes. There must have been something on Susan's face that made Mary feel the need to clarify. A look of repugnance. "I want you to understand that I never saw Gerald *touch* Lenny—do you think I would have stood by while he fondled a little kid?"

You let your husband do it to your own son.

"But the look," Mary said. "It was strange for a teenager. It was the way a young man of Gerald's age should've been looking at a *woman*."

"I understand," Susan said, focusing hard to keep her voice even. The whole thing made her feel violated, dirty.

"I knew then that Wayne was starting to influence Gerald—that if I didn't do *something*, Gerald would never have a chance at a normal life. So after I sent Lenny home, I went out into the field and picked those mushrooms. A couple days later, Wayne was dead."

Mary paused, adjusted her blanket. "But I can see now that I waited too long. Gerald had already been polluted by Wayne. Though maybe he was always polluted—maybe this *sickness* had been passed down in his genes."

The Nichols. What a group of utterly screwed-up individuals. And here Susan had been thinking that her own family had problems. The Nichols made them look like the Brady Bunch by comparison.

Susan nodded solemnly. "You mean because of the way Gerald turned out anyway—him going to prison?"

Mary gave Susan a funny look. "Yes, that, and because of what happened to Lenny."

Susan leaned forward on the sofa. "What do you mean? What happened to Lenny?"

"Oh, I thought you knew," Mary said with phony surprise, as if she didn't really buy into Susan's confusion. "He disappeared."

"When?"

Mary shifted in her seat.

"*When*, Mrs. Nichol?"

"The day after I saw him playing with Gerald. The day before I killed Wayne." Mary's voice was nearly a whisper.

"What are you saying, Mary? Are you telling me that Gerald had something to do with Lenny's disappearance? Or Wayne? Both?" Susan couldn't get the questions out quickly enough. "Is the body we found in your field Lenny Lincoln?"

"I don't know anything more than what I've told you," Mary snapped. Witnesses sometimes got that way, Susan had found. One minute, they were singing like canaries; the next, they lost their voices. Especially where their own children were concerned. "If you're expecting me to tell you that Gerald killed Lenny, then you're crazier than half the people here at the Meadows. He's my *son*, so I won't help you send him to the electric chair. All I know is that Lenny Lincoln disappeared while playing hide-and-seek with his brother."

"But you've got to admit, given Gerald's other crimes—"

Mary stared directly into Susan's face, her gaze cold. "If you want somebody to blame, blame *Wayne*. No matter who did what, he's the one responsible. *He's* the one at the root of all this evil."

"But—"

"I've said all that I have to say." Mary seized the needles and yarn from the basket.

"What I don't understand, Mary, is why come clean now, after all these years? Are you looking for some kind of absolution?"

"If you want to arrest me for the murder of Wayne, fine—you go ahead," Mary said, her needles clicking as she worked. "If not, I'd like you to leave. *Please.*"

Susan knew when badgering a witness was futile, when it was time to pack it in. She wouldn't be able to pull anything more from Mary. She toyed with the handcuffs at her hip as she watched the old woman work, her needles moving so speedily that their movement was almost blurred.

With a long sigh, Susan got to her feet. She thanked Mary for her time, and the old woman refused to look up even as she left.

Out in the cruiser, Susan sat staring out the window, grappling with indecision. Mary *had* just admitted to murder, a crime that had no statute of limitations . . . to arrest or not to arrest? She might be able to book her on obstruction of justice, if nothing else.

Susan found that she really didn't *want* to arrest Mary, and not only because the notion of hauling a frail-boned ninety-six-year-old woman down to the station in handcuffs was beyond distressing. And never mind the public relations uproar it would likely create: in today's climate of social media witch hunts where those targeted are guilty until proven innocent, police officers operate under unrelenting public scrutiny that slants toward hostility more often than not.

But still, that wasn't the crux of it. Though she'd never admit such a thing out loud—especially not in front of those who were familiar with her affiliation to law enforcement—the real reason she didn't want to bring Mary in was because, deep in her heart, she felt that Wayne Nichol had had it coming. While Susan had no children herself, she didn't have to strain too hard to imagine that she might murder anyone who'd violated any son of hers the way Wayne had Gerald. To hurt a powerless child in such a manner—in *any* manner—well, that was an extra-special kind of evil.

And maybe it had been Wayne who'd killed the boy next door and not Gerald, if the body was, in fact, Lenny Lincoln's. Though if it was, Susan was leaning more toward it being Gerald who'd done the deed, given the way he'd skipped town after the discovery of the body. Regardless, couldn't it be argued that the world had become a better place without Wayne Nichol in it—that the children of Perrick were just a little bit safer?

But that wasn't *her* argument to make. Such judgments weren't even in the dominion of her job—if anything, she was duty bound to treat suspects in a way that was impartial. Arguments and death sentences were reserved for lawyers and judges.

Thus far, Susan had managed to keep her nose clean on the job, but one of her biggest anxieties about being a cop (other than being killed in uniform) remained the perpetual risk of becoming dirty. If she let Mary slide, she wondered, where would she draw the line? Would she then become the sort of officer who'd let friends slide—a forgiven DUI here, a covered-up assault there?

Susan reached for the tumbler in her cupholder, remembered that it was empty, and sighed. It wasn't even noon, and she was already sleepy again, an exhaustion headache clouding over her brain. Maybe she was being dramatic, getting ahead of herself. Big decisions, she decided, could wait.

Mary had murdered Wayne over fifty years ago. A few more hours wouldn't hurt.

CHAPTER 7

Bodega Bay was even better than Eric had hoped, and he felt that the positive reviews he'd found online about the quaint (to use Maggie's word) little coastal settlement were well deserved.

After beachcombing the rocky coastline at Goat Rock Beach, he indulged in a hearty lunch of fish and chips at Currents Seafood—served the proper old-fashioned way, in newsprint (or at least in tissue paper that was meant to *look* like newsprint)—washing it down with a local draft called Seasick Sally's Ale. He took pictures of seagulls and met a polite shop owner named Bert while browsing kites at the aptly named Bert's Kites. He bought a five-pound bag of saltwater taffy at Lulu's Gifts, inhaling about half a pound of it before he even left the parking lot. From a quirky little roadside stand he bought a half dozen fresh oysters and a tuna steak to cook up later for dinner.

His heart was light and his belly full. All in all, it had been a damn fine day.

Eric didn't think his day could go any better until he spotted a splintery homemade sign along the highway a few miles outside of town. It read:

ANTIQUE SALE
SATURDAY 8AM–8PM
RAIN OR SHINE!
CASH ONLY

Eric nearly dismissed the sign because it was getting late, but then he allowed himself a smile as he remembered that he had nobody at home to answer to. Maggie had routinely hassled him about his antique fixer-uppers, as he had the tendency to start working on them eagerly—a bit of sanding here, a coat of paint there—but then lose interest about halfway through. Into the garage they would then go before oftentimes retiring to the dumpster. She'd call them his *half projects*, always with a snort.

What Maggie, like others who were baffled by the "picker" calling, didn't understand was that Eric had a connection to antiques that was practically otherworldly. The mere touch of an old piece of furniture could transport him back in time decades, centuries; he could smell the air of the forest where the tree had been cultivated, feel the power of the woodworker's hands within the carvings, connect with those who had owned and loved it. With a certainty he could never prove to anyone, not even himself, he could occasionally even determine whether the piece had been in a happy home or one that had been filled with turmoil.

Maggie would, of course, say that he was full of it.

Eric's foot eased off the gas pedal. It *had* been a while since he'd taken on a project. And if he wanted to fix up an antique or two (or ten), so what? A little distraction might even do him some good. Give him something to tinker with, keep him from dwelling.

Eric clicked on his blinker and then made a quick left turn down a scraggy gravel driveway that ended at a large barn—that was something he hadn't seen much of in Philly, barns. Gravel driveways, too, which these parts made up for aplenty. There weren't too many cars parked at the foot of the driveway, but there were enough to give Eric a panicked *What treasures have they beaten me to?* jolt that those who covet antiques are so often prone to. Since it was already past six o'clock, he wasn't too optimistic. Whatever was left was most likely junk.

Still, it wouldn't hurt to look.

The inside of the barn was well lit but dingy and full of cobwebs, with probably an owl or two using the rafters as a permanent dwelling. Eric knew that surroundings like this typically meant that the sale was either going to be really good or really bad. That either a land developer with lots of money but no interest in antiques had acquired the property and simply wanted to clear everything out before bulldozing the lot (really good), or a backwoods tweaker was hocking garbage to make a few quick bucks for his next score (really bad).

In the case of *this* barn, Eric discovered that it was neither.

The concrete floor had been swept semiclean, and tarps had been laid every few feet, with various items resting on top. Eric had been mostly correct in his assumption about the junk; much of what was left was ugly wood furniture from the 1970s, heavy desks and dressers, the occasional avocado-green pleather chair thrown in. There were also a lot of rusted car parts, most of which Eric was unable to identify. He supposed some of the other items were worth a decent amount of money, like the decorated dish sets, antique brooches, and unsettlingly lifelike porcelain dolls made with what looked like real human hair. But these were things he didn't want or need.

He'd already decided to leave when he saw the steamer trunk. It was sitting off in a corner, a little worn, looking about as sad and lonesome as any antique could be. *Ah*, Eric thought, *a kindred spirit.* Moving closer now, he saw that the trunk still had some life left in it.

He wanted it immediately.

Actually, Eric had *always* wanted a steamer trunk, but he'd never gotten around to buying one. This was mainly due to price,

(and Maggie)

as a decent trunk could set a buyer back hundreds or thousands of dollars—even tens of thousands of dollars, if a prominent designer had made it. This trunk, Eric imagined, would be in the couple-hundred range, which he probably shouldn't spend until after he started receiving steady paychecks again.

But he really, *really* wanted it. He had plenty of room for it inside his pathetically empty home, and it was calling to him the way no antique ever had. (Though Maggie might have argued against this claim.) He closed his eyes and ran his hands along its top, feeling connected to its history, bumpy ridges of wood pressing against skin. He could already see it at the foot of his bed, filled with records and old horror movies on VHS.

Eric figured that, like looking, it wouldn't hurt to *ask* about price. He had an honest face, and you could always count on people to trust a teacher. Maybe whoever was running the sale would take pity on a broke educator and allow him to pay it off in installments.

Outside, Eric located the person in question, a stooped old hippie with a long white ponytail and beard to match, whom everyone at the sale had been calling Rustler. He was sucking on a hand-rolled cigarette, flicking ashes dangerously close to the patch of dried yellow grass that clung to the earth near the barn's entrance. He didn't seem too concerned about the possibility of the whole place going up in flames. Maybe it was what he was hoping for.

"The trunk over in the corner," Eric said, bracing himself for the inescapable back-and-forth that was sure to follow. If these old junk geezers loved anything, it was dickering. "I'm just wondering how much you'd want for it."

Rustler shrugged. "How about twenty?"

Eric wasn't sure he'd heard right. "Twenty . . . dollars?"

"I don't want twenty cat turds for it," Rustler said and then barked out the sort of raspy laugh that must have taken decades of smoking unfiltered cigarettes to achieve. "Yeah, twenty bucks, and we'll call it a day. Cash only. I'm ready to go home. Back's killing me."

Heart thumping, Eric gave the inside of the barn a quick glance. They were now the last two people there. He'd pocketed a few pieces of sea glass at the beach, and they came flying out now as he scrounged for the two tens inside his jeans. And to think that he'd almost skipped going to the sale!

Sighing, Eric pushed the bills back into his pocket. He didn't believe in karma or hell, but he knew he'd feel guilty every time he looked at the damn thing if he didn't speak up. Curse of the Good Guy.

"I can't believe I'm about to say this," Eric began. "But you should know that the trunk is worth more than twenty bucks. *A lot* more." It was times like this that he wished he could be more like Jim. He'd have *no* qualms hustling the elderly.

Rustler shook his head, wrinkled turkey neck wobbling as he cleared his throat. "I appreciate you being honest, son, but I'm afraid not." With a wave of a knobby hand, he led Eric to the trunk. "Now it's *my* turn to be honest. You didn't look inside, did you?"

Eric smiled, sheepish. "No, I didn't."

"You might wanna stand back for this," Rustler warned, and then he wrestled the trunk open.

Eric clamped a hand down over his nose and mouth—*holy shit!*

"Stinks to high heaven, don't it? I can't imagine what was stored in here, but it sure as shit wasn't no roses." The old man's cackle ended in a few dry coughs. "When I started the sale this morning, I had it open with some of my wife's potpourri sprinkled in the bottom. She keeps a bag of it in the car 'cause she says my feet smell, though I think it's *hers* she's trying to cover up—Tuscan Breeze, I think, whatever the hell that's supposed to smell like. But then I started noticing the stink was driving people away, so I shut the lid."

"I can believe it."

"Anyway, I figured I should set you straight about its inside before you bought it. I like to run an honest business."

"I appreciate that," Eric said, fairly confident that Rustler would have taken his twenty bucks and let him leave without telling him about the stench had he not first spoken up about the trunk's worth. No honor among thieves, eh, old man?

"Also, there's a hole in the corner. It's real small, though. The wood's kind of warped around it, see?"

"So there is," Eric said, peering down into the trunk. "Mice?" He'd been holding his breath, so it came out sounding like *moose*, but Rustler caught his drift.

"Beats me, though there were no pellets inside when I got it." Rustler plucked a flake of tobacco off his lip and then snubbed his cigarette nub under a boot. "But I figure somebody could use the trunk as decoration, if nothing else. Add to a room's fang she or fig shoe or however you say it." He rolled his eyes to show just how much he did not subscribe to new age baloney like feng shui. "It'll be fine, so long as it's kept closed."

"Mind if I ask where you got it from? Yard sale?" Despite the stink, Eric found that he wanted the trunk anyway. Any smell could be scrubbed away with the right pine cleaner. If not, maybe Rustler was right, and it would enhance his bedroom's fig shoe.

"Nah," Rustler said, as if that were sufficient explanation. Eric allowed the silence that followed to float in the air around them, let it settle. Eventually, Rustler added, "Found it on the side of the road just up the way."

"You must have a good eye."

Rustler nodded noncommittally. "That's why I'm not too concerned with profit. When I saw it just sitting there, I was amazed that some-body would toss it out. I knew how much these trunks were worth even before you told me. Been peddling antiques probably longer than you've been alive, sonny. But when I opened it up and took a whiff, it made sense." He made a face and fanned a hand under his nose. "Lordy!"

"Still, you could clean it up and probably get a lot more than twenty bucks for it." With this comment, Eric felt his obligation to civic duty had been fulfilled. He wasn't going to twist the man's arm into charging him more.

Rustler snorted. "Take a look around. I could go on living another fifty years and still have junk to hock. I don't need any more, since I'll be lucky if I'm alive in fifteen."

Eric was thinking the dude would be lucky if he were still kicking in five, but he kept his opinion to himself.

"Antiques aren't moving as quickly as they used to. It's these damn millennials," Rustler said with a scowl. "They only want what's new. Spend a thousand bucks on phony mass-produced garbage that's meant to *look* old, when they could just as easily buy the real thing for a quarter of the price. Then they wonder why their houses look like every other place on the block. Course, maybe that's what some of 'em want."

Eric offered the two tens. "Well, okay . . . if you're *sure* you're fine with twenty, I'll be happy to take the trunk off your hands."

"Deal, long as you load it yourself," Rustler said, kneading his lower back. He pocketed the bills before Eric had a chance to agree. "That's all I really want the money for. My trouble, that is. Nearly broke my damn back trying to get the thing into my flatbed, so I figure I might as well get *something* out of it. How people used those things as luggage is beyond me. My suitcase has those wheelie-mabobs, and I *still* struggle, not that I'm doing too much traveling these days. But I got a daughter and grandkids over in Arizona we're planning to go and see over Christmas. Me and the wife restored a '73 Airstream that we're hauling down with us—it'll be its maiden voyage, so let's hope everything goes right! Hate to have it go kaput in the middle of Route 66; it's hotter'n hell out that way. Be withered like raisins before anyone found us. Ever been to Sedona?"

Eric shook his head. "Can't say that I have."

"It's real pretty, if you like rocks."

Eric opened his mouth to say that rocks just so happened to be his area of expertise but then thought better of it. As much as he'd been lonesome earlier, all the talking had exhausted him, and so what he wanted to say more than anything was that he needed to shove on.

As if sensing his eagerness, Rustler finally cut him loose. "Anyway, I'll quit jabbering so we can both get on home. My wife'll kill me if I make her keep *Wheel of Fortune* on pause too long. We got that new service that lets us do that. Pause it, I mean. It's our dinner show. That and *Jeopardy*."

Eric once again held his tongue, this time against the urge to share with Rustler that *his* wife hadn't allowed the TV to be on during dinner-time. She'd said it wasn't healthy for the marriage, if you could *believe* that an adulterer would have the audacity to make such a claim.

Eric moved to load the trunk, making sure the lid was latched down tight. The last thing he needed was the stench permeating the upholstery. Elbowing aside a pair of tennis shoes he'd forgotten to take into the house—he'd been wondering where they were—he hefted the trunk down into the back of the Jeep. He closed the hatch on his vehicle and then turned to face the antique dealer. "Kind of makes you wonder, doesn't it?"

Rustler looked up from the ample stack of cash he was counting, most of it tens and twenties, none of it taxed, unquestionably. "Wonder what?"

"What was in that trunk that made it smell so bad. Wish I could find its previous owner just so I could ask."

"Not me," Rustler said with a wry yellow smile. "If the dude who had this trunk before smells even half as bad as the inside, I don't wanna go anywhere near 'im."

At home, Eric moved the trunk out of his Jeep and into the garage, raring to get to work on his new fixer-upper. He made a mental check-list of all the cleaners and tools he'd need to pick up at the hardware store the next day.

"Screw you, Maggie," he said.

With a final glance at his sweet antique score, Eric turned out the light in the garage with a vow to prove just how wrong his ex-wife had been to underestimate his passion.

CHAPTER 8

To Eric, teaching a new class always felt a bit like going on a first date. He wanted to be liked, to show that he was interesting and easygoing—but not *too* easygoing, or else he'd run the risk of students thinking he was a pushover. Then they'd only try to get him to put out for them.

Eric typically didn't get first-day jitters, but today he was a mess, pulling at his hair and gnawing his nails right down to the quick. He wasn't sure if it was boredom, depression, his medication, or the new time zone, but he'd been feeling off since his relocation: sluggish but antsy, exhausted but wide awake.

Now he was feeling all these things *and* tweaky. He'd had more coffee than was probably prudent, which had only exacerbated his twitchiness. (He'd been shocked to find the pot empty before the machine had turned itself off automatically, a rarity typically reserved for end-of-semester grading sessions.)

He checked his watch for what very well could have been the hundredth time. More than two hours to go. He checked again. More like two and a half.

That was the problem with having classes that started at eleven in the morning and ended at seven at night, with small breaks in between. It made getting into a routine difficult. There wasn't enough time to accomplish much in the a.m., yet he'd be so tired once he was done at night that he'd have no energy left to do anything of significance. Eric supposed that over time he'd adapt. As he'd recently come to understand, it was amazing the things a person could get used to when they really had no other choice.

Complicating Eric's routine further was his staggered teaching schedule: Mondays, Wednesdays, and Fridays. Of course, he'd also have to grade papers during his "time off." A small college, Perrick City didn't have the budget to provide him with a teaching assistant. At Warrenton, he'd had two. Eric imagined the attendance numbers for his night classes would dwindle significantly once the semester got going—they always did at community colleges, from what he'd heard—but that didn't have any bearing on him, since *he'd* still have to show up.

Eric went to make another pot of coffee and then reconsidered; he'd give himself an ulcer if he didn't do *something* soon. He needed to use his hands to expel the nervous energy that had fizzled up inside him like a pop bottle ready to blow its cap. It used to be his old drum kit that he'd pound out energy on, but like a good many other things he used to own, it was

(gone, baby, gone)

back at the house in Philly. Eric wondered if he'd left the kit covered, because it tended to get a little grimy out in the garage. Scowling, he reminded himself that it didn't matter too much anyhow, since, like the house, coffee table, and plasma TV,

(and Maggie—don't forget Maggie)

it was no longer his.

After this thought came a much nastier one: Had Jim been using his drums, the shithead? Though he'd tried to hide it, Jim had always been jealous of Eric's musical ability. Why, Eric could never figure out, though he suspected it had something to do with the fact that it was the one domain where Eric held marked superiority over his brother. He wouldn't put it past Jim to steal his drum set.

(Though it's hardly stealing if you left it behind, now, is it?)

After all, Jim clearly hadn't had a problem stealing his—

"No, stop this shit right now," Eric commanded the murmurs within his brain. He'd been down this road before, and if he allowed himself to continue getting worked up, he'd spend the rest of the day with thorns of bitterness needling his gut.

(Good for you for taking control of your emotions! I'm proud of—)

"Oh, give it a rest, you insufferable goody two-shoes," Eric spat at one of the perkier voices and then let out a quiet chuckle. He wondered if all recent divorcés talked to themselves this much or if it was just his own brand of crazy. He supposed it was probably a little bit of both.

Mini–Dirt Devil in tow, Eric went out into the garage with the intention of vacuuming his Jeep's carpet. He'd taken a few hikes along the coastline—Tomales Point, Point Reyes, Bodega Head—and its floor was starting to resemble a sandbox. He'd never realized just how sticky damp sand was, having been an urbanite most of his life. He kind of liked it, having sandy carpets. It made him feel . . . Californian. He imagined the sand could be problematic over time, though, if he let it build up. All that brackish moisture in the air.

His little vacuum tended to run out of juice after only a few minutes of use, so he'd brought the charger base with him. Eric hadn't needed to plug anything in out in the garage previously, so he had to search for an outlet. He found one just behind the steamer trunk. A flitter of guilt tickled the underside of his belly as he moved it aside to reach; he was supposed to have started the restoration, wasn't he? He didn't even have the excuse of being busy at work. The trunk—his kindred spirit—*should* have been given his love and undivided attention, but instead it had turned into a

(half project)

chore he hadn't wanted to contend with. Eric wasn't at all surprised to hear Maggie's smug voice lurking at the back of his mind, and he was peeved that he'd proved her right once again. What irked him more was that his ex-wife's opinion on things still mattered to him at all, since it was unlikely that *he* had crossed *her* mind even once since he'd left town.

Eric went back into the house and grabbed a couple of rags and the bottle of wood cleaner he'd picked up during his last shopping trip. At the time of purchase, Eric hadn't even known if he *needed* wood cleaner, but it seemed like the sort of thing a responsible adult would have in his home. Back in Philly, it had been Maggie who'd bought all the innocuous domestics: paper towels, aspirin, dish soap, floss, air freshener. On this front, Eric was clueless. He supposed in time he'd learn.

Eric was planning on giving the trunk only a quick wipe down. Just to get the project rolling. He hadn't done any real research on steamer trunk restoration, and the information he had skimmed online had been laughably inconsistent. For every blogger that hyped a specific method of refurbishment as being the best out there, another would come along claiming that the same method had splintered their trunk's woodwork. Or scratched the metal. Or stripped the patina.

But a simple cleaning couldn't hurt, right?

Eric was once again reminded of the trunk's stink as he lifted the lid, which prompted another trip back inside the house to change out of his work clothes. That would be the worst, going to his first day on campus reeking like roadkill. His character was already shaky enough. He didn't need to *smell* weird too.

He'd found one of those sponge kneeling mats used for gardening back when he'd decluttered the cottage. It was hot pink and embellished on the edges with puff-paint daisies. Doris had left a few other things in the garage that she supposed Eric might need. He appreciated her thoughtfulness, but he didn't think he could ever bring himself to use a leopard-print beach umbrella out in public, or the folding chairs that matched. At least not while he was on his own.

In the privacy of the garage, Eric had no problem using Doris's daisy kneeling mat, which he pushed right up to the trunk so he could apply some real elbow grease. He was so eager to get started that the stink didn't even bother him much. Eric's initial task was to remove the dust, first with the vacuum and then with a dry rag. It was tedious work, but if he skipped this step, he'd only spread the grime around and make things worse once he started with the wood cleaner. He chuckled a little when he found a few chunks of potpourri at the bottom of the trunk, picturing that raspy-voiced old codger sitting in front of the TV with his pruned wife, the two of them heckling *Wheel of Fortune* contestants over pot roast.

He wrapped the cloth around his index finger and used it to scrape oily muck from around the metal studs and latches. It was fascinating, in an esoteric sort of way, touching all that history. He wondered how many owners the trunk had passed between during the century or so that it had been in existence. Where in the world had it been? What treasures had it held?

He closed his eyes and rubbed his bare hands against the wood, willing it to speak to him the way only old furniture could. He opened his eyes and frowned as he felt something splintery on the underside of the lid. What the hell?

It looked like . . . "Scratch marks," he said. Now, what would cause those? Would somebody keep a pet locked inside the trunk? With it flipped upside down so that its claws were resting on the lid? Maybe somebody had been smuggling an exotic pet way back when, and then the trunk had gotten tumbled around during transit. Eric pictured a sailor coming back from some exotic island in the South Pacific during the turn of the century, a Gila monster hidden among his belongings. A pet for his wife or child, maybe. Weird, though the trunk *did* smell as though an animal had been kept inside it.

Eric was so caught up in his ruminations that he jumped when his cell phone alarm chimed in his pocket, indicating that he needed to get cleaned up for work.

"Olly olly oxen free," he said as he silenced his phone. "Come out, come out, wherever you are."

Eric snapped his head back and permitted himself a nervous little laugh. Now, what would possess him to say *that?* Schizo, indeed.

A more important question Eric should have asked himself, had it only occurred to him, was why he'd been chanting the phrase from the very moment he opened the trunk.

CHAPTER 9

Susan was surprised when she awakened on Monday morning and discovered that it wasn't morning at all. She'd slept most of the day, but she had no regrets. Her head was volumes clearer, rational, after the much-needed rest. She felt like her whole self again and not the exhausted, cobbled-together individual she'd gone to bed as. Coffee and energy drinks were fine and dandy, but sometimes, what a person really needs is sleep.

She changed into her workout gear and then went about putting an hour in on the treadmill that she kept at the nook of her kitchen intended for a dining table. As a singleton, she ate the majority of her food, usually bits and pieces of chow in lieu of a complete meal (a couple of slices of cheese here, a few cold cuts there, crackers), parked on the sofa. Though she normally watched television while she ate, work remained at the back of her mind, as was the case now.

As Susan sweated and huffed, she thought about the wisdom Ed had imparted to her back when she was a rookie, that sometimes—*many* times—hunches paid off. Words that were ironic, given that it had been Ed who'd discouraged her earlier from going to Emerald Meadows to chat with Mary. Susan, despite the quandary that now weighed on her conscience, was glad that she'd ignored Ed's pessimism about Mary's mental state and gone anyway. Though she couldn't quite connect the dots now, she felt that the information she'd been provided by the old woman might later have some significance.

Susan found that she still did not want to arrest Mary Nichol. She couldn't see what good it would do, what justice it would serve. Even *if* a prosecutor was unsympathetic enough to bring a ninety-six-year-old woman up on murder charges, she would almost certainly be dead before she was convicted, as Mary herself had pointed out.

Still, Susan had her career to worry about. If it ever got out that she'd said and done absolutely *nothing* after hearing not only a murder confession but also a blow-by-blow account of how it had been executed, she'd be kicked off the force. Maybe even brought up on charges herself.

But *would* it ever get out was the question.

Susan pressed the button with the large plus sign a few times to crank up the speed of the treadmill's belt. Of course there was always the *chance* that it would get out. If not by Mary herself during a last-ditch deathbed confession, then by someone else she might have told. Susan would have bet a year of her salary that Gracie Hoguin had also heard Mary's confession. Still, it was unlikely that the nurse would talk even long after Mary was dead and gone, given how protective she seemed of the old woman.

Despite the humiliation it would cause Susan if she were fired or arraigned, what would bother her most of all would be the sense of betrayal Ed would feel. Her actions on the force reflected back on him. The man had, after all, been the one responsible for her becoming a cop in the first place.

It had been Ed who'd recognized Susan's potential back when she was a directionless seventeen-year-old with no real plans for college or a job after graduation; he'd liked her enough even way back then to fret for her future, the same way he'd fret for his own daughters' futures, if she didn't soon cultivate a plan for it. He'd been the one who'd noticed how often she'd gone above and beyond her required high school–internship duties down at the station, oftentimes staying long after her classmates had all gone home. It had also been Ed who'd fostered Susan's curiosity about the law when he could have as easily dismissed her as just another nosy, violence-obsessed teenager.

Later, at Susan's graduation from the police academy, Ed would claim that he'd simply acted as a map—that she'd been the one who'd done all the driving. Susan understood that Ed was only being humble. She suspected that he knew way down deep, just as she did, that she owed him everything she'd become. Chief Bender wasn't only Susan's mentor; he was the closest thing to a father she had.

Susan's real father had never been around much, at least not where it counted. Physically, Calvin Marlan had been present plenty when Susan was a young girl, every morning and evening, a mortgage loan officer with standard working hours at the local bank; emotionally, it was a different story. He spoke to his family only when addressed directly, a dazed look always playing at the edges of his features, as if he'd been jolted awake from a happy fantasy and was disappointed to discover the true state of his existence. The thankless job, the wife with her overcompensating cheerfulness, the morose little girl who wanted absolutely nothing to do with sports . . . surely, this couldn't be *his* life.

Calvin's exchanges with his daughter were stilted, plagued by aggravated sighs—*Why are you bothering me, and what do you want?* He dealt with Bonnie, Susan's mother, in much the same manner. Susan and Bonnie generally tried to stay out of Calvin's way. Susan spent much of her childhood holed up in her bedroom listening to music, an underage lodger who'd overstayed her welcome but was forced to remain because she had nowhere else to go.

Bonnie spoke badly of Calvin when it was just her and Susan, giving him the moniker Sir Lump—*He just sits there like a huge lump!*—her hollow giggles veiling evident pain. Eventually, Bonnie grew fed up with Sir Lump's indifference, about the time Susan had become old enough to remain at home unsupervised. She sought therapy, got a job in retail as the afternoon shift manager, left Calvin lickety-split, and took her daughter with her. Calvin put up embarrassingly little fight, but he'd paid every single child support payment on time, up until the day Susan turned eighteen. Which Susan figured was something. Susan and her father now spoke approximately three times a year: his birthday, a day near her birthday (he could never seem to nail the exact date), and Christmas. It was an arrangement that satisfied them both.

After her cooldown on the treadmill, Susan stretched out her tired muscles and then took a shower. She started to feel antsy even while she was drying off, absurdly disappointed that she wasn't due back at the station until Wednesday. She was having a difficult time taking her mind off Gerald's disappearance, as well as Mary's left field confession.

She now understood that she'd have to tell Ed about Mary's confession. There was just no way around it. She felt it prudent, however, to first do a little fact-checking, lest Mary had been fibbing about the disappearance of the boy next door as a means of further justifying the murder of her husband. She fired up the desktop computer in her home office, hoping Google would spin its usual magic.

She did not get as lucky as she'd expected. *Unsolved kidnappings 1960s. California kidnappings 1960s. California farm kidnappings 1960s. Perrick, California, disappearances 1960s. Unsolved child murders California 1960s.* And the list went on. She tried dozens of variations on the same key phrases and netted very few results that were even close to being relevant.

Finally, it dawned on Susan to search for something more specific, *Lenny Lincoln disappearance 1960s,* which she did without much hope. She let out a quiet *yessss* when she found the web page of a local historian, Ben Pepper, who blogged about notable Perrick events from the last hundred years: storms, droughts, sporting events, crimes. It was the only source on the net that mentioned Lenny Lincoln, so Susan felt fortunate to have found it, even if the newspaper clippings on the site were slightly blurry and faded.

She read on.

The first article, taken from the front page of *Perrick Weekly*, was dated June 13, 1964: Local Boy's Disappearance Remains a Mystery. Beneath the story was a large photo of Lenny Lincoln. Mary Nichol hadn't been kidding when she'd said that he was precious. Though the photo was black and white, it was obvious that his large, round eyes were bright blue, his lashes as long and lush as swan feathers. Across his nose was a smattering of freckles, the two bottom front teeth missing from his wide smile.

Susan's eyes misted. It was impossible to conceive that anyone would ever want to hurt this child.

Beneath the photo of Lenny was a smaller photo of Lenny's mother, Nora. She was coming down the stairs of the police station, clutching a lace handkerchief against her bosom. Her eyes were puffy from crying, and her mouth was contorted into a bloodless grimace. Below the photo was a caption. Grieving mother mourns: "I know in my heart Lenny is alive," said Nora Lincoln after county officials called off the search for her son. "I just want my baby home." Lenny Lincoln, age six, has been missing for one month. He is now presumed dead.

Susan scrolled down to the next article, also from *Perrick Weekly*. This one—Community Comes Together to Search for Lost Boy—focused on the search party that had been organized for Lenny the day after his disappearance. There was a photo for this one as well, snapped early during the hunt. It really did seem as if the whole town were there: farmers, high school students, volunteers from the fire department, police with floppy-eared dogs, other men and women of all ages. They'd searched the Lincoln farm, the woods, the schoolhouse, the park, the railroad tracks, and every store in town, even ones Lenny would have no interest in entering, like the fabric shop and meat market. They'd dragged the lake. They'd even explored the Nichol property, though obviously not underground, where Lenny might have been in a grave.

If Lenny Lincoln was, in fact, Overalls Boy, Susan reminded herself once more. There also remained the chance that she was grasping at straws, connecting two completely unrelated crimes.

There were no more articles on the blog, though Pepper had cited additional information about the Lincolns using indiscriminately placed asterisks. A *funeral was held for Lenny on July 1, 1964. A bodiless coffin was buried in the family plot after it had been filled with items Lenny cherished: toys, baseball cards, a marble collection, and his favorite food: sourdough bread that his mother had baked fresh. Lenny's father, *Henry, died the day after Lenny's funeral in what was reported as a farming accident (*though many locals believed that it was a suicide). The story was that he'd fallen off his tractor while plowing and had been crushed by the machine. It was the second farming accident on the Lincoln farm that had resulted in death. Nora's first husband, *William, had also been killed after a baler had torn off his arm. William was father to Lenny's half brother, Milton. *Nora died of heart failure in 1983.

Susan printed up a few screenshots from Pepper's blog and then closed out of it. For good measure, she ran another search about the Lincoln family, though she wasn't too surprised when nothing came up.

The evident setback she faced was that there had been no internet back in the sixties. Even Perrick PD hadn't gone fully digital until the early 2000s. Susan knew this empirically because of the volunteering she'd done at the station as a teenager. As one of the unlucky student helpers chosen to type up ancient handwritten files, she could attest that it had taken *hours* to get through just a few minor cases. As far as Susan knew, they'd stopped updating digitally around crimes that had occurred in the late seventies. All earlier handwritten files remained in boxes down in the station's storage basement, where they'd probably stay, ignored, until the end of time.

Printouts in hand, Susan went into the living room to find her cell phone to call Ed. He didn't pick up on his direct line at the station. His cell phone also took her straight to voice mail, which was odd; usually, if he couldn't be reached at one, he was available on the other. Susan called the main line to locate him, which she was loath to do, since it involved conversing with Officer Fran Terri, who made the notoriously ill-tempered parole officer Juno Tomisato look like Tickle Me Elmo.

Terri was pleasant as ever when she picked up. Somehow, she made even the standard greeting, "Perrick Police Department, how can I help?" sound like *Fuck you, what do you want?* Susan quickly stated her business—no pleasantries for this one.

"You should call Ed's direct line," Terri barked, as if that hadn't already occurred to Susan.

"I did. And his cell. No answer. Which is why I'm now trying you." *You crabby bitch.*

"He's not here."

Susan waited for additional information, which she should have known better than to expect. Extracting anything other than the bare minimum from the officer was like trying to pull crocodile teeth, though you'd have a better chance of having your hand bitten off with Terri. "Okaaaay. Any idea when he'll be back?"

"None. We've been busy here, with the guys from—" A man yelling in the background, followed by the sounds of a minor scuffle. "Look, I gotta go. Some drunk asshole's trying to tear up the place."

Have fun with that. Susan smirked to herself as the line went dead in her ear.

Despite her smugness, Susan felt oddly jealous of Officer Terri. If there was one thing that Susan couldn't stand, it was missing out on the action.

Chapter 10

For the second time that afternoon, Eric was questioning a group of twenty or so students: "How many of you are here because my class meets a science requirement for transfer?" He'd asked the question under false pretenses, as he knew most of them were only going to lie anyway.

He'd already gone through the first-day rigmarole of taking roll and reiterating key points on the syllabus that students could easily discern for themselves if they only bothered to read the damn thing: *No, I do not grade on a curve. Yes, exams are closed book.* With one class already under his belt, he was less nervous this time around, though still not feeling a hundred percent.

Like in the class before, very few students responded to his query. The ones who did venture to raise their hands did so shyly and with hesitation, as if they suspected Eric was trying to trick them and sniff out those who were only taking the class out of obligation.

Eric smiled his best *Don't worry; I was a student once too* smile. "It's okay, you guys. I'm sure not all of you are here because you just can't get enough of geology." This netted him a few nervous chuckles. "So let me ask again: How many of you are here to fulfill a transfer requirement? One, two . . . five. Ten. Fifteen . . . eighteen," he said, counting the newly raised hands. "Right, so most of you, then."

Though this was not surprising, Eric was still disappointed. He'd grown accustomed to the enthusiasm of his students back in Warrenton, many third- and fourth-year science majors. Like Eric they'd been geeky, and his classroom discussions had often been so animated that he'd had a hard time getting a word in edgewise.

Here at the community college, not so much. Eric hadn't been speaking for even five minutes when half the class turned back to their cell phones and laptops, the importance of social media trumping that of inexpensive public education. It had gone the same during his first class, and he imagined it would be ditto for the next one. His *other* students back in Philly, having shelled out forty grand a year for their educations, had paid attention.

Eric, who rebuffed elitism of any kind, would normally be the first to point out that a university degree was only as good as the student, and one did not necessarily need to spend tens of thousands of dollars to acquire knowledge. Still, he couldn't deny the substantial difference in the manner in which his previous students had conducted themselves. He tried not to take it personally—kids will be kids, as the saying goes—but he couldn't help smarting over the outrageously disrespectful behavior of his Perrick pupils. There were a lot of things Eric would have to get used to in this new teaching environment, and as far as he could tell, none of them were good.

Eric could feel that sharp, cheated bitterness creeping in, a sensation so familiar as of late that it had practically become like breathing. He knew it wasn't fair to those who actually *were* paying attention in class, all eight of them, and he made a conscious effort to squash his negative attitude. As much as he loathed coming to grips with the reality of his situation, this *was* his job and his life now, whether he liked it or not. It would be a long, miserable existence if he constantly dwelled on the past, and it would only make him feel like shit.

(*Don't you mean shittier?*)

"But we're also here because we *love* geology," quipped a heavily made-up blonde, attractive in a pornographic sort of way. She winked at Eric from the first row of seats. She was an older student—at least in relation to her classmates—around twenty-four or twenty-five. "Yes, indeedy."

Just perfect, Eric thought with an internal scowl. *A comedian.* He could feel a migraine blossoming at the crown of his skull. He pinched the bridge of his nose. It did nothing for him.

"Geology is *sa-weet*," jeered some deep-voiced jackass in the back. He was the kind of meathead Eric could picture doing keg stands to impress underage drinkers, the token lecherous older dude at high school parties. Driving a lifted truck with oversize wheels—shrill heavy metal music blasting, spike-collared pit bull slobbering out the passenger window, Confederate flag sticker pasted across the back windshield—taking up two spaces wherever he parked. Sporting a backward trucker hat and barbed wire bicep tattoo, T-shirt adorned with an ultra-classy maxim: NICE LEGS. WHAT TIME THEY OPEN? He was just the sort of asshole who'd chuck his dirty old mattress in front of Goodwill after they'd closed. Use speakerphone in a quiet movie theater. Swear in public in front of children.

Eric would never go so far as to say that he *hated* guys like this.

Though he wouldn't exactly claim to *like* them either.

Eyebrow arched and eyes locked on Eric, the porny blonde bent forward and extracted a glittery notebook from her backpack. She did it in such a way that it provided Eric a perfect glimpse down her shirt at her very large and very shiny

(*fake?*)

breasts, which were now mashed up under her chin by her knees. Slowly, she eased back into her seat. Eric couldn't be positive, but he thought she'd flashed him a smirk. He quickly averted his eyes, already sensing that this one might be trouble.

It wasn't the first time a student had flirted with him, and it surely wouldn't be the last. Back when he was fresh on the teaching scene as a young and single man, Eric had instituted a personal career policy: Shoot it down from the get-go. To not even *flirt* with going *there*, since nothing good could ever come from student-teacher relations. It simply wasn't worth the risk. If things soured, best-case scenario was that he'd have to contend with drama inside the classroom; worst case, he could find himself the focus of a sexual harassment investigation, maybe even a lawsuit. And try getting a teaching job with *that* on your record.

He'd lost count of how many female students had made passes at him in Philly, though none of them had been as brazen as the shiny-breasted blonde. Maybe California girls were just more brazen in general. When he'd first started wearing a wedding band to teach at Warrenton, Eric had assumed the flirting would cease. Much to his bafflement, the ring had only added fuel to the fire, since his marriage implied to young women, fed up with young male immaturity, that he was a real man capable of real commitment. It had only gotten worse after the time Maggie had stopped by his classroom to drop off his forgotten wallet. Clearly, he *must* be a catch, if he could get a woman like *that*.

Even though Eric looked a good five years younger than his true age, he felt ancient when stacked up against his students, most of whom were just a couple of years beyond legal driving age. He liked his women, well, *womanly*, and though they were undeniably cute, to Eric most girls at an undergraduate level seemed teenagery, on the brink of becoming women but still not quite there: pimpled and wrinkle-free, scrawny waistlines and birdy legs. It didn't strike Eric to view them in a sexual realm—to him that would be just plain creepy, like perving on his seventeen-year-old cousin. Eric also liked having a partner he could actually *talk* to, and conversing with a member of the opposite sex got tiresome fast if they weren't on his level intellectually or were too young to get cultural references from his own era: the childhood annoyance of rushing to find a cassette tape to record a song off the radio only to have the DJ start yammering over the end of it, or what he meant when he joked, "Be kind, rewind."

Eric asked, "Are there any of you here who actually *are* geology majors?" Those who did bother to look up from their electronics furnished Eric bored, vacant stares. "Anyone at all?" he added, cringing at the desperation he heard in his own voice.

Finally, a kid sitting in the second row raised his hand. He, like the blonde, was an older student, but shorter. Way shorter. Eric guessed that his height wasn't much taller than four feet—now, what was it you were supposed to say? *Midget* was just as taboo these days as *retard*, not that Eric, himself a veteran member of the mentally challenged brotherhood, would ever use such a derogatory term. Little person? But little people were technically taller, he thought, but then again he could be wrong. Was it . . . dwarf? Yes, that was it. *Dwarf.*

"What's your name?" Eric said to the kid, hoping to get a class discussion rolling. He nearly cursed out loud when he peeked at his watch and saw that sixty minutes remained of the class. The whole damn thing was only an hour and twenty.

"Jake."

"Hi, Jake. Thanks for being here," Eric said conversationally. "Do you have an idea how you'd like to use your geology degree . . ."

Do not pass flashes of light. Do not collect pills. Go straight to crazy. This was a saying of Eric's from way back, a private joke he'd used during times his schizophrenia had reared its ugly head violently, unexpectedly, and without prodromes.

Prodromes, Eric's most valued tool against insanity, acted like a warning system inside his head. Like many schizophrenics, Eric's prodromes were as personalized as a fingerprint; in his case, it was the phantom smell of fresh-cut grass and the sound of parrots squawking. When he imagined either of these two things, he knew to hunker down fast, because shit was about to hit the fan. Big time. It had been quite some time since he'd experienced visual hallucinations without prodromes—ten years at least, probably more like fifteen—but he was now evidently amid a real mental shit storm.

Deep, *way deep*, Inside the Curve.

There was a young boy hovering at Jake's shoulder. He was a cute but grimy little guy,

(I saw you peeking, you cheat!)

dressed like a prairie kid in denim overalls. His clothes were older: worn, yes, but also old-fashioned. He was staring straight at Eric, unsmiling. Eric stared right back—stared right *through* him, as the kid was translucent.

Eric blinked. He blinked a few more times, hoping to flutter the hallucination right from the room. The little boy remained, swiping a hand under his wet nose as he started to sniffle. Eric grimaced. The kid's fingers were bleeding, knuckles exposed down to the bone. With growing horror, Eric noted that his visitor was rotting: skin shriveling and flaking away, eyes sinking back into sockets, hair dropping to the ground in clumps. Flies began to buzz around his small balding skull in a gruesome black halo.

Despite his great many years of practice keeping cool in public during schizophrenic flare-ups, Eric was entirely unaware of his mouth dropping open. The dry-erase board pen he'd been holding tumbled from his fingers, cracking down on the shiny gray linoleum and rolling halfway across the classroom floor. Roused by the abrupt silence, a few students glanced up to give their mute professor their eyebrow-puckered attention. Eric *knew* he should finish his question to Jake. He *understood* that he should still be speaking, but shock had stolen the words from his brain before they'd even had a chance to develop on his tongue.

Pull it together, Eric commanded himself with desperation. Letting the crazy hang out at home was one thing, but in his professional life? Unacceptable.

Slowly, he let out his breath. *It's all right. Breathe.*

The kid nestled up next to Jake, who was now glaring at Eric with an expression that was somewhere between confusion and indignation. The little boy's withering hand jerked up in a swift, unfeasible motion: before at his side, now at Jake's head—an old eight-millimeter movie skipping over a few frames.

The kid gave Jake's earlobe a good hard flick.

Jake didn't exactly *react*, but what happened next was nonetheless astonishing: he shifted in his seat, then rubbed his earlobe, frowning.

He felt it, Eric thought. *Goddamn, he felt it.*

A bystander sensing his schizophrenic hallucinations. Now there was a first.

The kid vanished as suddenly as a dandelion blown apart by a shift in the wind.

"What?" asked Jake, sounding not quite perturbed but getting to be.

Now Eric had the undivided attention of the entire class. The room had grown so uncomfortably silent that, had a mouse farted at that precise moment, it would have reverberated off the walls like a foghorn. Jake seemed understandably offended, since he was probably assuming Eric was gawping at his dwarfism. The idea of offending somebody over what some deemed a disability appalled Eric, but just what could he say? *Don't take offense, Jakey Boy. I wasn't staring at your smallness, but at the rotting kid lurking beside you—by the way, how's your ear?*

"It's nothing," said Eric to Jake with a tight smile. "I . . ." *You what? Hate your new life and have an ex-wife whose Jim-screwing antics have driven you to hallucinations on your first day on the job—you sure you want to be sharing this?*

Jake raised his eyebrows, as if to demand, *Yes, what?* He reached up and rubbed his earlobe, and suddenly Eric wasn't so sure that he *had* felt the little boy.

Then, by sheer dumb luck, Eric caught something that he'd previously overlooked: Jake's clothing. He nearly laughed out loud. It was his T-shirt that was going to redeem Eric, if not to the whole class, then at least to poor Jake.

"Sorry, I was taken by surprise," Eric explained to the confused faces staring him down. He plucked his collar and then gestured toward Jake. "I don't want to get too much off the topic of geology, but I noticed your shirt."

Jake glanced down, perplexed. "Uh . . ."

"Swindled 5. The band?"

He nodded slowly, gave Eric a hint of a smile.

At least he no longer looks so pissed off, Eric realized with some relief. "Two of their members were my students in Philly, way back when. The bassist and the lead singer." Eric hesitated, not sure that he wanted to get so personal. Oh, what the hell, he thought and then added: "We jammed together a couple of times, before they got really big. I play drums—or I used to play drums. Now it's more like an occasional hobby."

A wide grin spread across Jake's face. "Get out of here! They're *so good.* Crazy good."

"They are. Nice guys too."

At that, the students began to relax. A few more even started paying attention.

Maybe, Eric thought, *I might live through this after all.*

After class, Jake shyly approached Eric, who was busying himself with organizing the syllabi for the next round of students. "You know, I'm a musician too."

Eric tapped the packets against the desk to straighten the stack and then set them aside. "Is that right?"

"Yep," Jake said. He raised a hand up to his shoulder and mimed moving a bow back and forth across strings. "I play violin for a band called Augustine Grifters."

"Oh, I like the name. Catchy."

"Thanks. We've got a gig coming up this weekend here in town—well, we're *supposed* to play this weekend, but we've kind of hit a snag."

"Oh no."

"Here's the thing, Professor: I think you might be able to help."

Eric arched a brow. "Is that right?"

"That's right," Jake said with an impish smile. "But before I get into it, I need to ask you a question: Do you believe in fate?"

CHAPTER 11

Yawning noisily—a positive of living on her own, being able to yawn obnoxiously—Susan shuffled into the kitchen to make coffee. It was back to work tomorrow, so she was going out of her way to take pleasure in the simplicity of just *being*: the underlying scent of sweetness amid bitter as she doled six heaping scoops of caramel-flavored coffee grounds into the french press, the relaxed feel of the soft, baggy pajamas that hugged her skin, the crinkle of the morning paper.

In the living room, she turned on the television and flipped through the channels until she found her morning news station. She took a step back toward the kitchen to retrieve her coffee before she wheeled back around to peer at the screen, her mouth ajar.

The hairs on the back of her neck stood at full attention. She *knew* that place, that field and farmhouse. Only she'd been there at night.

She quickly scanned the banner that ran along the bottom of the screen. *LIVE BREAKING NEWS: GRISLY DISCOVERY IN PERRICK, CALIFORNIA.*

"Son of a bitch," she muttered. Immediately, she felt . . .

She didn't know *what* she felt—disgust, anger, and even a bit of embarrassment, she decided, that *her* case had been scooped by a news station. Despite it having occurred over fifty years ago, the murder of Overalls Boy was still a pressing matter and under open investigation. It would only delay her search for answers if she had to waste time, which she now undoubtedly would, responding to inquiries from the nosy public.

She felt a trifle confused.

A news exposé about a body from the 1960s—really? Susan couldn't imagine why a murder that dated so far back qualified as "breaking" news. The disappearance of Gerald Nichol, a convicted sex offender currently loose on the streets, seemed as if it would have precedence. It would certainly be a bigger scandal to exploit.

Susan's frown deepened as it dawned on her that the news station didn't only cover Perrick stories or even those that had occurred all over California. It covered all of the United States. The station itself was based out of New York.

Susan groped for the remote on the coffee table, turned the volume way up.

"... are scheduled to hold a press conference later today," the news anchor was saying in the gravest of tones, though she was wearing a contrastingly bright canary-yellow blazer that seemed far too loud for "serious" reporting. "According to local sources, the bodies of nine children have been discovered on the property so far, and the search will continue . . ."

"Holy shit," Susan whispered. *"Nine?"* How was that possible—had she missed more bodies by the telephone pole? She was sure that she'd been thorough in her search of the property. Then again, she'd been tired, cold, eager to get home. Her blood ran icy at the notion of her negligence, which might now be exposed on a public platform.

Who had actually *found* the bodies? That's what she wanted to know.

Of course, Susan thought with a great deal of irritation, what *she* wanted was clearly not a top priority down at the station. She'd been trying to reach Ed for the past three days, to no avail. She imagined that he'd been busy, but it was strange that he hadn't at least *called* her as a professional courtesy to give her a heads-up about the discoveries. Such oversights, unfortunately, were sometimes a part of the father-daughter-type relationship they shared. Ed probably assumed that she'd always forgive him, which she probably would.

The reporter continued. "Also according to our sources, many of the murders do not appear to have been recently committed, and in fact, the bodies of some victims might date back decades."

Susan sank down into the sofa, her legs as useful as two wet noodles. Nine child murders? Her brain was still having difficulty processing it. How could such gruesome acts have taken place in her seemingly safe little town? Perrick was no stranger to crime, of course, but it had nowhere near the amount as neighboring San Francisco, and murders were few and far between. And when the rare murder *did* occur, it typically stemmed from too much alcohol between acquaintances and heat-of-the-moment lovers' quarrels—rarely in Perrick did citizens murder strangers. The town had certainly never ever experienced anything as horrendous as *this*, the senseless murdering of children.

Susan was wondering if she should reconsider her earlier assumption about Gerald. If the news station was correct, and the murders had not transpired recently, the likelihood of him being responsible was remote. Sure, he might have been sly enough to have gotten away with one or maybe two murders as a teenager, but *nine*? Seemed an unlikely feat for a high school kid living with his parents to pull off.

So *had* it been Wayne all along—was Gerald innocent of the murders? If he was, why had he fled after the first body, Overalls Boy, had been found? Could it be that he was so terrified of returning to prison that he'd simply panicked when he'd seen a police cruiser in his field? It was certainly plausible. The picture Juno Tomisato had painted of Gerald's prison stay had been gruesome enough that even Susan had felt terrified.

There was also the possibility that Gerald had aided Wayne in the killings. A father and son bonding over murder. What a charming thought.

Susan shuddered.

An even more shocking question surfaced: What if Mary was the true killer, and she'd made up that story about her husband being a pedophile to throw everyone off her scent?

Susan shook her head. No, that was a pretty far-fetched theory. Statistically, in 80 to 95 percent of pedophilia cases, the perpetrators are male. Also, Sal had informed her about the town rumors concerning Wayne's creepiness toward kids before Mary had even offered up her confession.

She turned her attention back to the news.

"The first body was uncovered late last week, when R&G repair crews were doing ground excavation due to an unrelated auto collision. We have confirmed that the FBI is assisting Perrick police on the case . . ."

The FBI! When had the FBI gotten involved?

And how was it possible that a news station on the other side of the country knew this before she did—who in the hell were these "sources" feeding the media information?

". . . property's owner, convicted sex offender Gerald Nichol, is at large. Authorities are asking for anyone with tips that may help locate him to call the hotline listed at the bottom of the screen. We will provide updates as we receive them."

Susan hurled the remote down on the sofa. Her hands were shaking badly, though she hardly noticed them through her indignation. She began pacing around the living room, stung that she'd been left out of the loop. The lack of respect!

She had to do *something*, or else she would lose her mind. She decided to start with more coffee. She went into the kitchen to pour herself a cup, spilling about half of it because of her quaking hands. She'd been the officer present for the discovery of the first body—how had nobody down at the station thought to call her? *She* would have made the call, had the roles been reversed.

She marched into the living room, where the information previously given by the sunny-jacketed woman was now being repeated by a man in a somber gray suit—perhaps the woman had gone to change into something in a grimmer shade—and snapped off the television.

Right. To hell with her last day off.

She was going to get some answers.

Chapter 12

Outside the police station was pure pandemonium.

The entire building was surrounded by news vans with their dubious claims—KTLO 2: *Breaking news you can trust!* XTB 10: *Number one eyewitness news delivered!* KIT 5: *Get it here first!*—most from out-of-town stations. Nearby reporters preened for camera close-ups as they practiced lines. While their deliveries varied, the story remained the same. It wasn't every day that a mass grave of children was unearthed—particularly not in a town as wholesome as Perrick—so naturally word had spread fast.

Susan hadn't come in uniform, so thankfully, they let her be.

Inside the station, it was just as chaotic, with people milling about *everywhere*—more than Susan had seen in the building during the last six months combined. Maybe ever. The majority were ghoulish busybodies, in attendance only to glean details about the murders. They were aggravating in their very existence, as their main goal seemed to be to get in everyone's way, Susan's included.

There were, however, some legitimate visitors. Just past the entrance, a couple of stressed-looking officers, arms waving overhead to be seen through the throng, were shouting directions to the volunteers who were gathering to help answer phones for the tip hotline. Wrapped around the front desk was a line of about thirty well-meaning locals coming forward to provide information about the case. Near the back corner of the station congregated a cluster of mostly couples, their voices hushed and eyes red from weeping. Desperate parents of missing children.

Susan quickly averted her gaze when they noticed her staring.

She snaked through the crowd to find Ed. She located him just outside his office, where he was finishing up a conversation with a very tall man in his mid- to late forties. Judging by the way the man was dressed (smart), as well as his manner of speaking (authoritative), she guessed he was high-ranking FBI. He had the *look*. Or at least how she imagined they'd look based on what she'd seen on TV.

Trying to disguise exactly how much she felt like a caricature of a feeble underling, Susan maintained a respectful distance until their conversation was over, pretending to study a text on her phone that her mother had sent earlier that morning about a children's birthday party a friend of hers was throwing for her grandkids. Her mother was helping out with the preparation. **What do kids like these days: ice cream cake or regular?** she had asked. As if Susan knew. She wondered if the text was a veiled dig at her childlessness. *This is what I'm reduced to, throwing parties for children who are strangers, as I have no grandkids of my own.* It was better than her asking about the case, she supposed, though Susan had to wonder if her mother hadn't heard the news yet. If she had, Susan's phone would have been inundated with a dozen or so texts, which would have only added to her vexation. Being scooped by a national news station was one thing, but her own mother . . . well, that just might have pushed her completely over the edge.

The fed, while lean, was intimidatingly muscular, with skin the color of pure coffee and kiwifruit fuzz for hair. *Streamlined* was the word that first came to Susan's mind. A Dyson vacuum cleaner personified. The blindingly white smile he offered Susan as he glided past her in the hall deepened her trepidation. *Hey, we're all friends here. But you'd best stay out of my way, understand?*

Susan offered a polite smile in return, though she didn't mean it. Sure, *he* was smiling—why wouldn't he be? She could already see how it was going to pan out. The FBI. *They* were running the show now, which Mr. Smiley Face had made crystal clear with that smirk. Now all she'd have to do was wait for them to start treating her and her fellow officers like bumbling yokels who couldn't hack working with the big dogs. Just see if they didn't.

Frown deepening, Susan made a beeline toward Ed, who didn't seem all too surprised to see her. "Aren't you off?" he asked just the same, leading her to his office with a lazy step. He closed the door behind them and then took a seat behind his desk.

Susan didn't bother to sit down before she started in with the questions. "So what gives?"

Ed gave her a patient look and waved an upturned hand out in front of his midriff, indicating the crowd outside. "As you can see, we've been busy."

"Why didn't you call me in?" she demanded, sounding far more petulant than she had intended. Or maybe she had. She felt she was justified in her anger, and she wanted Ed to know it.

"Last I checked, I wear the stars," Ed snapped, pointing to the brass pinned to his collar. "I don't report to you."

Susan took a seat and leaned back in the chair, stung and chastened from her verbal dressing-down, remembering her place despite her resentment. He had never spoken to her so harshly, as if she were just some run-of-the mill subordinate.

They *were* like father and daughter, but even Ed had his limits. Apparently.

What stung Susan most was the way Ed had indirectly pointed out her lowly standing on the force by highlighting his seniority, which she could hardly be *blamed* for. It was, as Susan so often reminded herself, one of those things that was entirely out of her hands. For her age and number of years on the job, Susan should have possessed a higher ranking. Much higher. And had she been at a station in a larger city, she probably would have already made detective. But in Perrick, it simply wasn't possible. It wasn't that she'd been passed over for promotions; it was that there were no promotions to give. They were a small force with small-time crimes (until now), and their allotted staff budget reflected this. The only way to move up, it seemed, was to wait for a higher-up to quit, transfer, retire, or die. When Susan had first started at the station as a rookie, a fellow officer—who, coincidentally, was slated to transfer to LAPD at the end of the following month—had made a joke when Susan had professed her ambition to move up quickly through the ranks. "You want to know the fastest way to get promoted at Perrick PD?" he'd said with a laugh that was more than a trifle bitter. "Quit."

In their silence, Susan studied Ed's face, which looked a good ten years older than when she'd last seen him. He appeared edgy, exhausted, his hair a little more gray. Susan was only now realizing just how much Ed had gotten on in years. He *looked* like an old man, which, she supposed, he kind of was. As worked up as she was, she felt sorry for him. Getting on his last nerve was not going to help matters. She said, "I'm sorry. It's just . . . I thought this was sort of *my* case, Chief. Or that we were going to work this one with county?"

"Well, we were," Ed said with a shrug. The edge in his voice had faded. "But once all the bodies started turning up, the sheriff's office handed everything over to the FBI. It's out of my hands now."

"That's what I don't understand—how *did* the bodies start showing up?"

Ed arched a brow. "What, did you think everyone was going to pack it in at Gerald's place just because it was your time off?"

Susan did not enjoy being zinged. "Of course not," she said stiffly. "I'm just surprised nobody called me."

"You were off."

"But I still would have liked to have been called. Who was working in my place?"

96

"Flynn."

"But . . ." *But Flynn's an idiot*, she nearly said.

"But nothing. Other officers also have to put their hours in. I can't reserve all the exciting work for you."

That's hardly the point, she thought.

Susan's anger was threatening to make an encore. It irked Susan—not just being left out of the loop but also how lackadaisical Ed was being about the whole thing.

How could he *not* feel the same indignation that she did? Wasn't the FBI taking over its way of insinuating that they didn't think Perrick PD was competent enough to handle the case on its own?

Susan had heard a few officers call Ed "ROD" behind his back, and the nickname had always pissed her off royally because of its unfairness. Ed had become somewhat listless, sure, but he still did his job. Now, though, *retired on duty*—policespeak for an apathetic cop on payroll—seemed to be a pretty accurate summary of his attitude.

"Frankly," Ed continued, "if the FBI wants the headache, they can have it. We're in no way equipped to handle this sort of thing."

Speak for yourself, she thought.

"We just don't have the resources."

Translation: the Gerald Nichol murders were a colossal mess a man just a few weeks shy of retirement had no interest in cleaning up.

Or maybe it was Ed who doubted the competency of the officers at Perrick PD.

Susan felt like grabbing Ed by the shoulders and giving him a good shake. The biggest case Perrick PD had ever seen, and Ed was passing it off to the FBI like it was infected with smallpox—he couldn't get rid of it fast enough. Ed may not have cared about establishing himself as a crime solver, but Susan did. It was embarrassing to still be at the same position that she'd been at as a rookie, despite the circumstances that had kept her there. A case like this would have given her real clout, catapulted her standing within the force.

After a measured exhale, Susan said, "The thing is, I've still been working the case."

Ed grew very still. "Meaning? You were off, so I don't see how." Suspicious, even.

Susan flapped a hand, exasperated. What did it matter? "This was *before* I was off—on my half shift a few days ago. I went and talked to Mary at the Meadows, remember? She told me some very interesting things. Things I would have told you, had you called me ba—"

"Oh, I'll bet she did," Ed said with the same dismissive tone he'd use with a person claiming they had proof of life on Mars.

"Don't you at least want to hear what she said?"

"Will any of it lead to the apprehension of Gerald Nichol?"

"Well . . . no."

"Then, honestly, I have no interest. Sorry. The priority now is apprehending that son of a bitch before he has the chance to hurt another kid." Ed made a move to stand, a clear indication that he wanted her to wrap things up. "And the sooner the FBI catches Gerald, the sooner they'll be out of my hair. It's been nonstop around here."

Susan wasn't done talking. "So, what, they've just come in and taken over?"

Ed let out an amused chuckle that bordered on sarcasm. "This isn't Hollywood. The FBI doesn't 'take over' police cases. They're *helping* us."

Susan folded her arms across her chest and asked tartly, "Was that a *helper* out in the hall?"

Ed nodded. "Came up from San Francisco. Special Agent in Charge Denton Howell. Works closely with VCAC. Nice guy."

Denton? Sounds pretentious, Susan thought, determined not to like the man. "VCAC?"

"It's a program within the FBI's Violent Crime unit. Don't feel bad; I didn't know, either, until Howell told me. It stands for Violent Crimes against Children," Ed clarified. "They focus on abductions, child pornography . . . really, any kind of violent crime targeted at kids. You can see why they're needed in this case."

"Do they think there are *more* bodies? On Gerald's farm?"

"They've still got agents over there working." Ed shook his head, as if he could hardly believe it himself. "We've just got to wait and see, but there very well could be."

"Jesus."

"I hear ya," he said, looking a little worse for wear. His skin was the color of paste. "I just can't believe that this is happening in *our* town."

"So what now?"

"If or when Howell needs us, we'll make ourselves available. Until then, it's back to our regular duty." Ed must have sensed Susan's disappointment, because he added, "Look, I know you'd like to make a name for yourself, but trust me when I tell you that now would not be a good time. You'd be out of your depth on this one—hell, *I'm* out of my depth, and so is county. Screwing up would be far worse than doing nothing—believe me."

Susan nodded in reluctant agreement, but still. It would have been nice to have at least been given the *chance* to screw up.

Chapter 13

Eric glanced at Jake from the corner of his eye and then brought his attention back to the road. "I still cannot *believe* you talked me into this," he said with a shake of the head.

But really, had Jake given him much of a choice?

The kid had been so earnest in his request that Eric could have hardly said no.

And then there was the whole fate thing Jake had proposed back in the classroom earlier that week, which even Eric, so scientific in his thinking, had to admit was a pretty fortunate coincidence. Jake's band, they of the great name Augustine Grifters, had a show coming up on Saturday—the gig had already been advertised in the local papers, and tickets had been sold. The only problem was that one of their members, Chuck, had sprained his wrist, leaving the band without a drummer. So what great luck it had been for Jake that his new professor *also* played drums, and could Eric please-please-please stand in for a onetime gig (though it would also require a couple of additional nights of practice to learn their songs), because it would really help them out.

The truth was that Eric was more than happy to oblige. He hadn't realized exactly how lonely he'd been until Jake's small measure of companionship had been extended to him. Given the gruesome vision with the boy in the classroom, Eric was beginning to have serious concerns that isolation was literally making him crazy (well, crazier). He knew it would do him a world of good to get out and socialize, and it had. He was feeling far less depressed after getting out, even if it was only band practice.

"Oh, believe it, friend," Jake said with a wicked laugh.

Were they *friends*, though?

After a moment's contemplation, Eric supposed they were. Or at least he suspected that they *would* become friends soon enough; he hoped so, anyway.

Eric tended to take solace in others who'd had weirdness thrust upon them early in life—physical or mental characteristics that would forever place them on the fringe of society no matter where in the world they went, whether it be Perrick, Paris, or Panama City. In Eric's case the weirdness was mental illness; in Jake's it was height, or his obvious lack thereof. It was an existence the average person, no matter how sympathetic, could never understand. The weirdo existence. Eric had discovered that weirdos tended to gravitate toward each other intuitively, as if they released a unique pheromone only others of their kind could detect.

The two men had had a few seconds of awkwardness loading into the car before practice as Jake struggled to reach the passenger seat from outside the Jeep. Eric had stood by with alarming indecision, wondering if he should give Jake a boost or if that would be emasculating or insulting or what, but then Jake finally managed to climb in. After buckling his seat belt, a smirking Jake had offered Eric a suggestion: "If you want to check out my sweet ass, next time just ask." Soon, they were both laughing. It felt natural, their camaraderie, and Eric was more at ease than he'd been for a very long time.

"You know, I'd taken it with a grain of salt when you said your band was its own category," Eric said. "But I've got to give credit where credit is due; I really haven't ever heard anything like you guys." He glanced over at Jake. "And I mean that in a good way. It's like . . . like classic rock, blues, and British rock—more Stones and less Beatles—got together and made a baby. That baby's your band."

Jake let out a throaty laugh. "Thanks, man, I appreciate it. And thank you—again—for helping out. You really got us out of a jam."

"You sure I don't sound terrible? It's been ages since I've played."

"Well, you're no Travis Barker," Jake replied.

Eric pretended to make an invisible note on his hand, muttering, "Okay, that's an F on Jake's next homework assignment."

Jake laughed. "You didn't let me finish! I was going to add a *but*— but you don't suck either. You're good. Tell you the truth, you're a lot better than I'd expected."

"For such an old guy?"

Jake shook his head. "You're not *that* old—I'm practically your age."

"Humph," Eric said with a teasing grunt. "I doubt *that*."

"I'm twenty-eight."

"Seriously? I never would've guessed."

"I get that a lot," Jake said with a sigh. "Must be because I still dress like a teenager."

"Must be it."

Bringing them back to their original topic, Jake said, "No, I was surprised you were so good because you'd said you hadn't played in a long time. You caught on to our songs fast."

"Been listening to you guys' CD. It's helped."

"Why did you stop playing, if you don't mind my asking?"

Eric shrugged. "Eh, you know how it goes. Life gets in the way— work, marriage, obligations."

"I didn't know you were married."

"I'm not," Eric said grimly. "Not anymore." Eric did not elaborate further on his situation with Maggie. Even if he did want to get into it—which he absolutely did *not*—he wouldn't have known where to start.

Jake, thankfully, took the hint. "I just broke up with someone too."

"I'm sorry."

Jake flapped a hand. "Nah, it's all good. It was for the best; we both wanted different things. Kelly, she wants the whole package: marriage, stability, kids, a picket fence. She's ready to settle down."

"And what do you want?"

"Freedom," Jake said and then laughed. "I know it probably sounds selfish, but I need to focus on myself, now that I've gone back to school. Also, we—the band—are starting to book gigs out of state. It's nice to be able to just pick up and go without having to answer to anyone."

"There's nothing wrong with being on your own," Eric said, nearly sounding like he believed it. Changing the subject, he said, "Back when I was in the Complete, we played out of state sometimes. Good times."

"The Complete?"

"That was the name of our band—this was during my college days. We played a few small gigs along the Eastern Seaboard, mainly for the girls and free drinks," Eric said with a little chuckle that was loaded with nostalgia.

"What was your sound?"

"We were pop punk, with a little ska thrown in sometimes, if we could persuade our horn player to travel out of town with us."

"Why'd you guys break up? Creative differences—isn't that what they always say?"

Eric smiled lopsidedly. "No, it was nothing dramatic—for a band, we actually had surprisingly little drama. We just sort of lost momentum after graduation. We joined the masses, got real jobs. Became responsible adults: Engineers. Doctors. Teachers. Husbands. Parents."

The two men went quiet.

Jake broke the silence. "I think you're going to like the bar we're playing on Saturday—Luna's. It's smaller, probably like what you played in college. Mellow crowd. Low key."

"Good, because I'd rather not make an ass of myself in front of a colosseum full of people."

"Oh, stop," Jake said. "You're not going to make an ass of yourself. I'm telling you, you're *good*."

"How about you, though? You're amazing! When you play, it sounds like the violin is actually *singing*." Eric placed a hand over his heart. "It brought tears to my eyes, man. Honestly."

"Aw, thanks," Jake said with the kind of confident modesty one uses when they've been praised so many times for something that they recognize their skill as fact. "Been playing since I was six."

"It shows."

Jake brought a hand up and tapped the windshield. "Oops! Almost forgot that I was giving you directions. Take this next turn. Just up here on the left."

Eric squinted. Although they hadn't been driving that long, they were out in the country now. "What? Down there—is that even a road? We doing a body dump or what?"

Jake chuckled. "I'm showing you a local shortcut. You've got to start learning back roads around here, or else you'll waste half the day farting around in town traffic. It gets even worse in the summertime, when tourists drive through to the coast."

It disheartened Eric to hear Jake talk about shortcuts for locals as if he were one. He supposed he'd have to face facts: he *was* a Perrick local, just like he was also a divorcé and community college professor.

Still, the unintentional sucker punch delivered by his well-meaning new friend smarted, since it solidified his situation. Made it real through vocalization, permanent. It endorsed the idea that Eric's time in Philly was now merely a facet of a former existence he'd never return to—and that all events that transpired henceforth could only occur *if* he got off his ass and started rebuilding his life. That, out West, everywhere he'd go, everything he'd see, and anyone he'd know, love, and fuck (though sex was the last thing on his mind) would be new to him. His friends, his lovers, his hangouts, his possessions, and, yes, even the local directions he learned would all be foreign. *Everything.*

Eric made the turn and saw that there was a long, sprawling field to his left. It had just turned twilight, and the horizon was swallowing up what remained of the sun's rays. "I heard it can sometimes get pretty foggy outside of town," he commented. The field was quite pretty, with an old windmill and a rickety fence that ran across its base. Seeing down-home properties like this in Perrick still struck Eric as amusing, as he'd always imagined California as it was shown in the media—all glamor, beaches, surfers, celebrities.

"Sometimes it gets so thick out this way that it's like driving through a cotton ball," Jake said. "I remember this one time . . ."

Eric's teeth came together with a painful click. He gaped at Jake, who had broken off abruptly and was staring intently out the window.

Eric held his breath, listening. *That sound!* He gave his earlobe a rough tug, and the world went silent.

"Sorry, Jake. I missed that last—"

More screaming! Coming from everywhere inside the car: exploding from vents, blasting from the radio, whooshing up from the floor. It wasn't merely screaming; it was a cacophony of agonized children *wailing*, a soundtrack befitting a kindergarten slaughterhouse in the blackest of nightmares.

Jake placed a hand on Eric's shoulder. "Hey, man, you all right?"

Me? Only hearing a bunch of kids being tortured. You know, just another day in the life of a schizophrenic.

Eric made a controlled effort not to shout as he spoke, since the car would seem quiet to Jake. "Sorry. I'm fine."

"Are you hearing it too?"

Eric's neck cracked as he whipped his head sideward to peer at Jake. "What are *you* hearing?"

"I don't know—it's coming from really far away. It sounds like . . ." He shook his head. "I don't know."

Can he hear it? Eric wondered. Like with the rotting kid back in the classroom, Jake could sense *something*—maybe—but he didn't get the whole picture. *Could* there actually be a metaphysical side to life that only fringe-dwelling weirdos like Jake and himself could detect, some uncanny connection they all shared . . . or was that just crazy tinfoil-hat thinking?

"I'm going to stop so we can get a better listen," Eric said.

As he made a move to pull over, the screaming ceased. Like a switch that had suddenly been flipped.

Then they saw it: the police barricade near the end of the road. As they approached, an officer stepped out and stopped them. He shined his flashlight into the vehicle and then waved them through. A few more official-looking individuals were walking a grid in the field, speaking into walkie-talkies, waving metal detectors. Something big was going down.

"Well, *that's* weird," Jake said. "I wonder what the hell's going on?"

"Way weird. Looks like they're searching for something. But the screaming, I wasn't sure if . . ."

"Sure if?"

Eric bit his lip and then blurted, "I hear things sometimes because I'm, um, a little . . . schizophrenic."

Eric wasn't sure why he'd revealed his dark secret, but he found that he did not regret having done it. If he was truly forming a friendship with Jake, he figured he might as well go in whole hog.

Eric braced himself for what would surely follow, exclamations of *Yeah, right!* or *Are you joking?* (because having schizophrenia is *hil-a-rious*) or, the crowd favorite, *Are you dangerous?*

Jake surprised Eric with his reaction. "That sucks, man; I'm really sorry" was the extent of it, but Jake said it with such solemn sincerity that it nearly made Eric burst into tears. He couldn't recall a time, ever, when somebody he hardly knew had given such a reaction. He was touched.

Eric said, "I've had it for years now, so it really doesn't bother me so much anymore. But listen, nobody at the school knows, and I'd really like to keep it that way since—"

"Hey, your secret is safe with me." Jake made a zipping motion over his lips with his index finger and thumb. "We freaks need to stick together."

"Freaks till the end!" Eric exclaimed, though he didn't know exactly what he meant and felt more than a little corny after saying it.

Jake understood perfectly.

CHAPTER 14

Eric dropped Jake off and arrived home twenty minutes later. He would have made it in ten had he not taken the long way around, but he'd wanted to avoid driving by the field again, with its screaming-kid noises and officer waiting on the side of the road to shine a flashlight in his face.

He parked inside the garage, humming an Augustine Grifters ballad he'd learned during rehearsal. He was in a happy, humming mood—really, he was just happy to be happy.

Inside the house, however, his joy wavered.

Immediately, he sensed something wasn't right. It was the feeling of *otherness*.

He was not alone.

Or he'd had uninvited company while he was away at band practice. He went very still and listened, the feeling that someone had been there lurking around his home but had only recently left intensifying.

Stomach brick heavy, he quickly groped his way to the hallway light, holding his breath as he flipped it on, expecting to find that Doris's cheap television and his expensive turntables (the only big-ticket items he'd brought from Philly) had been liberated from the living room.

He was shocked to find everything still in its place.

But there was a *scent*. A scent so unmistakable that half the Western world could probably identify it in less than three seconds flat. Bread baking.

Eric's initial concern was that he'd left the oven on, which was absurd, since the last time he'd baked up a loaf of bread was never. The only time he *ever* operated the oven was to heat a frozen pizza, and he hadn't had one of those in over a week.

Still, he checked.

Off.

He shrugged. Maybe the scent was coming from a neighbor's place, though it had to be some serious sourdough if it could be detected clear across the yard.

Eric discovered the spilled sugar as he rounded the center island in the kitchen. He felt an immediate pang of violation, the same as if he'd pulled open the blinds and discovered a Peeping Tom goggling back at him. He wrenched a butcher's knife from the block on the counter and searched the house room by room.

It didn't take long. The place was empty.

He now stood in the kitchen looking down at the mess on the floor, realizing with some wonder that he was feeling rather tranquil about the incident. And why not? Whoever had broken in hadn't taken anything—not that there was much *to* take, other than a few minor possessions and Doris's bizarre bric-a-brac out in the garage. It wasn't exactly a death threat, was it? It wasn't even an *implied* threat, only a single name squiggly scrawled in sugar: MILTON.

Having dwelled in metropolises for most of his adult life, Eric was no newbie to home invasion. He'd rented some seriously dodgy apartments as a broke grad student in DC, the sort of low-rent lodgings where robbery might as well have been included in the lease. One place was so sketchy that he'd been robbed twice in the same day: his apartment burgled in the morning while he was at school and then his vehicle hit later at night while he was in bed. What had bothered Eric most about the double theft was the senselessness behind the crimes: they'd taken a dump in his bathtub after discovering that he was out of toilet paper (and boy, you should have *seen* the shower curtain) and busted the $200 driver's side window in his seven-year-old Nissan to steal a pack of gum and $30 worth of CDs.

The sugar mess was clearly the work of kids and not hardened criminals, and a scrawled name was certainly a hell of a lot politer than feces in the bathtub. Probably a bunch of drunken guys out raising hell on their friend Milton's twenty-first. But surely there were better ways to celebrate reaching drinking age than breaking into a random house and vandalizing the kitchen? That was behavior more indicative of teenagers—*young* teenagers at that.

Then again, it wasn't like Eric was still living in Philly. Maybe townie kids were strapped for boozy venues . . . no, that wasn't right either. He'd seen a few decent-looking bars down near the town center—bars like the one he'd be playing with Augustine Grifters. Maybe it was some kind of fraternity hazing: break into a professor's home and make the kitchen floor sticky? But did his community college even *have* fraternities? Maybe it was just a group of bored neighborhood children looking to rebel.

Maybe it was the sugar bandits, he thought and then barked out a demented laugh, though he couldn't figure out why this was supposed to be funny.

He thought about it some more and then laughed again, picturing a group of nervous, pimply-faced preteens standing around his kitchen, brandishing skateboards and plotting their sabotage: *Right, first we're going to toss a bunch of sugar on the floor. Then Milton's going to write his name in it. Asshole won't even know what hit 'im!*

The sugar bandits hadn't even broken a window or jimmied a lock—that was what Eric found peculiar. The house was still locked up tight, so how had they gotten in? And even if he had forgotten to lock up, would the sort of kids who'd toss a whole bag of sugar on the kitchen tiles be so courteous as to secure the house when leaving?

Maybe he should stop playing gumshoe and call the cops already. Yeah, and here's what he'd say: *Quick, send help! I've been victimized by a nefarious posse of sugar bandits! And y'all might want to send for backup—I think they might be diabetic!* Surely Perrick PD had bigger cases to attend to.

(How can you be so sure it was a break-in?)

"Because it was."

(If it wasn't a break-in, then what else could it—)

"No way," said Eric with a shake of the head. Just what, exactly, was being suggested—that he'd vandalized his own house?

"No way," Eric repeated, though not quite as firmly as the first time around. "I don't believe it."

But . . . he *had* heard kids screaming out of the vents in the car, hadn't he?

(And don't forget about the rotting dead kid in the classroom.)

"No." Eric folded his arms across his chest. "No. I'm fine. Just fine. Happy, even."

Eventually, his impatience won out. No matter *what* had happened, he couldn't very well stand there in the kitchen all night, arguing with himself over a mound of sugar.

What he did next was snap a few photos with his phone. Proof, just in case. *Say cheese, Milton.* He then swept up the mess; it was almost like it had never happened. He added *sugar* to the grocery list he kept taped to the fridge and then called it a night.

He'd had such a nice evening up until that point that he saw no reason to spoil it by getting worked up over nothing.

CHAPTER 15

Susan was already five steps into the break room before she noticed Special Agent in Charge Denton Howell and one of his FBI cronies congregating by the area reserved for making coffee. They, too, had noticed her in return, or else she would have quietly backed out the way she'd come in.

Since they were now both giving her a quick tip of the head as a way of greeting, she figured she'd better commit to that cup of coffee she'd planned on making. It was that or stand there in the middle of the break room gaping at them like a simpleton, empty handed.

They scooted off to the side so that she'd have access to the immense variety of coffee trimmings—creamers, raw sugar packets, honey sticks, syrups—the station now had on offer. There was also a fancy machine that made coffee from prefilled pods, and not just run-of-the-mill french roast, either. These were *blends* with jazzy names like Bright Eye Bold, Smooth Italian, and Vanilla Bean Cream. Susan had no doubt that the FBI visitors had something to do with the upgrade, as the selection at the station prior to their stay had been Folgers, plain powdered creamer, and take it or leave it. She was impressed, though she tried hard not to show it. Who were *they* to turn their noses up at Perrick PD's humble coffee?

She selected Vanilla Bean Cream, which she flavored with hazelnut syrup and a dash of cinnamon. She put it in one of the handy to-go cups that were also now available.

As Susan capped her cup, she did a quick once-over of the break room. She'd always known that it wasn't the most elegant of places, but now, with the FBI in their tailored suits standing off in the corner, it felt especially shabby. The walls, last updated when lava lamps were fashionable, were desperate for a lick of paint. The veneer of the only table in the room was chipped in numerous places. The artwork . . . what artwork? Unless a vintage McGruff the Crime Dog poster—TAKE A BITE OUT OF CRIME!—qualified as art.

She picked up a newspaper from the counter and took a seat at the table. She hunkered down close to the page and peered at the title of the first major article she came across—something about a 4-H event happening at the county fair over the weekend—pretending not to listen to the conversation Howell and the other agent were having. They were all business—no chitchat about wives and kids and weekend plans for these guys—discussing the body count at Gerald's place, which had now risen to thirteen. No identifications of any of the victims had been made as of yet, they said, and the majority of the bodies had been found near the house. All of them, in fact, but one.

Overalls Boy.

"It's weird," the agent said to Howell. "That one body is about a football field's distance from all the others."

Howell asked, "Any theories?"

The agent shook his head. He did not seem entirely relaxed in Howell's presence. He seemed eager to impress, to offer up at least *something* that was better than *I don't know.* "Got a couple profilers down at the scene now. They think that maybe the kill was special in some way, maybe his first."

Howell's expression didn't break from the unchanging mask of austerity that Susan had seen him wearing around the station. "Maybe."

"I might have an idea about Gerald," Susan offered before she had a chance to think better of it. Slowly, she lifted her eyes from the paper— she hadn't actually *verbalized* that thought, had she?

The agents were frowning in her direction.

Okay, so she *had* opened her big mouth. Fantastic.

"Gerald?" The agent whose name she did not know smirked.

"Gerald *Nichol*. Sorry, I should have clarified," she said pleasantly. "We tend to use first names around here, if the guy's notorious enough around town, which he is."

"Right." The agent gazed at her with a look that bordered on incredulity. *Why are you, piddling Small-Town Officer, speaking to us? Because if a team of highly trained FBI agents can't come up with a theory, I'm sure you'll solve the case now with all your infinite wisdom of traffic stops and emergency house calls over stolen apples.*

Denton Howell was harder to read. His eyebrow raised a millimeter. *Maybe* a millimeter. "What's this theory of yours?"

Now Susan wasn't so sure of herself. Or her theory. "Well, it could be nothing, but I interviewed a witness a few days back, Mary Nichol. She's Gerald's mother—"

"At Emerald Meadows, right?" the smirking agent said.

Susan swallowed. "That's right."

"We tried her already," he said dismissively. "Got nothing from her that made any kind of sense. She's senile, thinks the year is 1955."

Susan frowned, the back of her neck feeling hot enough to fry an egg. Senile? No, that wasn't right. Mary was sharp as a tack—sharper than half the so-called witnesses who'd come forward with "tips" about Gerald. Seemed Mary had put on a little show for the FBI. "Well, no, actually—"

"Hello, agents. What are we discussing?" Ed asked as he came striding into the room, all smiles and false cheer.

Uh-oh, Susan thought. *Look what you've done now.*

"What else?" the agent said in an obnoxiously jokey fashion, as if the answer was obvious. Which, Susan supposed, it was. The Gerald Nichol case was all anyone seemed to be discussing down at the station. And in town, for that matter. A person couldn't stand in line at the market or run on the treadmill at the gym without overhearing at least one person talking about it. "Officer—" He looked at Susan, his eyebrows raised, and she gave him her name. "Officer *Marlan* here was just telling us about her witness interview with Mary Nichol."

Ed snorted. He glanced at the new coffee installation with a look of marked disdain and then poured himself a cup of black coffee from the Mr. Coffee machine that out-aged Susan by about ten years. "Mary? Hell, I'd take anything she has to say with more than a grain of salt."

The agent nodded as if to say, *My thoughts exactly*. Howell didn't really seem to have an opinion on the matter.

On his way back out, Ed stopped in the doorway and said over his shoulder to Susan, "A quick word?"

Susan knew how bad it looked, as if she had gone into the break room with the intent of going over Ed's head to speak directly with the FBI. She didn't dare look at the two agents as she left, but she could feel their eyes boring into her back. Well, that was just great; they thought she was an idiot.

Ed shut the door to his office, which was never a good sign. He sat down behind his desk with a long sigh, as if the movement itself was a strain to his bones. "What, exactly, did you think you were doing in there, Officer Marlan? I thought I made it clear to you that you no longer were working the Nichol case."

He'd addressed her by title. Also not a good sign. Susan spoke fast—a little too fast. "I know it looks bad, but I promise you that I was not trying to be sneaky." She quickly explained that she hadn't even known that the agents were in the break room—that she would have, in fact, actually avoided going in there, had she known they were present. She went on to say that she'd inadvertently heard them discussing the case (which wasn't *entirely* untrue) and figured that she'd offer up the information that had been provided to her by Mary.

"Which was what?" Ed said, exasperated. *Go on—drop on me this load of bullshit*, he might as well have said.

"It was what I tried to tell you before, but you didn't want to listen."

"I'm all ears now."

Susan seriously doubted that, but she continued anyway. "Which part do you want to hear first: Mary's confession of the Wayne Nichol murder, or the part where she said that her husband or son—or both—probably murdered the kid next door in the sixties, who I believe might be Overalls Boy?"

Ed muttered something under his breath that sounded a lot like *Jesus Christ*. He shook his head in evident frustration. "You shouldn't be wasting the FBI's time with this stuff—these ravings from an old woman. And she didn't *kill* her husband. It was an accident—bad food or something."

So you think. Susan did not want to waste time debating the logistics of Wayne's demise, though she found it odd that Ed could recall specifics about it when he so often claimed ignorance about other cases when he was not in the mood to discuss them. Especially once they'd already been closed, which in Ed's mind was the equivalent of the crime having never occurred. Selective memory, she imagined. "That's the thing. They're *not* ravings, Ed. A farm kid *did* disappear. The Nichols' *neighbor*, in fact, a boy named Lenny Lincoln, while he was playing hide-and-seek with his brother, Milton—"

"Now that's enough!" Ed roared, the veins under the skin of his neck bulging. Susan could have sworn that the window rattled in its pane. He sat up very straight in his chair, rubbing his temples with his eyes closed.

Susan froze in place. She could hear the second hand ticking in the clock on the wall, the phones ringing at cubicle desks. She couldn't find her words. Here was a side to Ed that she'd never seen, a truculent beast that the FBI had unleashed with their presence. Ed was too stuck in his ways, aggravated by intrusions. For the first time that day, Susan was noticing how bloodshot his eyes were. She hadn't really given it much thought before, but now she realized exactly how much Ed needed to retire. If he stayed on much longer, she feared the stress might kill him.

How is your heart, Ed? she wanted to ask. Instead, she said, "I was only trying to help."

"Here's the thing: The FBI don't *need* your help. They've got about a dozen agents working here in Perrick, including the head honcho himself, Howell. They've got dogs and forensics—and even a botanist, I heard—out in the field and everything else they could ever possibly need." Ed sat back in his chair, his voice scolding but soft. "I know you're only trying to do some good; I understand that, but the last thing they need is another chef in the kitchen. And believe me when I tell you that any new information you might *think* you have about Gerald and his neighbors—they've already got it. They're the *FBI*, for Christ's sake! Their reach is a lot longer than ours; they have resources we can't even *dream* of."

"Okay, I'm sorry," Susan said quietly, her voice quaking.

Sorry that Ed was under stress, sure, and sorry that he felt emasculated by the FBI's presence, but not sorry for trying to do her job.

She was having a hard time letting go, and the reason for that was because she felt as if she shouldn't *have* to. Not with it being her case to begin with. She pushed just a little more. "It's just with the kid disappearing *right next door* . . ." She sat back in her chair, shook her head. "Doesn't it seem like a massive coincidence?"

Ed sighed, but not unkindly, his expression now pitying. "I've said it a thousand times to other officers in the station, just as I've already said it to you, and I'm going to repeat myself now: It's always tough when kids are involved. And it never gets easier."

Susan felt almost dizzy from the emotional roller coaster she was being forced to ride on Ed's behalf. Was he pissed off or sympathetic to her plight? And what did the bit about cases involving kids being difficult have to do with the price of tea in China?

Susan opened her mouth to speak, and Ed held up a hand to silence her.

He continued. "But that doesn't mean that you should lose your head whenever a case involves one."

A rod of indignation heated up at Susan's core. She resented the implication that she was somehow being hysterical by sticking to her guns, following through with her investigative work. "I hardly think I'm *losing my head*, Chief. I was simply trying to relay information that a witness provided. It pertains to a current case."

"How does Mary Nichol's alleged"—*alleged* again like *bullshit*— "murdering of her husband pertain to the case?"

"Well, not *that* part. I'm talking about the missing neighbor kid, Overalls Boy."

"You don't even know if the neighbor *is* Overalls Boy! In fact, there's a greater chance that it *isn't* than it is."

Susan folded her arms across her chest. "How's that?"

"Look, it's probably hard for you to imagine, having grown up with modern parenting." Ed took a sip from the coffee cup steaming on his desk. "Now, I can see you're getting offended, Susan, but I mean nothing by it. All I'm trying to say is that kids weren't coddled in the sixties like they are now. Parents did things back then that would probably land them in jail now—hell, I remember my own dad sitting me on his lap in our truck to let me steer through downtown. I thought it was a hoot! I got smiled and waved at by other drivers. My point is that it was a different time. Kids were left alone at a very young age, and if they had a slightly older sibling, hey, great, that meant babysitter. Usually, things were all right, but not always."

Susan sat forward on her chair. "Meaning?"

"Meaning that a kid disappearing back then was not as uncommon as you think. Now, I'm not saying it was unsafe for kids in a predatory way, but more in an environmental way. You think Perrick is 'country' now; you should have seen it back then. Everywhere you looked, there were fields—fields for miles and miles—and just as many wooded areas. Kids sometimes got lost in them and were attacked by animals or froze to death before they were found. People also had these giant pits behind their houses that they used to throw all kinds of stuff in—old tires, refrigerators, rotten wood. They were deep, like swimming pools, and they *became* like swimming pools after it rained, with the sides all slippery. Sometimes kids would fall in one of those, not be able to climb back out. They'd drown in the mud."

"Jesus."

"So you see now why you should just forget what Mary told you. I don't want the FBI sent on a wild-goose chase because of something that woman *thinks* she knows." Ed took another sip of coffee, cracked his neck. "And I can't have you going around the station convoluting the facts with gossip and false leads. The biggest way you can help out on the case is to *not* help out."

Susan raised her hands so that her palms were facing her boss. "Okay, okay," she said, doing her best to sound amiable. Like she was simply going to let things go, give up the search for answers. "Request received loud and clear."

"That wasn't a request; that was an order."

But giving up had never been Susan's strong point.

Chapter 16

Eric was pulling into the garage when his cell phone vibrated in the cupholder. He scowled when he saw the caller ID. "Oh, fantastic. *Just* what I need."

He took a breath and then tapped answer.

She was off before he said hello. "Eric? Is that you?"

"Yes, Maggie, it's Eric." He tried not to sound condescending, but the way she said his name in that skeptical tone had wound him up even back when they'd been together. What did she think, that he had hired an imposter to field his calls for the occasions she rang? If only. "Is there something wrong with the papers I sent? Because if there is, you should really talk to the mediator—"

"What are you doing right now?"

Eric cut the engine and hit the clicker on the rearview mirror, closing the garage door behind him. He placed a hand on the door handle but then pulled it away quickly, as if the metal were hot, opting to stay inside the vehicle until their exchange was over. He didn't want to bring poisons from the past into his home, even if it was only a phone conversation. Thus far, his house had remained Maggie-free, and he intended to keep it that way.

He would have avoided talking to her altogether, but there was still the matter of the divorce. To move the process along faster and cheaper and to save themselves a trip to court, they'd hired a mediator at Eric's suggestion. He was hoping now that this wasn't a mistake.

"Actually, I've just pulled in from my new job." He'd said *from my new job* with such contempt that he could have added *and fuck you for being the reason I had to take it* and achieved the same level of vitriol. Sighing, he pressed the heel of his palm into his left eye socket and gave it a couple of grinding twists. His migraine from earlier was back with interest. "I haven't had the best day, so—"

"I lost the baby."

Eric curled his free hand around the steering wheel. "What baby?" he said, just to say something. As if he didn't know.

"My baby!" she shrieked, the subtext being *How are you such a goddamn idiot?*

"Oh." He paused to let the information sink in. "Okay." He wasn't sure how he felt about the news—no, the truth was that he didn't *want* to know how he felt about the news, because he suspected a trifling part of him might feel more than a little joyful about it. He cleared his throat, stalling, formulating what to say next. "So . . . thanks for telling me."

Maggie exhaled sharply, and Eric could just *see* her face scrunching up into an ugly twist of fury. They hadn't been married long, but he knew her well enough. "Is that all you've got—'Thanks for telling me'?"

He was tempted to remind her, *Hey, you're the one who called me, toots*, but he let it slide. He could hear her crying. She was doing it softly but right into the phone so that he'd know. *Soothe me. Say all the right things and make ME feel better. It's all about me. Me. ME!* So typical Maggie.

Eric unclenched his jaw. "Maggie, I'm so sorry this has happened to you—"

(Liar, liar, pants on fire.)

"—but I really don't know what to say."

"How about a little sympathy, you robot!"

Eardrum ringing, Eric pulled the phone away and gave his ear canal a quick swirl with his pinkie. He returned the phone to his cheek and said with strained calmness, "You can't be serious. You were pregnant with *my brother's* baby."

She sniffed. "How can you be so cruel?"

Eric's hand tightened around the steering wheel, choking it. He could sense that he was taking her bait, being manipulated like a doofy little puppet. Maggie always knew exactly which strings to pull—and how to pull them *fast* for maximum frustration.

"H-how can *I* be so cruel?" he sputtered, and then he was off, brittle scabs ripped clean from his emotional wounds in one fell swoop. "Do you actually *hear* yourself right now? You were mine! Mine! Not his! You vowed to love and honor *me*, honor *our* marriage! What I can't figure out is why you even bothered staying married to me when half the time Jim was . . ."

Eric clamped his teeth together until the temptation passed. He'd nearly finished with *sticking his dick in you*, but that sounded vile even to him. Despite the misery Maggie had caused and continued to cause him, he didn't want to strike her below the belt. He supposed it was because some part of him—a part that dismayed him more than anything else about his character—still loved her. Even after all she'd done, and even though he'd never get back with her no matter how much she begged (though he suspected he'd be rolling snowballs in hell before *that* happened), some secret, shameful part of him still loved the woman.

A rush of memories: Laughing in the snow, Maggie cupping his fingers under her mouth, warming them with her steaming breath, teasing the tips with her tongue. A lipstick-kissed Post-it Note on the pillow: *Gone to work early. Love you more than ice cream! xoxo*. Making love in her studio, bright canvases towering above, smudges of orange and yellow paint coloring their skin. Gripping her hand in the doctor's office, a saltwater fish tank humming softly in the wall behind them; no, there was nothing they could do to help ease the pain in his dying father's cancer-riddled bones. Maggie rocking him as he sobbed against her breast. "Shhhh-shhh, hush now. It's all right. We'll get through this, E. We'll get through this. Hush, baby, hush . . ."

Still, Eric couldn't help drifting back in time to the afternoon he'd discovered The Affair. He remembered how he had struggled to relieve himself of his wedding band during the sprint back to the home he and Maggie would never share again, not even for one more goddamn night. Because of the thrashing Eric had administered to Jim, he couldn't get the ring to wriggle up past his engorged knuckle. After a quick swap of jackets—he'd already traumatized far too many of Philly's fine citizens during his blood-soaked flight from the Moonflower Café—he high-tailed it to the nearest mall, where he had a jeweler cut the ring off his finger with what looked like a miniature version of the Jaws of Life. He wept the whole time.

Later, he wept some more as he sat alone at the kitchen table polishing off the eye-wateringly expensive bottle of champagne they'd been saving for their five-year anniversary, longing with each harsh gulp for Maggie to come skulking through the door, begging for his forgiveness. She never showed. In true coward's fashion, she stayed away for six whole days. When she finally came around, it was only for short bursts of time and conveniently while Eric was at work so that she could snatch armloads of toiletries and changes of clothes like a cat burglar trying to evade arrest. It hadn't required much speculation on Eric's part to gather where she was hiding out.

Eric opened again with "Look, you've caught me a little off guard. Like I tried telling you before, now is not the best time for this conversa—"

"Right. Like there ever *is* a good time for you." Maggie spat a curt, bitter laugh. "You really *do* believe that you can avoid dealing with us until the end of time, don't you?" She did not specify if the *us* in question related to the two of them and their failed marriage or her and Jim and their upcoming one.

That is the plan, my dear ex-wife.

"Well, you can avoid me all you want—and I hope that isn't what you want, since I'd like for us to move forward in a positive way, and because I'm here to stay. But you can't cut Jim out of your life—he's your *blood*." Ah, so it was Maggie-Jim "us."

Eric was on the brink of saying something constructive when a childish "ha!" beat him to it, projecting from his mouth a fine spray of spittle that settled on his chin hotly. He didn't bother wiping it away. What he *did* wipe away were the tears that had begun to sting the corners of his eyes, first with his index finger and then with the back of his hand when he needed something larger to get the job done. He would *not* shed one drop over Maggie and Jim. Not *one*. Were they sitting around crying over what they'd done to him? Hell no. Too busy getting pregnant and planning a wedding.

Eric said, "*Sure*. That explains why Jim hasn't called *once* since I kicked the shit out of him. And rightfully so, might I add."

"I don't think he really knows what to say," she said, and Eric thought, *Well, that makes two of us.*

"Okay, Maggie, I'll play ball," Eric said at last. "But first, how about you tell me exactly what it is that you're hoping to get out of this conversation. Is it: *No hard feelings about everything? Let me know when the wedding is; I'll send a gift? No, it isn't* at all *creepy and incestuous, you now being with my brother?* Because if that's what you're after, I should probably tell you now that it's *never* going to happen."

She made a loud, breathless sound, as if she'd been smacked. "Don't you talk to me like that! You don't *ever* get to talk to me like that!"

There was only one color Eric was seeing, and it was red. Bleeding, violent red. "I mean, Jesus Christ, Maggie! Did it ever occur to you what you were going to tell that poor kid when it grew up? You two are like some kind of *Springer* episode: 'Pregnant with My Husband's Brother's Baby.'"

"You're *not* my husband anymore!" Maggie screamed. "When will you get that through your *thick head?*"

(And the hits just keep on a-comin'!)

"You won't have to worry about changing your last name again once you and Jim get married. So that's a plus." When her string of obscenities ended, Eric said, "I'm guessing I was still with you when it happened."

"When *what* happened?"

(Are you sure you want to go there? You may not want to know the answer to this one.)

"When *he* got you pregnant."

Since learning of the pregnancy, Eric had been telling himself that he'd been out of Maggie's life long before Jim had made her a mother. He couldn't wrap his mind around the other grotesque possibility, which was that they'd shared a bed while Jim's spawn was growing inside her. He'd never confronted her on the subject before today.

Call it morbid curiosity; now Eric *had* to know. It was a need he felt on such a deep level that it was almost cellular, and if she chose to withhold, he imagined it would feel like something close to torture. "You and I were still living together as husband and wife when Jim got you pregnant."

Her silence gave him the confirmation he'd been seeking. So she'd been further along in her pregnancy than he'd previously assumed. He started to do the math and then felt too sick to continue.

"I'm so sorry, Eric," Maggie sobbed. "We never set out to hurt you. If it makes you feel any better—"

"Nothing you have to say, Maggie, could possibly make me feel better. Not about anything. Not now and not ever."

"Things have been tense with Jim," she continued. "Since we lost the baby."

"When *did* you lose the baby?" Eric asked in a flat tone, not particularly needing to know but asking anyway. The conversation had become like hideous airplane-crash footage he was seeing on the news, and he couldn't find the will to change the channel.

"About a week and a half ago."

"A week and a half ago," he echoed.

"I just . . . I thought I should tell you before you heard it from somebody else." She sniffed.

Eric opened his mouth to ask her: *Who do you think would provide me with such information?* Before he could form the words, she was speaking again.

"He's not like you. Jim. You were always so . . . *nice* about things. Jim can be . . . he's just . . . *distant.*"

"I am *not* hearing this." The phone started to quake against his ear, his knuckles going white from how tightly he was gripping the thing. "Are you actually *fucking serious* right now?"

Sobbing. "I'm so sorry about everything! If I could take it all back!"

Eric took in a long breath before he spoke. "My advice to you, Maggie, is to go on the pill before Jim has a chance to knock you up again." He was stunned by how smoothly the words had seeped out, like scalding soup dribbling from his lips. Eric knew with absolute certainty that he'd later feel guilty for saying such an awful thing, but damn if it didn't feel amazing in the moment, when he was positively *drunk* with outrage.

"And you think Jim's distant now? Give it a few years," he powered on. "Let's see how he's treating you when you're no longer a novelty but his newest coeds are. Actually, I bet there already are at least a half dozen pretty young things lined up to take your place. How old *are* you now, come to think of it?"

Maggie was crying so intensely that her words came out in garbled jags. But Eric understood her, all right. *I hate you.* As if to clear up any confusion, she shouted down the phone: "*I hate you* so much *right now!*"

"You should consider yourself lucky on that one," Eric said with a mildness that sounded remarkable even to him. "At least you only have *one* person to hate. I have to worry about two."

Click.

"Hello? Hello?" Eric lobbed the phone at the passenger seat with all his might, and incredibly, it bounced back, cracking him square on the chin. "*Fuck!*"

Eric snatched up the phone with one goal in mind: he was going to call Maggie back if only to experience the satisfaction of hanging up on *her*. If there was one thing he hated—the one act that could truly drive him to murder, he reckoned—it was when a person hung up on him. The ultimate disrespect, as far as he was concerned.

As Eric was about to go through with the call, however, he stopped to consider what he was going to say once she picked up. *You're a bad person. Thanks for ruining my life. How could you?* Because when it came to Ye Olde Fucked-Up Situation of Eric and Maggie, all that could have been said—and all that probably should *not* have been said—had pretty much already been stated.

With that thought, Eric pocketed his phone and exited the Jeep.

On the way into the house, he stumbled over the bottle of wood cleaner he'd carelessly left in the middle of the walkway. He dropped his satchel and seized the bottle, and like the phone, he nearly lobbed it . . .

Before he knew it, he was rolling up his sleeves and pouring a splash of cleaner onto a rag. His belly hitched when he neared the trunk. Eric patted a burp out of his chest; his fast-food dinner, combined with the lingering stink inside the trunk, had given him a slight case of the queasies.

(Or it was the conversation with Maggie.)

Okay, fine, it was probably the conversation with Maggie, though he wasn't going to dwell on it now. Nope. Eric took a seat and wedged the daisy kneeling mat under his rear, his brain focused on finding a topic unrelated to his ex-wife. He settled on the upcoming show at Luna's.

The nausea soon passed, and Eric went about scrubbing the trunk's inside. He removed remnants of lining that remained in the seams, balling shreds of faded blue silk on the ground by his thigh. When it was all gone, he stepped back to behold it. The trunk was cleaning up quite nicely, and for the first time since purchasing it, Eric could discern its hidden beauty: rich wood grain, solid brass hardware, an overall robustness. It had come from an era when things were built to last, and he could imagine it living on for a few more centuries. It was a shame he didn't have kids,

(Jim and Maggie might)

since it would be a fantastic heirloom to start passing down through the generations. Even with the hole in the bottom, and even with that stench (which was finally starting to dissipate, thank Christ for small miracles), he'd still gotten an amazing deal for twenty dollars. Once it was fully restored, it just might be the nicest thing he owned.

(Though that's not too great an achievement, considering you don't own much now, anyhow.)

Eric flapped the rag down at his side. "What *is* your point?"

Right away he thought: *If anyone walking by outside earlier didn't think I was nuts when I was shouting at my wife*

(ex-wife)

over her having my brother's baby, then they certainly do now after hearing me snap at my invisible companions.

He surprised himself by snickering. Really, what else *could* he do at that stage but laugh?

Eric fell silent as his phone vibrated against his hip. He knew who it was before he even checked the caller ID to confirm. Maggie, adding insult to injury, now calling from home—*his* former home.

This should be good, he thought and then spoke with sharp meanness he felt high up in his scrotum. "Yes? What *now*?"

"Hi, Eric . . . I know you don't want to talk to me, but . . ." A nervous clearing of the throat.

Eric's grip loosened, and the rag sank to the floor in a woozy, chemical swirl. Then so did he, knees groaning as he fumbled back on his haunches, joints alarm-slackened, dropping, dropping, until the bones of his butt felt the coldness of concrete pressing up through the seat of his pants.

"Eric? Just listen, all right? Please."

Eric rooted for anger, finding it effortlessly in the pit of his belly. He seized it hard. "The *fuck* I will—"

"I'm an asshole, all right? I don't deserve you as a brother. And I don't deserve any sort of forgiveness—"

"Not in *this* lifetime."

"I crossed the line. What I did . . . it was unconscionable. Deplorable—"

Jim's groveling, Eric thought. *He only uses big words when he grovels.* "Fuck you, Jim! *Fuck! You!*"

A pause. "Okay, well . . . I can't say I didn't expect this."

He sounds amused—uncomfortable but amused. The cheeky bastard is relishing this. "If you have something to say, I suggest you get on with it. Because after this conversation, I don't ever want to talk to you again. You *or* Maggie."

"We've been through tougher things than this. Mom and Dad—"

"Don't you *dare*."

"I miss you, little brother. I'm so, *so* sorry," Jim said with what sounded like genuine remorse. "If I could go back in time . . ."

Throat tensing, Eric felt his grudge-holding resolve began to slip away. Maybe it was purely the sound of his brother's voice, which he realized how much he'd been missing now that he was hearing it. He was still light-years away from forgiving Maggie, but maybe he *could* try burying the hatchet with Jim . . .

His eyes fell to the nearly faded band of white flesh that marred the bare ring finger on his left hand, and he bristled all over again. He shook the idea from his head. He was not ready to forgive and forget. Not even *close*.

Jim responded to Eric's silence with a long sigh. "Fine," he said, as if that settled it. "I was calling about Maggie, anyway."

"What about her?"

"Look, I know I'm in no position to ask for any favors—"

"You've got that right."

"Can I please finish?"

Eric's curiosity got the better of him. "What is it?"

"Maggie has been having a hard time lately—you've heard about the miscarriage." Jim paused, probably anticipating some type of response.

Eric wasn't going to give him the satisfaction of one.

"You might think that she doesn't feel guilty about . . . about what happened, but the truth is that she does. She's really hurting over the whole thing. You know what she's like; she can't stand having anyone upset with her." Jim paused. "She hasn't been eating or sleeping. She's been depressed. I've been worried about her . . ."

"So?" As much as Eric had been loath to accept it, and as much as he wanted to imagine that Jim was still out cruising the field like the player he'd been all through his twenties and thirties and even much of his early forties, he was now starting to wholly comprehend that his brother's interest in Maggie ran deeper than a cheap fling.

My God, he actually loves *her*, he thought with more than a little astonishment. *Jim is* in love *with my ex-wife. My Maggie.*

"So maybe you could go a little easier on her?" Jim asked. "We—*I* . . . I'm in no position to ask for sympathy, but this is serious. She lost a baby, and I'm worried that it was because—"

"I'm going to stop you there," Eric said. He was utterly drained, no longer sad or angry. He was done. Just *done*. "I can't do this right now, Jim. I just can't. I *will* go easy on Maggie, but that's only because I won't be taking any more of her calls. Yours either. I don't forgive either of you, and I doubt I ever will. You're going to have to live with that, just like how I've learned to live with what you've done to me."

"Come on; at least let's—"

"I've said what I have to say. If you and Maggie are as sorry as you claim, then you'll both respect my wishes. If the time ever does come when I feel like reaching out to you, I know where to find you. You are, quite obviously, now living in *my* house."

Eric could hear Jim speaking fast as he disengaged the call.

"Prick," he muttered as he pocketed the phone once more. He shook his head. "Jesus Christ, what a day."

(She was right earlier, you know. Maggie. You can't avoid this Jim situation forever.)

"But I can avoid him for the time being," Eric said, scooping up the ball of tattered blue silk. He deposited it into the garbage bin and slammed down the lid. "And you can't call olly when you're the one hiding . . ."

Eric stopped dead in his tracks. Now, what the hell was *that* supposed to mean? And who the hell was Ollie?

Hands on his hips, Eric asserted to the quiet, empty room: "Okay, enough is enough. You need to get a grip."

He was done dealing with Maggie and Jim. Done debating with invisible companions. Done feeling like shit. Though his life was still not perfect (though when was it ever?), he'd finally managed to get it (slightly) back on track and to a point where envisioning some semblance of a future without his ex-wife was not entirely incomprehensible.

With a childish stamp of a foot, he added: "Humph. That's right. Tonight, right here, *right now*, you're going to get a grip."

Eric believed himself too. But as he approached the trunk to get back to business, his guts bubbled up in his throat. He stumbled over the bottle of cleaner once again as he sprinted inside to throw up.

CHAPTER 17

When Eric was a young boy, he had a cocker spaniel named Lucy.

Lucy was intended to be Jim's, too, but shortly after their father had brought her home as a puppy, it became clear which son the dog favored. Despite Jim's repeated attempts at bribery—squeaky toys, bones, beef jerky—it was Lucy and Eric who became thick as thieves, the two inseparable on days Eric wasn't in school.

Lucy used to pad into Eric's room every night while he was sleeping and jump up on the bed, where she'd curl herself into a furry little ball and nestle down into the quilt Eric kept for her near his feet. Lucy never awakened Eric when she did this, but some part of him always knew she was there, her breathing and her warmth never failing to bring him comfort.

This pleasant childhood memory was brought to Eric's mind as he now felt a weight resting at the foot of the bed. However, unlike Lucy, it brought him no comfort whatsoever. The mass emitted an unhealthy charge, the itchy radiation of a heated laptop cooking skin. Whoever—*whatever*—it was also breathed differently than the gentle manner of his beloved pup. It wheezed, drawn-out gasps suggesting that each pained breath might be its last.

It was all wrong, unpleasantly *off*.

Eric thought of Maggie. At the core, she was a free-spirited artist, so the way she'd insisted on making their bed with suffocating hospital corners had always struck him as ironic. Maggie's feet were tiny for a woman of her height, and so the pull of the sheet hadn't bothered her. It had irritated Eric immensely. It had not only pinched his size twelves, sore from walking campus all day, but also made him feel mummified. The hospital-corner battle was constant during their marriage, and it was one Maggie typically won, since Eric had run late most mornings and thus hadn't concerned himself with minor troubles like making the bed. Now Eric got up early each day to tidy the bedroom, smoothing blankets over mattress with spitefully sloppy edges.

Eric kicked a foot up and over to loosen the sheet, an instinctive maneuver he'd executed nightly during his marriage. The movement didn't alleviate the tension, and now Eric was rising up, up, up through waking layers of fitful slumber. He'd gone to bed early, his uneasy stomach continuing to bother him to such a degree that he'd begun to worry that he'd caught the flu from one of his students—and wouldn't *that* just be the icing on the shit cake of his new job? He rolled onto his back lazily and peeled open his eyes, giving the ceiling a resigned sigh. A tickle caught in his throat, and he coughed dryly, parched from vomiting earlier.

He needed water.

Eventually thirst won out over laziness. It was as Eric turned to ease himself out of bed to go and get that cold drink that he finally noticed his two intruders.

The creature was what he spotted first, floating in front of the bedroom's long windows. Hidden within the gauzy white curtains at an impossible height, its pointy, deformed silhouette started about four feet up, as if it lacked a head and legs but possessed a narrow, protruding chest. A grotesque alien form gurgling and snorting in a manner no human is capable of.

The second visitor was somebody with whom Eric had already formed an acquaintance. The little boy from the classroom. He wasn't rotting or partaking in any ear-flicking antics; now he played a game of jacks at the foot of the bed, bright-red ball bouncing high before his freckled face, moving sluggishly, as if floating through gel. When the ball came back down, the boy's grubby hand vanished right into the mattress along with it, materializing again with a scoop of silver and red.

For the first time since awakening, Eric became aware of the boy's wheezing, which his tired brain had previously dismissed as wind beating against the house and which now seemed as if it were blasting right against his ears. The excitement of the game had agitated the boy, and he sounded on the brink of a fatal asthma attack.

He played on, taking no notice of Eric.

Eric had frozen midmotion: head tilted back; bicep, hip, and foot pressing against the mattress on one side; bent elbow aimed toward the ceiling and leg hovering on the other; midsection twisted. It would be a painful pose for anyone to hold for even a few seconds, worse with the boy's weight pressing down against the blankets. Eric, muscles cramping and starting to quake, wasn't fazed. He was too focused on the creature, which had begun to sway within the curtains.

The creature, with its strange, frightening, inhuman sounds.

A small voice at the back of Eric's mind implored him to squeeze his eyes shut so that he wouldn't have to gaze upon whatever monstrous abomination was emerging. Like with the plane-crash exchanges with his ex-wife, he couldn't bring himself to look away, not even when terror caused his bladder to let go and he wet the bed, a humiliating act he hadn't carried out since he was seven.

It was a horse's head. Backlit by moonlight, it jutted from the window, neck up. It was decomposing. Badly. Its death stink could be smelled from clear across the room, yet underneath the rot there was a whisper of a richer scent: fresh dirt. Eric's mouth dropped open in a startled, silent scream as the horse clomped forward, its putrid rust-colored body materializing from thin air with each new step. When it was fully formed, it occupied the entire space in front of the bed, nearly from one end of the wall to the other. Snorting, it turned its neck slowly and blinked at Eric with milky eyes, only it looked like it was winking because its left eyelid had decayed. Its mane was scant and tangled, patches of maggoty scabs clustered at the roots. Beyond its bony rib cage, Eric could see his coat and umbrella dangling from a peg on the wall, and it was then he realized that the horse was flickering in and out of existence with a strobe light effect, solidifying and dissolving and then solidifying again.

His eyes shifted to the foot of his bed, and he saw that the boy was flickering also.

Eric's stomach somersaulted. *Makeitstopmakeitstopmakeitstop.*

The boy whinnied as he met Eric's unblinking eyes.

Behind him, the horse stamped its foot on the hardwood floor, whispering, "Tweeeenty-twoooooo, tweeeenty-threeeeeee." Its speech was childlike, yet molasses slow and full of static—a tired phonograph dying a slow, painful death.

Crazily, Eric thought of a late-nineteenth-century doll he'd read about in a random toy collectors' magazine he'd flipped through at the dentist's. Edison's Talking Doll, invented by Thomas Edison, had been produced with a tiny phonograph of sorts, chanting rhymes like "Hickory Dickory Dock" with such realism that it had frightened Victorian children half to death. Intrigued, Eric had later found clips of the doll's voice on YouTube, and it was ghastly, indeed.

The horse's chanting was a million times worse—times infinity.

I don't know how much more of this I can take—

The horse's counting intensified in speed and volume. "Twenty-two, twenty-three . . . twenty-two, twenty-three . . ."

Eric's throat tightened, and his mouth watered. He belched. *Just make it go away. I can't do this. I can't. I can't—*

"Twenty-two, twenty-three! Twenty-two, twenty-three!" High pitched and chipmunk fast.

I'm going to be si—

"TWENTY-TWO TWENTY-THREE TWENTY-TWO TWENTY-THREE!"

Eric launched up from bed and sprinted toward the bathroom. He made it to the toilet just in time. He cracked his elbow on its edge as he kneeled over and heaved what acid he had left inside his stomach into the bowl. The horse stopped shouting, thank Christ, but the kid started neighing again in its place, mocking him, Eric was certain. Eric bent over the bowl and spewed again. By the time he finished gagging, the house had fallen silent.

Eric wasted no time running through the house and turning on all the lights. Except the bedroom; that one he ignored as he held his breath and squeezed his eyes shut, groping the door closed from behind the safety of the wall. Now he stood in the living room under the spotlight of the ceiling fan, panting, his face glistening with postvomitus sheen, foul vinegary breath tasting of sick, hands trembling against his thighs, heart hammering in his throat, balls constricted as two grapes, crotch embarrassingly soggy.

He had no idea who to call or where to go or what to do. None. Zip. Zero.

It dawned on Eric that the person he wished to seek comfort from most was Maggie, maybe simply out of habit but maybe out of something else entirely. Jim, too, since he'd know what to say and do better than anyone, having been around when Eric's disease had first manifested.

But *fuck that*.

He'd rather stand there under the fan all night, half-naked and shivering, scared out of his gourd, than ask *those two* for help. It was this revelation that delivered Eric the small amount of irritation he needed to get moving . . . three steps to the sofa, where he now sat calming himself, pondering what had just happened and what he was planning to do about it.

As far as schizophrenic episodes were concerned, he'd had some doozies. He'd been so deep Inside the Curve for a few in his early twenties that he'd thought he'd never make it back around the bend again without suffering some form of permanent trauma. But *this* . . . to compare *this* episode to his others would be like equating a microwave-dinner meltdown with nuclear devastation at Chernobyl.

He wondered just what had brought this on.

The answer came to him quickly enough. Maggie and Jim.

And let's not forget the other enchanting activities that had plagued his life as of late: Divorce. Finding a new, lower-paying job. Moving across the country to a state he'd never once traveled to, let alone had any true friends in. These were all major life changes, and he was experiencing them concurrently. It was a wonder he hadn't lost the plot sooner.

Hell, even if he *had* started out stable, he'd probably be questioning his sanity by now.

At least this incident could be explained as stress induced. It was when an episode came out of left field that he should *really* start to worry.

You mean like coming home from band practice to find sugar on your floor but the house locked up tight? Eric shook his head, assuring himself once again that he'd been a victim (an *unharmed* victim at that) of vandals.

Besides, just what was he supposed to *do* about any of it? He wasn't living in Philly anymore. He was living in a small town on the other side of the country, where he had absolutely no one to vouch for him. People tended to get a little cagey once you dropped the sch-word. They started having all kinds of prejudiced ideas about semiautomatic rifles and clock towers and tinfoil hats, particularly when they didn't know you from Adam. If word got out that he was seeing a dead kid in the classroom, or an even deader horse in the bedroom (he couldn't decide which sounded more outrageous), he would become a pariah in no time. Worse, he could jeopardize his job. They might even try locking him up. One trip to the loony bin was already one trip too many in his lifetime, thank you very much, and he had absolutely no interest in going back.

He wasn't feeling aggressive, suicidal, or more depressed about his situation than usual. (He wouldn't dare try to pretend he wasn't feeling depressed *at all*.) And he wasn't a danger to himself or to others. So . . .

So *this* was what he was going to do: He'd hold his horses (though probably a poor choice of words at that precise moment) and not jump to ridiculous conclusions about losing his mind. He'd wait it out—give his life some time to regain balance. If after that the situation got any worse, *then* he'd make a call to his doctor back East and have a talk about switching up his meds.

Tonight, however, he'd be doing his waiting from the sofa with the lights on, since even he wasn't crazy enough to believe that he'd be able to catch one wink of sleep back in the bedroom. What he was going to do first, though, was change out of his soggy underwear and take a shower.

After cleaning himself up, Eric made a cozy little bed on the sofa using spare sheets (electric blue and tropical fish patterned) he'd found mixed in with Doris's towels. He set the alarm on his cell phone—thankfully, he'd left it charging in the kitchen—and then stretched out, thinking that it would be hours before he'd fall asleep. He was comfortably snoring within minutes.

Eric woke in the morning with the sun glowing on his face through the front blinds. He was surprised to find that he felt okay, other than having a slightly stiff neck after his night on the sofa. He felt pretty damn *great*, actually, whether it was the sun or the few hours of sleep that had been responsible for lifting his mood.

Grinning, he went into the bathroom to start his day.

Eric's feelings of optimism continued, and so he tried not to think too much about it when he saw what could have been hoofprints on the hardwood floor as he went in to strip his bed of its pungent sheets. An unfamiliar sensation of positivity had taken him over, and he did not wish to question much of anything for fear that it might go away completely. He whistled his way into the garage, grabbed a broom, and then gave the bedroom floor a few rapid sweeps, overlooking entirely the sun twinkling against a tiny object on the windowsill: a silver jack.

CHAPTER 18

Logging on to the computer at her desk, Susan peeped over her shoulder, looking about as guilty as any man would if locked away in a study watching a live webcam-girl show, prim wife tending to the kids in the other room. She saw that there was nobody lingering in close enough proximity to decipher what she was up to.

Slowly, she relaxed, let her shoulders unravel.

Most of the station's officers were gone, off answering calls. Ditto on the FBI, who were out poking around on the Gerald Nichol farm. There were blissfully few civilians as well. The more credible citizens of Perrick had already delivered relevant information about Gerald Nichol during the first few days after the initial discoveries on the farm. Which left mostly crackpots, who, without steady jobs to go to, usually slept in late and didn't start rolling in with their "tips" until much later in the afternoon.

Susan had no idea where Ed might be lurking, so she had to be especially careful. For as old and achy as he complained of being, the man was surprisingly nimble; he could sneak up on a person as quietly as a ninja.

Not that she necessarily had to *hide* what she was doing.

Not exactly.

Ed had told Susan that all information that pertained to the Overalls Boy case now belonged predominantly to the FBI and that she needed to cease interviewing any witnesses who might be tied to Gerald Nichol.

Okay, she was *forbidden*, if you wanted to get technical about it.

He had not, however, forbidden her from learning about local history. Which, for all Ed and the FBI knew, could be a hobby of hers. She was on her lunch break as well, so it was really of no concern to anyone other than herself how she perused the internet. If she wanted to spend her downtime studying the blog of a local historian who just so happened to know a thing or two about the 1960s disappearance of a certain overalls-wearing boy named Lenny Lincoln, so be it.

Susan clicked through Ben Pepper's blog until she located the contact section. It featured a photograph of Pepper standing on an ocean cliff at sunset with a gargantuan Saint Bernard at his side, as well as a brief bio: I'm Ben Pepper (but you can just call me Pepper—all my friends do), a Perrick lifer with my finger on the pulse of the town since 1944! He was, it seemed, quite the busybody. If 1944 was indeed the year he was born, that made Pepper a ripe seventy-five, though he was fit enough to pass for fifty. Susan imagined there must be more than a few town secrets locked within Pepper's brain, lots of skeletons rattling around in his skull. She filled in all the required information on the contact form, providing her personal email and cell number. She also added a quick note about why she wished to speak to him, deliberately omitting that she was a police officer. She hit send. Pepper's last post on the main page had been only the day before, so she was hopeful that she'd hear back from him relatively soon.

After another look over her shoulder, she pulled from her handbag the stack of *Perrick Weekly* articles she'd printed from Pepper's blog earlier that week. Highlighter in hand, she began reading each article over again, a lot more slowly this time. She didn't know exactly what she was looking for, but she suspected that there was a vital piece of information that she was overlooking in the pages.

It struck her once she got to the section marked with all the asterisks. As Pepper had notated, Lenny Lincoln's mother and father were both deceased. But there was nothing on the status of Lenny's brother, Milton, whom Lenny had been playing hide-and-seek with on the day he'd disappeared. At the top of the page, Susan jotted a note: *Milton Lincoln still alive / living in town? Possible interview?*

If Milton *was* in town, she wouldn't need to search too hard to find him. Interviewing him would be a little trickier. If Ed and the FBI found out, she'd likely—no, she *would*—be in serious hot water. Meeting up with a historian to discuss the good old days she could explain away easily enough, but she drew a blank on what line of BS she could possibly use to justify meeting with the man who was—oh, what a coinkydink—the brother to the boy she suspected the R&G guys had unearthed.

If she were caught this time, she suspected Ed might even go as far as formally reprimanding her. He'd been acting as if her interest in the case were some kind of personal slight against him, which was ridiculous, since she was only trying to do her job. She was disappointed that he'd assumed that she would give up so easily.

She was even more disappointed that Ed was behaving so apathetically toward the murdered children of his town. Where was his sense of duty to the community that he'd been living in his entire life? The FBI were on the case, but they hadn't *taken over* Perrick PD like rogue Viking invaders. Which Ed, himself, had gone out of his way to clarify. Had Ed asked to work with them, they most likely would have obliged or, at a minimum, kept him abreast of what was happening. But Ed, it seemed, wanted to be kept out of things completely.

Susan tried to be fair by putting herself in Ed's shoes. She hadn't even racked up ten years on the force, so it was only natural that she veered toward the gung ho side of crime fighting. After a few decades of police work, her perspective might change. Maybe instead of feeling a rush when catching a criminal, she would feel sickened by the state of humanity. Perhaps, like Ed, she'd finally reach a point where she'd had enough.

As aggravated as Susan was about Ed's apathy and refusal to let her help out, she could understand his stress over her meddling. When subordinates ignored orders and went off on their own half-cocked missions, it made him look bad. Ed had done a lot for her. Apathetic as he was, he still deserved to retire with the dignity he'd earned during all his years on the job. The last thing she wanted was to cause him disgrace in front of her fellow officers and the FBI.

Which was why she had absolutely zero intention of getting caught.

Susan was just logging off her computer when her phone chimed with an email alert. It was Pepper. He was out of town for the day, but he had some free time later in the evening. If she fancied a chat, he could meet up with her at, say, Coolie's Coffee Shop downtown around eightish? If it worked for her, he could give her a buzz when he got closer to town limits.

Susan wasted no time replying. Yes, it certainly worked.

"*Shit*," she muttered as soon as she set her phone down on the desk. She'd all but forgotten about the Augustine Grifters show she'd meant to catch after work. She shot off a quick text to her friend Cyndi, with whom she was attending the show at Luna's, and let her know that she would be leaving the bar early. She didn't think Cyndi would mind in the slightest being left on her own, as she was the type who regularly went to watch movies alone in the theater. And it wasn't as if they wouldn't know half the people in the crowd anyway, which reflected less on their regular attendance at bars and more on exactly how small a town Perrick actually was.

She would have postponed with Pepper, but she knew how it went when trying to question the public. You had to strike while the iron was hot, or else the interview might never happen. Schedules changed, leads left town, and people suddenly stopped feeling so chatty. She didn't know quite what yet, but she sensed Pepper might have some valuable information to impart—though she had no doubt that much of what he'd have to say would be based on speculation and rumors.

But sometimes, a grain of truth could be found in even the most outrageous of tales.

CHAPTER 19

Based on Jake's description of its "vibe" (Eric had found that many Californians openly conversed about things that would likely be considered fruitcakey around his old stomping grounds—vibes, energies, auras), the inside of Luna's Pub looked exactly as Eric had predicted. West Coast cool met East Coast blue blood: heavy, dark wooden tables; brushed-chrome stools; industrial light fixtures. It smelled rich and boozy, but not unpleasantly so—more aged whiskey barrel than dirty frat house.

Eric liked the place and was hoping it would like him and his drumming in return.

As Eric had come to learn while playing in the Complete, there really *is* no limit to a drunk's assholery potential. While onstage, the Complete had had drunks heckle them, throw bottles onstage, and grab at their instruments. The weirdest of all was the stumbling middle-aged woman who'd demanded the all-male group to "Show me your tits, you sluts!" before jumping onstage to flash the crowd her own. Still, he probably needn't worry; Luna's was considerably more upscale than most of the dives his college band had frequented.

The crowd at Luna's behaved itself. People cheered when appropriate, bought the band endless drinks, and even hollered song requests. Apparently, Augustine Grifters had quite the local following. A few of those followers were even cute women, duly noted by Eric and Jake.

After a few minutes onstage, Eric started to feel a markedly unfamiliar sensation of contentment coursing through his veins. What struck him most was exactly how foreign it felt. It had been *months* since he'd felt so good, so weightless.

So *alive*.

Unfortunately, Eric's eyes had fouler ideas about how the night should play out. They were just two songs into the set when he had his first vision, a lightning-fast flicker across the tall mirrors that ran along the back wall of the bar.

Eric, who was accustomed to dark flashes in his vision—his floppy brown hair—was not alarmed. His natural assumption was that a lock of it had fallen over an eye, his aggravation being that he was using both his hands to drum. Jake, who could plainly see that Eric's sweat-dampened hair was pasted back from his face, looked over as Eric puckered his lips and began to blow upward. He caught Eric's eye and threw him the classic *What the hell you doing, man?* expression. It made Eric laugh.

But then . . .

Then Eric was remembering the time he'd gone skydiving at age twenty. Skip's Sky Adventures had offered two basic types of jumps for first timers. The first, more conservative option, tandem, entailed jumping from the plane with an instructor strapped to his back. The second, far more reckless option, the AFF—which Eric learned stood for *accelerated free fall*—entailed Eric pulling his own rip cord, with two instructors at his side instead of attached to him. With the blind impulsivity of youth on his side, Eric jumped at the AFF. He'd had to sign a lot of papers, as there was a risk of *splat* if he panicked or screwed up. Once in the plane and climbing toward the jump height of fifteen thousand feet above ground level, Eric was seized by a terror that iced him all the way down to his bones. He was *compressed* by fright, an invisible vise grip cinched down tight across his chest, guts, and groin. Shivering, he'd thought: *If I piss my jumpsuit, will it dry before I touch ground?*

Looking at those mirrors now, Eric suddenly felt as if he were back on that plane. Though supremely happy only moments ago, he sensed a foul terror crackling inside his chest, expanding but at the same time compressing. The air was thin and cold, and he was giddy, shivering as if he'd just been shoved into a meat locker and splashed in the face with a bucket of slush.

The horse-creature.

He saw its tail first, then its scabbed, maggoty midsection, and then finally its large, dead-eyed head. It was galloping backward within the mirrors on a loop, vanishing between the gaps of wall and then reappearing in each mirror that followed, starting over at the beginning after it reached the last.

In his shock of seeing his stinky friend, Eric fell off beat. It was only a momentary lapse, but it was drastic enough for Jake to turn around and furnish Eric with yet another classic expression, the old *Are you on crack?* Madison, the band's lead singer, also gave Eric a look over her shoulder, though hers was more of the annoyed *Will you get it together?* variety. Eric didn't have to observe either look long; it was at that very moment that the lights went out inside the bar.

The crowd hooted and whistled good-naturedly. Eric did not. Within the throng were glowing children apparently only he could see. So many children, well over a dozen.

All of them dead.

They, like the ghostly boy in overalls, who was also in attendance, were in various states of decay. Dressed in clothing from decades ago, they held various childhood memorabilia: girl about seven, baseball glove, blue-and-white-striped uniform, left eye and ear missing; boy about five, Ping-Pong paddle, cowboy costume, skin yellowed and pruned; girl about four, plastic doll, corduroy bell-bottoms, skull rotting . . .

All of them, with their sad, dead eyes, were staring directly at Eric.

With them was an adult woman, whom Eric had initially dismissed as one of the spectators in the crowd because of her wobbly stance. She was swaying, as if still hearing music, like drunks in bars often did long after the band had stopped playing. Now Eric could see that she was as dead as the kids, though she must have been quite beautiful alive. Her long black hair, parted down the center with a daisy tucked behind an ear, draped down to just below her waist in two glossy curtains. Her russet-colored frame filled out her long dress like a song. Unlike the children, she wasn't paying Eric attention. She was smiling down at the boy at her side, humming to him softly, her tresses obscuring the left side of her face in a screen of dark silk. She was pressing him against her moldy hip, as if to protect him from lurking danger. Her arm was only skeletal from the elbow down, the bones of her fingers tapping the boy's shoulder in time with her melody.

Why now? Eric thought. *Why, right now, am I seeing this—*

The woman raised her head and caught Eric's eye. It was then that he saw the black void where the bottom-left part of her face should have been. It was gone—not decayed but utterly *gone*, as if it had been dissolved, evaporated, blown to smithereens. The remaining right side of her rotten mouth curled up into a hideous sneer. Then came the surge of blood, spurting out from the hollow of her face, showering the living with shards of teeth and gobs of oozing red: blood clumping hair, clouding beers, dribbling into cleavage.

Nobody noticed.

But to Eric, it was so bright, so vivid—

His mouth fell open, and he steeled himself to belt out a good long shriek. *I don't care if people think I'm crazy. I'm losing it, I'm losing it—*

The lights powered back on, and they were gone. No woman, no decaying kids, no blood.

Eric rubbed his eyes. They had only been there for an instant, but they *had* been there, and he *had* seen them. They were so real—how had nobody else seen them?

Eric yelped when a small hand fell onto his forearm.

It was Jake's. "So I just talked to the owner," he said. "It's going to be about ten, fifteen minutes until we can get rolling again—blown fuse or something. Care to join me at the bar for a pint? Our freebies have gone piss warm. Such a shame. Alcohol abuse, really."

It took Eric a moment to process what Jake had said. "Do I . . . want to join you at the bar . . . ?" He managed a smile. "Sure. Just going to hit the head quick. Meet you over there."

Jake's face clouded with concern. "You all right?"

Eric flapped a hand. "Just, you know, haunted by old ghosts." He chuckled flatly.

"The ex, huh?"

Strange—he hadn't even *thought* of Maggie.

Eric hesitated. "You, um, didn't see anything weird when the lights went out, did you?"

"Weird? Like what?"

Like a pack of dead children glaring at me. A sexy dead woman with half her face gone, perhaps? Eric shook his head. "Never mind. See you in a minute."

Pull it together, he commanded himself as Jake walked away. *You are fine. Because not being fine might suggest that you aren't as in control of your schizophrenic brain as you think. Is that what you want—to be out of control?*

No, that wasn't what he wanted. Not *at all*.

When Eric got to the bar, Jake was surrounded by a group of fans offering lots of backslapping praise. Jake, though modest, was obviously relishing the attention. Smiling to himself, Eric ordered a drink from the cheery, spiky-haired bartender, whose bulging biceps were thicker than both of Eric's thighs put together. Eric wondered if the guy also moonlighted as a bouncer. Or a lumberjack.

As he settled back with a beer, a voice to his right said, "You guys are playing *really* well tonight."

Eric turned toward the source of the statement and discovered that it had been uttered by a gorgeous blue-eyed brunette. In front of her on the bar was a tall, fizzy soda with lots of crushed ice and the biggest platter of deep-fried food he'd ever seen: mozzarella sticks, fries, chicken strips, popcorn shrimp, and what looked like fried zucchini (because vegetables). She was chowing down unabashedly, which rendered her even more attractive in Eric's eyes. He liked a woman who could eat.

"Thanks." Eric smiled. "But don't give me too much credit. I'm only standing in for tonight."

"I know," she said with a wink. "I've seen these guys play tons. But I like your modesty." She elbowed the platter toward him. "Here, help yourself. I think my eyes were bigger than my stomach when I ordered this monster."

"Thanks," he said and pinched a fry. A fat gob of ketchup fell down his front as he went to pop it into his mouth. Of course it did.

"You've got red on you," she deadpanned in a faux English accent and then chuckled self-consciously.

He laughed with her as he dabbed a cocktail napkin at his shirt. "Ha! I love *Shaun of the Dead*."

Her eyes widened. "I can't *believe* you got that! Nobody *ever* gets my film references."

"Come on, Cornetto Trilogy? Classic," he said. "Though *Hot Fuzz* is my favorite."

"Mine too—though I also love *The World's End*."

As the woman dropped her hand from her chest, Eric noted that she was not wearing a wedding ring. She nudged the platter. "Have more, if you want. Just try to keep it in your mouth this time."

"I'd better not. I still have to finish our set."

"Yeah, might put a damper on your performance if you upchuck mozzarella sticks on the crowd."

Eric laughed. Hot, and she kept it real. *And* she liked horror films. He had to get to know this dream woman. Even if she ended up rejecting him, he still had to *try*. "I'm Eric," he said, extending a hand.

They shook. "I'm Susan."

"That's a big plate of food, Susan. Were you planning on eating it all by yourself?"

Susan threw back her head and cackled. "Was that your sly way of asking if I'm here on my own?"

Eric flushed, but still he asked, "*Are* you here alone?"

"Maybe." She smirked. "Are you hitting on me?"

"Maybe."

"Then maybe I'm here alone."

In his mind's eye, Eric was imagining her back at his place: first on the sofa and then in his bed. She seemed into him, so . . . he did a quick mental scan of the state of his bedroom and bathroom—not spotless but not so messy that he'd be embarrassed to bring a woman home. Did he have drinks to offer? Yep. He'd bought a case of Heineken when he'd gone to the store that morning. He didn't have wine or any hard stuff, but she'd probably be okay with beer, given how she'd plowed through those chicken tenders. He didn't have to work in the morning, which was good, since it would save him from having to engage in an awkward conversation about her needing to leave so he could lock up before—

"Yes," she finally confirmed, leaning close to Eric so that he could hear her over the rowdiness of the crowd. "I'm here by myself. My friend actually bailed on me last minute." Her skin brushed against his, and he practically ached with want. She picked up the cell phone next to the platter on the bar and gave it a small shake. "Which is good, I guess, since I'm waiting for a call that's kind of for work. Then *I'd* be the one bailing."

Eric was having a difficult time hearing her above the chatter of those lined up behind them waiting to be served by the lumberjack. "Oh, you're on call? Are you a doctor or—"

"Eric! Eric!" Jake calling him to the stage. "Get your ass up here! It's time to plaaaaaay."

Eric laughed and waved at Jake, who was wiggling his fingers at him impishly. To Susan he said, "Will you still be here, you think, when we're done?"

Susan checked the time on her phone. "Should be."

"Eric!" Jake again.

"Okay, let's talk some more when I'm done?" Eric said, making a move toward the stage.

"Looking forward to it," she said with a wink.

As Eric neared the stage, he glanced back at Susan. She frowned down at her phone, lifted it to her ear, and left the bar in a hurry.

Well, so much for that.

Back at home after the show, Jake beeped the horn as he pulled away, leaving Eric tottering on the front porch. He realized just how plastered he was after six failed attempts at getting the damn key to make contact with the damn lock, stumbling over the doorstep once he made his way into the house.

Eric was being a *very* naughty boy. He wasn't supposed to drink heavily on his meds—really wasn't supposed to drink much at all, according to his doctor—but he'd wanted to let loose after their set. Let loose he certainly had, and he was now feeling pretty damn fine because of it.

He'd be feeling even finer if Dream Woman Susan had gone home with him, but . . .

"But fuck it—that's life!" he chortled loudly in the stillness of the empty house.

As he headed toward bed, he followed up with a silent consolation: *It's a small town. Just a matter of time before I see her again.* He didn't realize how true this would turn out to be.

Chapter 20

Two chamomile teas and a hot bath later, Susan was still feeling wound up from the night. She moved around her house edgily, confused and a little frightened about what had happened at the show now that she was all on her own in a quiet house, and never mind the town's darker history that she'd discussed with Pepper.

She put on music but found it too loud even at the stereo's lowest volume, then turned to the TV for comfort. She settled on a made-for-television rom-com playing on a station known for its sappy love tales and bad acting. This wasn't her sort of entertainment, but tonight it suited her just fine. She needed the silliness of melodrama, the guarantee of a happy ending.

She'd *liked* the part of the night where she'd met Eric. He was cute and sweet enough that she was now kicking herself for not sliding him her contact information before he'd gone back onstage. She hadn't expected Pepper to call so soon, but he did—a whole hour early—so she'd had to rush out to meet him. She was glad that she had, despite the missed opportunity with Eric. She'd learned a great deal of interesting, albeit unnerving, information that might be of use in her unofficial investigating. Although she now had a few reservations about the things Ed had been telling her.

The part that she *hadn't* liked about her evening was what had happened when the lights had gone out at Luna's. It was about as close to a panic attack as she'd ever come in her entire life: shortness of breath, the feeling of being closed in on, and an irrational urge to cry out. It had all vanished as soon as the lights had come back on, which was odd, since she'd never been afraid of the dark, not even as a child. It had happened so fast that it had been easy enough to brush off at the time. But now, in the quiet of the night, where every creak and groan of the house conjured images of a hidden boogeyman, the feeling was creeping back, instilling an anxiety within her, when usually home was where she felt the most relaxed.

Perhaps her chat with Pepper had something to do with it.

Pepper himself was jovial enough. He was the type who exuded energy even while sitting still. Susan pictured how he'd be first thing in the morning versus very late at night, and the vision was pretty much the same. He probably eschewed coffee for wheat grass and was a part of some kind of raw-food diet movement.

He was also the type to overshare. After conversing for no less than ten minutes, he'd somehow managed to fit bowel movements into the conversation, toilets specifically. "They're doing it right in third world countries with their squat toilets," he'd begun his rant. "Western toilets are bad for the body because they force users to sit at an odd angle, thus pinching the intestines. You're never really emptying yourself out this way." Susan had provided him a noncommittal "How interesting," hoping that he'd take the hint and drop it. He'd powered on. "So the next time someone accuses you of being full of crap, they're right!" Then, without pause, he'd switched topics to his Saint Bernard, who she'd learned was named Truffle.

Things got a little stranger from there. Later during their chat, Pepper had endorsed Ed's claim that kids *had* gone missing in Perrick frequently back in the 1960s. But his follow-up offered a contradiction: they or their bodies had always been found.

The one exception being Lenny Lincoln.

Susan was now feeling uneasy about this new knowledge because of its implications. Either Ed was more burned out than she'd thought and was misremembering facts, or he'd gone out of his way to mislead her, probably in an attempt to dissuade her from further meddling in the Gerald Nichol case. Both possibilities did nothing to put her mind at ease.

She flopped down on the sofa, resting her chin in her hands. There was something else Pepper had said that also did not sit right with Susan. Lenny Lincoln's disappearance, at least according to Pepper, had been a *massive* (eyes widening as he'd said it) *deal* back in the day. Kids back then did not simply vanish without a trace, he'd assured her. It was, he'd said, one of the most talked-about stories in town history, and any local who'd been alive at the time should remember it happening. So why had Ed downplayed it so much—was this yet another way he'd hoped to deter her investigation, or was he protecting her from something—like getting herself fired?

Pepper, though, would have been older than Ed at the time of Lenny's disappearance; he would have been in his early twenties. After running some quick numbers in her head, Susan figured that Ed must have been around eleven or twelve years old at the time of Lenny Lincoln's disappearance. Would the event have been significant enough to a young boy that he'd remember it over fifty years later as an adult? Susan herself had never heard the name Lenny Lincoln until the day Mary told her about his disappearance. But she also hadn't been alive when it had occurred.

Pepper had also told her a great deal about the life of Milton Lincoln, Lenny's brother, the most pertinent detail being that he was still very much alive. He was, in fact, still living in the same home that he had as a kid. The farm where Lenny Lincoln had gone missing.

Chapter 21

Passed out.
>drunk
>restless
>freezing
>pillow soggy and sheets damp with sweat and
>thirsty
>*wants a drink of water more than anything but he is too weak to move
and if he could just have one sip of water just one sip is all he needs he'll be
good and he won't kick and he won't bite and he won't scream he promises
to be a good boy if he could just have some*
>coughing
>suffocating
>*can't get air and he can't see and it's so black and things scratch and
slither against him and bite at his toes and crawl into his ears when he
sleeps and he sees nothing only darkness and he's buried alive and the bad
stranger snatched him and he'll never see his mommy and daddy again and
they warned him never to talk to strangers but he didn't there was only a
shadow and stranger danger*
>pulling
>*what are you doing to my sister please don't hurt my sister I won't tell I
won't tell I promise if you let me go I*
>Pulling

won't say a word I won't tell if you let me go please let me go please
PULLING!

"I won't tell! I promise! I promise! Please just let me go home . . ."

Sobbing, Eric scrambled back on the bed until his spine slammed hard against the headboard. He clawed at the shriek blustering up in his vocal cords, hands flying instantly to his throbbing head. He felt drunk, thick, tired, and scared, and the blazing light he'd left on in the bedroom wasn't helping.

Eventually, he caught his breath. He groped for the quilt that had gotten bunched down at his feet and yanked it up roughly. Shivering, he covered his naked, goose-pimpled flesh—

The quilt whooshed back down over him and off the bed completely.

Eric's mouth dropped open, and a small, surprised yelp escaped him. He gaped at his curled fingers and then down at the foot of the bed, his brain about five steps behind his eyes. It was there a second ago, and then . . . ripped away . . . ?

???????????

Eric rubbed his scratchy eyes, jaundiced and wild. He'd hoped that he was still locked in a nightmare but now suspected he was very much awake when the familiar wheezing started below his feet and drifted higher, higher . . .

Higher.

The boy in denim overalls floated up from beneath the foot of the bed. In his small hands he held the patchwork quilt Eric's mother had made in 1991, the year before a residually drunk driver on his way to the early shift had struck and killed her while she'd been taking a morning jog through their quiet suburban neighborhood. Eric could see the pink tint of fruit punch he'd spilled on it when he was ten, the hole he'd singed into it while smoking his first joint with Jim at sixteen, and he thought then with sharp, hysterical clarity: *People do not imagine details like Kool-Aid stains and marijuana burns on their dead mothers' quilts when they are hallucinating. This is* real.

The boy released the quilt and drifted over the footboard, a squat, slatted rectangle of ugly forest-green-stained pine. A shockwave of nuclear unnaturalness discharged from the boy's feet as they touched down on the bed.

Eric commanded his leg muscles to move—pleaded with them to run him right the motherfuck out of Dodge—but it was as if he'd been bound against the headboard by unseen ropes that bristled at his wrists and ankles, holding him upright and fetal positioned. He could *feel* them, these invisible bindings, cutting deep into his raw flesh.

The boy dropped to his hands and knees and crawled toward Eric, catlike. Slowly, slowly. His palms left reeking imprints of pus and rotten skin on the sheets. Insects squirmed at the surface of his tiny features. Closing in, the boy's cold, pungent wheezing tickled Eric's bare skin, a grotesque contrast to the bloated warmth emanating from the boy's decaying insides.

Eric wanted to scream—he *tried* to scream—but when his lips parted, a clump of dirt came tumbling out onto the sheets. He gagged as he saw a worm wriggling within it.

The boy sat back on his haunches. He reached deep into the pocket at the center of his overalls and pulled out a handful of . . .

If there is any mercy or goodness left in the world, I will faint. Or some magical force will swoop down and knock me right out, because if I see what that kid has in his hand—rat carcass, some other poor dead kid's eyeballs—I will go insane and stay that way for a very long time. Maybe forever.

Eric, frightened to such a degree that he'd started to convulse, tried desperately to turn his head. It was as if it had been cemented in place. He groaned. *Look away! Why won't you look away?*

The boy uncurled his hand.

"What d-do you want?" Eric sobbed. "Why do you k-keep . . . why don't you t-t-ell me . . . w-what is it . . . oh God . . . oh God . . . w-w-what is it that you w-w-want f-from m-me?"

The boy rooted around his palm and pinched a spiky silver object between his thumb and forefinger. A jack. He cocked his arm back like he was aiming to pitch a baseball and then let it fly. The jack seared toward Eric comet fast and then stopped six inches from his face, floating directly between his eyes. It hovered there for only a second or two and then exploded like fireworks. Eric screamed. He tasted dirt on his tongue, and grit itched in his throat, but this time, he *screamed.*

The boy pitched another jack. Then another. Another.

Eric squeezed his eyes shut—pinched them together so tightly that his eyeballs watered and he started to see stars. *This is not happening. There is no dead kid, and there are no jacks exploding in my face like little microbombs of death. Nope. Nuh-uh. After everything that's happened these past few months, it was only a matter of time before I cracked up. Ticktock, baby, and now I've finally gone and lost the plot! The men in white coats can come take me away and electroshock the dead-kid hallucinations right from my loony brain—hell, they can zap all my memories, if that's what they demand. Anything is better than this. Anything at all.*

The wheezing got louder. No, Eric realized, it wasn't getting louder. It was *closer.* He unscrewed his eyelids and found the boy's face so close that they could have kissed.

The boy leaned in closer. *Wheeze-wheeze, kiss-kiss.*

Eric squeezed his eyes shut.

Closer . . .

Closer . . .

So close now that Eric could detect two cracked lips brushing against his cheek like rotten twigs, frigid exhales raising the hairs on the back of his neck.

Suddenly, Eric thought of nothing. He became nothing. He was frightened beyond comprehension and sensation and reaction, frightened out of his very *humanness.* He simply existed, a skeleton covered with tissue, some guts mixed in between, nothing more.

"Tell . . . them . . ." *Wheeze-wheeze.* "Tell them . . ."

Eric flickered back to awareness: Head throbbing. Heart pounding. Nakedness. Scratching sliminess at his cheek. Spinning and spinning around in his mind, he whirred back into himself, eyes flashing open, horrified all over again when he locked eyes with the boy corpse.

It had to stop. It had to stop *right now*.

"Who?"

"Tell them . . ." *Wheeze-wheeze.*

"Who? Tell me *who*, God dammit!"

Wheeze-wheeze. "Find . . . Milton."

The boy lifted a putrid hand and stroked the bone of his index finger across Eric's forehead. He pressed his lips to Eric's ear.

Sleep.

Eric fell slack as a sack of jelly. He melted away from the headboard, eyes rolling back into his head, a pool of a man spreading across the mattress. From the ground his mother's quilt lifted, unfolding in the air above him. It dropped down softly over his body, tucking him in like a child.

He slept.

Upon waking, Eric found that his memory of the young undead visitor was foggy. He had an overall feeling of anxiety, his mind struggling to grip the foggy nightmare. He could recall it as horrific, yet its subject matter was fleeting, like trying to grasp a fistful of sand.

It came crashing down on him when he entered the kitchen and saw the writing that was literally on the wall . . . and the floor, cupboards, and ceiling. The name that had been repeated dozens of times, squirted in ketchup, mustard, salad dressing. Honey. Chocolate sauce. Doodled in a dense layer of coffee grounds spread across the countertop. Carved into a stick of butter that lay melting in the center of the floor. Every terrifying moment of the corpse-boy's visit was remembered in a half blink: the quilt whooshing down off the bed, the rotten handprints on the sheet, the unholy smells, the clump of wormy dirt upchucked, the rotten, bony finger sliding over his forehead.

All because of one name: Milton.

Everywhere: MILTON, MILTON, MILTON.

Eric stood gaping at the mess, naked except for the sauces smeared up his arms. The television had turned itself on at full blast—or had he left it on and just not noticed? The news updated him that the FBI had unearthed five more children on Gerald Nichol's farm. Images flashed from a helicopter's bird's-eye view: body bags, barking German shepherds, a swarm of FBI agents. A tally of the latest body count blinked in the corner of the screen like an athlete's stats: 14. The media had now given the site a moniker: Perrick Death Farm.

Tell them, the boy had said. And now he'd shown Eric whom he meant.

And if he *didn't* tell the authorities, then what?

It was a question Eric did not want answered.

Shivering, he rubbed the raw rope burns on his wrists (he had a matching pair on his ankles). He was at a loss as to what had caused them, but he was certain they'd surfaced sometime during the night—during the night*mare*.

Eric couldn't understand why any of this was happening to him, but even he, so dismissive of the otherworldly, was having a hard time rationalizing all the phenomena he'd experienced since his move to Perrick.

And then there were his prodromes.

Eric cocked his head to the side, frowning. *What* about *my prodromes?* he thought.

(Your recent so-called hallucinations have come on without them. No warning whatsoever. One minute you're fine, the next: shit storm. Funny, that.)

Okay, sure, but which possibility seemed more likely: that a certified schizophrenic (he had papers to prove it, too, you'd better *believe*) was seeing things that did not exist or that there was a greater conspiracy taking place in his very home?

Eric was also a Man of Science—hell, he was a *science teacher*. There were lots of folks out in the world who thrived on finding mystical origins to the mundane—attributing creaks in the house to the dead communicating, a dove flapping by as a sign of good fortune—but Eric was not one of them. If he started entertaining the possibility of

(What, psychic visions?)

such *nonsense*, he might as well pour his meds down the drain now and start walking through the house burning sage and waving crystals, speaking in tongues.

He briefly toyed with a wild theory that involved Jim and Maggie: they'd hired a child actor to pose as dead, broken in to his house while he'd been at work, and switched out his meds with an LSD-based hallucinogenic. Eric understood such ideas were ludicrous even as he was having them (pure idiocy, really) and were the sorts of paranoid delusions he would have entertained when schizophrenia had first afflicted him in his late teens. Furthermore, Jim and Maggie were the wrongdoers, so if anyone should be plotting a fantastical revenge, it was *him*.

It seemed there *was* no rational explanation for what was happening. Perhaps, Eric thought, such occurrences might be studied in a century or two by more enlightened humans. Maybe his so-called phenomena (for want of a better term) could easily be justified by mere cosmic occurrences that were beyond the world's current grasp of physics. What if his visions were simply glitches in time, imprints created when the past or the future overlapped with the present? It all sounded very sci-fi, but it wasn't so long ago that society had been in the dark about things like how gravity worked. Less than a few centuries ago, humans—*scholars*, no less—were finding hidden messages in the stars, dismissing earthquakes and floods as punishment from the gods. Times when a guy like Tony Hawk probably would have been burned at the stake in Salem if a Puritan had seen what he could do on a skateboard.

But Eric wasn't out to solve any of the world's great mysteries. He only wanted to put an end to the ghastly visions of dead kids and that god-awful horse. For his house to stop being vandalized, even if he was the one doing it while in an unfathomable fugue state. And even if it *was* all a manifestation of his schizophrenia, maybe going to the authorities would have a placebo effect, cure whatever the hell was ailing him.

CHAPTER 22

Susan checked the clock, saw that there was still plenty of time left until her shift started—after yet another fitful night of no sleep, even being at work early was preferable to her eerily quiet, empty home—and made her decision about the phone call.

She could land herself in a spot of trouble for contacting the morgue again, but she was so tired that she hardly cared, her biggest hope being that her inquiry would put her troubled mind at ease, provide some answers to the confusions that niggled at her brain. Ed and the FBI were being tight lipped as ever. If they weren't going to let her into the loop, she'd have to find her own (extremely covert) way inside.

Medical Examiner Salvador Martinez picked up after the first ring.

"Your mouth sounds full," she said. "Are you eating in the morgue again?"

"Guilty as charged. Chocolate croissant."

Susan snickered. "You are *so* gross. Easily the grossest person I know."

"Ha! Well, I'm proud that you think so." Susan could hear the smile in his voice. "You're lucky you didn't call yesterday—was eating spaghetti. You don't even *want* to know what I was up to then. A busload of tourists had rolled over on the highway—"

"You're right. I don't want to know," Susan said hurriedly, in case he was thinking about expanding his story. She could picture Sal's family at dinner, listening intently as he regaled them with narratives from his day: scooping brains and cracking ribs, sawing chests. It wasn't that the Martinezes were gruesome people; they were just the sort of family who approached life with a wholesome exuberance Susan felt bordered on the macabre, as if they'd react to news about their house burning down with the same unflinching optimism they'd show when learning that they'd won the lottery. Boy Scouty to the extreme. Here was a man who wore *family man* like a badge of honor.

"So what can I do you for?"

"I'm . . ." Susan wasn't quite sure how to phrase her request without making it obvious that she was sidestepping Ed and the FBI, though it was a bit too late for that now, anyway. She had already called the morgue a couple of times earlier in the week, not exactly pumping Sal for information but also not stopping him when he felt like divulging details that higher-ups would probably feel that she did not need to know. Information like how they'd found jacks and a ball in the pocket of one of the victims. Or the true number of bodies found. The news kept getting it wrong, lowballing the count.

Susan settled on being direct, though she kept her voice low, cognizant of potential eavesdroppers. "I'm calling about the Death Farm." The Death Farm. Susan hated the term, but it was what everyone was now calling it.

"FBI still withholding?" Sal deduced.

"Well . . ."

"Yeah, they've pissed off a lot of people over here too. A couple of their guys came up from Frisco last night. What a pleasant bunch *they* are." He sniffed. "Coming in here swinging their dicks around like they own the place. I may not have trained at Quantico, but I didn't get my medical degree out of a Cracker Jack box either."

Knowing that Sal was being excluded made Susan feel a little better about being left out of the loop herself, though she suspected much of his aggravation stemmed from him being a scientist and wanting his workstation laid out exactly as he favored. Medical examiners had a reputation for being territorial.

"What's their issue?" Susan said.

"They think that we're moving too slow—well, they *used* to think that, but their tune has changed fast now that they've seen the state of the bodies. Would it be unprofessional of me to say *I told you so* while giving them the finger?"

Susan chuckled, trying to imagine Sal ever doing such a thing. "And here I'd been thinking it was just me they hadn't warmed to."

"*Warmed* has nothing to do with it. I bet some of these guys would toss their own mothers in Millstone if it meant advancing their careers."

"Ha."

Sal cleared his throat. "What sort of information are you looking for?"

"I don't want to put you out if you're busy . . ."

"Suze, come on. Don't you go playing coy with me. After what you did for my papa, you know I'll always bend over backward for you."

Susan flushed. She always did whenever Sal brought up the time she'd saved his father's life. It had happened while she was off duty and in the park having her lunch. She'd just *felt* there was something bad happening to the older gentleman sitting quietly on the bench across from her. Sure enough, he was having a stroke. The medics later said that he would have died had she not performed CPR. "You don't owe me a thing. It was nothing, Sal."

"It wasn't *nothing* to my papa. The man would be dead if it weren't for you."

"I just don't want you to think that I'm trying to cash in on a favor." To lighten the mood, she joked, "Maybe I call so often because I happen to find that deep Latin voice of yours enticing."

"Ay ay ay, girl! Ha! That must be it!" Sal let out a throaty laugh. "Seriously, though, I'm always here for you, day and night."

"Okay, okay," she said, self-conscious. "So I'm wondering, Is there anything new? You still at twenty-one bodies? I know they're still out on the farm searching."

"Twenty-one *kids*, yes."

"What do you mean, *kids*? Are there other kinds of bodies too?"

"We found an adult. A woman."

"Old? Young?"

"Our guesstimate: twenties to thirties. Decomp is severe. No signs of sexual assault—at least from what we can tell. The decomp is better on some of the bodies than it is on others, but the woman is one of the worst."

"This awful case keeps getting weirder," Susan said. "A child molester would probably have little interest in raping an adult woman, so I wonder where she came from. I'm glad for her, whoever she is—that she wasn't raped, I mean. *Do* they know who she is? The FBI?"

"They haven't a clue," said Sal. "My guess is that she's probably collateral damage, the mother of one of the kids Gerald snatched. She probably intervened during the kidnapping, and he bashed her for getting in the way. Her body is one of the older ones, so it's going to take some time before we get an ID, if we ever do."

"You said she's older. What *is* the age range of the bodies?"

"You mean the age range of the kids themselves or how long they've been dead?" Sal asked, confused.

Susan took a second to think. "How about both?"

"Sure, but again, this is only our best approximation. The kids range in age from about five to eleven. The majority are in the five-to-eight range."

"Jesus Christ," Susan said, disgusted. "He certainly liked them young."

Sal made a grunting sound in agreement. "As far as how long they've been dead, some for decades. Some are newer, though."

"How much newer?"

"None are recent, but we think the latest ones died within the last seven to ten years. The FBI wants us to focus on identifying those kids first—the newer ones," he said. "They want us to be thorough, but it's been slow going."

"Why's that?"

"The biggest problem is that not every kid has been fingerprinted or gone to the dentist, especially the really young ones. So identifying them has been practically impossible. And there's been *a lot* of decomp. Gerald didn't seem to care too much about body preservation."

"The first body—Overalls Boy," Susan said. "You still think he was from the sixties?"

"That's right," Sal answered. "And we're all in agreement that he's still the oldest of the bunch."

"Gerald's first kill."

"Mm-hmm." Sal sounded tense. Susan could only imagine how horrific it would be, examining the bodies of so many dead children, especially for a man who had four of his own.

"Were any of the other bodies moved like we think Overalls Boy was?"

"No. He was the only one."

"Odd," Susan muttered and then paused. "Wait, you said 'bashed her' earlier. The woman. What did you mean?"

"Oh. We've got a cause of death for her, at least: blunt force trauma. We found grit embedded in the wound on the lower half of her skull, probably from a large stone, which is why I don't think it was a premeditated attack. Usually with premeditation of this type you'd see the use of a tool—a hammer or baseball bat, something of that nature, which would result in a cleaner injury. The back of her skull was also fractured up near the crown, and we found the same pebbly grit up there, so the same object was used. Gerald really went to town on her—her mandible's obliterated. Seems he was covering his bases. He must've been in a real rage, which makes me wonder where he's taking these kids from."

"What do you mean?"

"Well, if the woman is the mother of one or more of the kids, they must've been taken from a place fairly isolated. You couldn't just roll up to a public park and beat a woman to death without somebody noticing."

"But I doubt that he's been doing the killing at the kidnapping sites, since he's been burying them on his property. My guess is that he brings them home, has"—Susan swallowed down the bile that was rising in her throat—"his way with them, and then kills them once he grows tired of them."

"Good point, but that doesn't explain the woman. Why would he bother bringing a woman all the way home? There'd be the chance that she could overpower him, make an escape. You'd think that it'd be easier to just kill her on-site."

"And drive her dead body through town, with the kid still living, all the way back to his farm?"

"It's a strange one, I know. Here's something else—and here's where it gets *really* weird. Two things, actually."

"Do tell." Susan's stomach growled, upset from her morning diet of all coffee and no food. She reached into her desk and rooted around for the jar of Skittles she kept hidden—it was better than booze, she figured, though her dentist might disagree—in the bottom drawer. Breakfast of champions.

Sal's voice grew quiet as he said, "But first you have to promise that you won't share this information. I could get in a *lot* of trouble if anyone found out that I've been talking to you. The FBI would probably see to it that I was shitcanned."

Susan could understand Sal's trepidation, being at risk for a serious reprimanding herself. "I promise that I'll keep my lips zipped about whatever you tell me. Have I ever blabbed before?"

"No, and that's why I continue to trust you," Sal answered. "Okay, the first thing is actually kind of good news. I guess *good* is the wrong word, but—"

"Focus, Sal!"

"None of the kids were sexually assaulted."

Susan released the Skittles she'd been holding onto her desk. Her palm was rainbow colored. "*What?* Are you sure?"

"Positive."

"Let me get this straight: a child sex offender murdered those kids but didn't touch them? What the hell was he doing with them, then?"

"Your guess is as good as mine," Sal said. "Of course, some of the bodies are far too decomposed to one hundred percent confirm that no sexual assault took place, but on the more current victims there's absolutely no trace. Which is weird, right, because those old creeps typically get worse with age."

"So if he wasn't doing it lately . . ."

"He probably wasn't doing it back then," Sal said. "Of course, this is pure conjecture on my part. I'm really no expert. You'd need to talk to your FBI-profiler pals for that."

Fat chance of that happening, Susan thought. "Gerald was busted for child pornography, though, so maybe he used them in videos or something . . ." She felt sick even saying it. She swept the candy off her desk into the garbage can, wiped her hand on her pant leg.

"I thought the same thing," said Sal. "But there are absolutely no signs that any of the kids were even *undressed*. I haven't seen a ton of child murders, but typically if there was any kind of sexual abuse, there'd be signs of it: pants bunched, underwear torn or inside out . . . buttons ripped off clothing, that sort of thing. But with these kids, there's nothing. No internal trauma of any kind either. No pelvic or femoral fractures."

Susan considered the new information as she jotted down a couple of quick notes on the pad on her desk. She came up blank for a theory and wondered what the FBI profilers were making of the information. No wonder they seemed so edgy. Denton Howell, though always cordial toward her whenever they encountered each other around the station, was a walking ball of tension. The pressure was on to find Gerald Nichol, who might, it seemed, enjoy killing kids for the sheer sake of killing.

"I don't know how you can stand doing what you do all day, Sal," said Susan.

"You and me both," Sal agreed. "But I try to remind myself that all the work I do will help put Gerald away. Hopefully."

"Right, *hopefully*. If we catch him."

Sal said, "I'm surprised he's been able to stay hidden this long. Half of America is looking for the creep. You know how many vigilante groups are tweeting about him online? I can't imagine *what* kind of scumbag lawyer would be willing to represent this guy once he's caught."

"I think even the FBI are a little stumped. They're running out of places to look. Ed mentioned that they might start having me help out today with interviews and weeding through tips. If they're turning to the public, they must be getting desperate."

"Gerald Nichol might be one cunning motherfucker after all. Pardon my French."

"Stop apologizing for your filthy mouth and tell me the second bit of fucking information," Susan said. It probably wasn't appropriate, joking around while discussing dead children, but crappy bons mots sometimes helped dull the horror people like she and Sal had to contend with every day.

"The only physical damage the kids show seems self-inflicted."

"Explain."

"I mean that they weren't beaten, they weren't shot, they weren't poisoned, burned, choked, or stabbed. It's the damnedest thing."

Susan frowned. "How did they die, then?"

"It's very difficult to determine, again because of decomp, but it is my medical opinion that they were asphyxiated."

"Like smothered with a pillow or something?"

"No, we found no foreign fibers in the nasal cavities to suggest that type of smothering. It's more like they were locked somewhere and ran out of air. It makes the most sense, given the self-inflicted injuries I mentioned."

"Which were what?"

"This news isn't so great," Sal said. "Most of the kids had damaged hands. Broken fingers and split nails. Like they'd tried to punch or claw their way out of something. Probably in a panic as they were running out of air."

Susan shivered. "It makes me sick. Those poor kids."

"Yes," Sal agreed. "Those poor kids."

Well, this is one way to start the morning, Susan thought as she hung up.

After a contemplative moment, she reached into her bag and pulled out the printouts from Pepper's blog. She found the page with Lenny's photograph and studied it, thinking about the conversation with Sal.

Finding the identities of the newer bodies was the priority; that was what the FBI wanted. Which meant that putting the true name to Overalls Boy was the least of the FBI's concerns. Susan suspected they'd lose interest in the case fast once Gerald Nichol was apprehended and the accolades started rolling in for bringing a child murderer to justice. Never mind the victims, as long as there was a monster to string up.

If the American public loved anything, it was seeing criminals *pay*.

Susan knew how it would go: once the FBI left Perrick, the task of identifying the earliest victims would go straight to the back burner. Of course it would; it wasn't like they didn't know who the murderer was. Focus on identifying corpses decades old when there were so many kids coming up missing every day? Taxpayers would lose their minds.

Overalls Boy might not even have any living relatives left, his murder having occurred so long ago—it wasn't as if she *knew* that he was, indeed, Lenny Lincoln. She was only reaching, at best. If he wasn't Lenny, there might not be anyone on earth left who cared to see that he was identified.

Well, *she* cared, maybe because she'd been there when he'd been found, or maybe simply because she wanted to help identify a poor soul who might otherwise remain forever nameless. She wasn't allowed to have direct involvement with the Death Farm case, but Susan couldn't see the harm in doing a little digging on her own time, off the clock. Really, it would be like she was providing Perrick a community service by working for free.

Her eyes drifted up to the clock on the wall and then down toward the stairway that led to the old records room in the basement. There was still a lot of time left before she started her shift. Perhaps, she thought, it wouldn't hurt to have a quick gander at some old files, which would only back up her recently acquired hobby—wink-wink—of exploring Perrick town history.

Susan took the stairs down to the basement with nonchalance she had to force. Unlike at larger, big-city stations, the records room at Perrick PD was not manned or even locked. She walked right in and discovered that she was entirely on her own, barring the few moth corpses that sat upturned on the ledge of the room's single window.

Though eerily noiseless and coated in a hefty layer of dust, the space was well organized. This probably had something to do with its lack of use, which gave Susan a small flare of hope. Less in and out meant fewer misplaced files.

She counted twenty rows of metal shelving, each four levels high. Easy enough to follow. The records were kept in uniform cardboard boxes, dated chronologically. She walked to where the first box was kept at the very back of the room, not surprised to see that it was dated 1954, the year Perrick PD had opened its doors. Each year of the 1960s was marked by a single box—except, she saw, the year 1968, which had two. It must have been especially hot that year; nothing brings out a town's naughty streak quite like intolerable heat.

Right. So with the extra box, that gave her eleven boxes to sort through, 1960–1969. She figured she'd focus most on 1964, the year Lenny Lincoln had disappeared, but she still wanted to cover all the sixties, in case there was additional information that might offer clues.

Susan sighed, already feeling overwhelmed. Best get cracking.

She brought over the step stool that was by the door so that she could reach the first box that she needed, placed on the very top shelf of the third row in. She sneezed as she slid it off, crying out and nearly losing her balance as a papery daddy longlegs carcass dropped down onto her chest. She didn't stop until all the boxes were down at her feet.

The crimes from 1960 were, overall, petty. Stolen farm equipment. Noise complaints. Grade-schoolers shoplifting candy, high schoolers shoplifting booze. Disputes over property lines. Not a single report of child neglect or abuse, though this wasn't surprising. Here were archives from an era when children had been taught to be seen and not heard. Few children probably would have had the nerve to report their parents to the police if they were being beaten or molested. And even if they had, would help have come?

After a while, Susan got a system down, and her sorting quickened. A few names she encountered in the files more than once. If she saw Ralph Combes, she knew it was going to be a complaint related to Neil Luchsinger's livestock wandering into his yard (they liked to munch on his cabbage and tomato plants). If it was Louise McClatchy, it was the noise the mechanics made—*swearing like sailors!*—in the shop next door to her house. A man named Mel Bancroft filed no less than fifteen complaints about teenagers doing burnouts in the gravel lot behind his barn.

Susan made a significant discovery about a quarter of the way through 1964. She'd been so fixated on the fact that she'd seen so few reports filed on children (other than for candy theft and their other bothersome habit, loitering inside the town's only comic book store without ever buying anything), that she'd nearly forgotten the main objective of her search. Now, the hairs on the back of her neck were rising, and her skin was breaking out in gooseflesh as she scanned the reports on one little lost boy, Lenny Lincoln.

Susan's excitement brought her to her feet, pacing. Attached to the thick stack of files were several photos of Lenny, as well as his home address, right next door to Death Farm. She quickly read. On May 13, 1964, Lenny and his brother, Milton, were outside playing hide-and-seek when Lenny went missing. Ultimately, it was assumed that a wild animal—used to be lots of coyotes and mountain lions in the area—had run off with the boy. The body, as she knew, was never found.

Susan frowned at what she initially dismissed as police ineptitude. How was it that the whole town had suspected Wayne Nichol of harboring unsavory feelings toward children, yet they'd never thought to arrest him when a child living *right next door* had gone missing?

She soon found the answer: On the day Lenny had disappeared, Wayne, along with his wife, Mary, and son, Gerald, were away visiting Mary's parents down in Fresno. Their alibi was airtight, investigated and confirmed. So it was claimed.

Wayne Nichol's death report was also at the very bottom of the box. An accidental poisoning, officially. *Bad produce.*

So *if* Overalls Boy was truly Lenny Lincoln, how could it still be Gerald or Wayne who was culpable, given that they both had alibis for the day he'd disappeared?

Susan pulled up the stool and took a seat, balancing the file on her knees. Okay, so if *Gerald* had skipped the Fresno trip with his parents and then murdered Lenny while he'd had the farm to himself, was it so far fetched to assume that his immediate family would lie to keep him out of prison?

As Susan knew from experience, no, it wasn't. People lied all the time, and it wouldn't have been the first time a family had orchestrated a cover-up to protect their own. She'd observed dozens of civilians committing perjury on behalf of their relatives in ways she couldn't have conceived, had she not seen it for herself. Parents lying about their offspring driving drunk, selling hard drugs from their very homes, sons beating wives and girlfriends nearly to death. Not too long ago, Susan had worked a statutory rape case that involved a middle-aged man and a fourteen-year-old girl. The man's sister—his so-called "character witness"—had claimed that the victim was lying for attention, that she had never even *heard* of the girl. Yet there were the sister and the girl all over Facebook, celebrating the brother's birthday together, arms linked over the liter of cheap vodka they'd been guzzling straight from the bottle.

The strangest part about it was that many of the perjurers had appeared quite wholesome. Their houses were tidy, decorated with cookie jars shaped like teddy bears and embroidered *Home Sweet Home* plaques. Blood. People will do almost anything for their blood, even if it betrays their own principles, even if they risk sending *themselves* to jail in the process.

Susan flipped through the file, not entirely convinced of the Nichols' alibi. Had Wayne and Mary produced gas or meal receipts to verify the trip? Had testimony been given by anyone other than Mary's family? There was nothing in the files to confirm or refute. Perhaps Mary had internally justified the lies to the police by later poisoning Wayne. Susan would have loved to ask Mary directly about the alibi, but she absolutely couldn't. Not without alerting Ed and the FBI to her snooping.

Susan studied the files spread out in front of her on the floor, shaking her head. There was the FBI with all their clout, all their flashy databases, all those Quantico credentials, yet *she* just might be closer than they to identifying Death Farm's first victim after only an hour of digging through old boxes in the station's basement. The FBI obviously hadn't even thought about checking old records; it was evident that nobody had been in the records room in weeks, months. Her shoes had left footprints on the floor, there was so much dust.

But.

But she might be getting ahead of herself. She'd proved nothing yet. And there were problems.

She drummed her fingers on her chin. Problem number one: If she *was* onto something, how was she going to justify to higher-ups coming across information she'd been forbidden to search for?

Problem number two was a lot bigger: she'd need DNA to prove her theory, samples from both Lenny—assuming Overalls Boy *was* Lenny—and Milton, since he seemed to be the only living relative left.

Problem number three: There was *a lot* of assumption happening on her part. She'd need something a lot more concrete than a flimsy alibi from the sixties before she could go to higher-ups with her theories.

CHAPTER 23

Eric began to have second thoughts about going to the authorities as he was mounting the steps outside the police station. He'd seen enough cop dramas on TV to know that it was typically attention seekers who went to the cops with so-called insider information they claimed would just *blow the whole damn case wide open!*

Not that Eric was going to make such an assertion. He was merely going to provide what little information he had, despite how cryptic it was. He was beyond mortified and felt like a caricature of a schizophrenic, showing up at the station with his half-baked theories, but he didn't know what else to do. He had to find a way to make his undead visitors go away before they incited a full-blown relapse.

There was also the most pressing possibility that he could help save some poor kid's life. Milton. The dead boy in his nightmare had said to *find Milton,* who might be suffering at the hands of that child predator, Gerald Nichol. Eric had thought more about it on the drive over, and it was what he ultimately had to assume—that his (visions? hallucinations? nightmares?) *insights* somehow related to Death Farm. It was the only thing that made sense, though it didn't make much sense at all: the screaming he and Jake had heard near the field as well as the news report that had played itself out on his television both pointed to Death Farm. Why *him,* when he had absolutely no connection to the farm, or even to California, for that matter?

The biggest obstacle Eric faced was getting the police to believe him about the potentially missing kid, particularly when he hardly believed it himself, if at all. Moreover, he had no concrete information to back his claims. It would have helped him greatly if the corpse-boy had told him *where* to find Milton or had given him a hint as to how long he'd been missing. An age. Physical description.

There was also the sketchy way Eric had been delivered his information, via a dead child and condiments. The most plausible story he could cook up for the police was that he sometimes had visions while he slept—that his dreams occasionally provided valuable insight about important events. And that was the *least* nutty explanation he could come up with, though it sounded exaggerated even to him.

Maybe they'll buy it, Eric reassured himself.

(Not a chance in hell.)

No, Eric thought miserably, *not a chance in hell.*

Though it was nippy out, a small cluster of sweat beads had formed along his hairline. Eric stopped on the second step from the top and shot a longing look over his shoulder at his Jeep, parked less than fifty yards away at the end of the street. He cupped his keys inside his jacket pocket and gave them a jingle. If only.

With a long sigh, he pulled open the station's thick glass doors and stepped into a warmth far too balmy to be comfortable. He was sweating profusely, his shirt clinging to his back and armpits unpleasantly. It was very possible that he would faint. He gripped his keys, sharpness bringing the world back into focus.

"Here goes nothing," he muttered and then smacked his lips. He'd brushed his teeth twice, but he still couldn't get the taste of sweet lemon out of his mouth. Which was funny, since he couldn't recall having eaten anything containing lemon for weeks.

The station's interior was small, ugly, and packed. Stale, like an old house that hadn't been aired out in decades. Its decor (if it could be called that) was industrial and outdated, gray and unwelcoming, though that was probably how police stations were *supposed* to look. Make things too nice, and the criminals just might keep coming back.

Eric approached a surly woman manning the main desk—the only employee there, or he would have gone to someone else. She was very large and very solid, with drab brown hair pulled back into a bun so tight that her forehead shone. Like the station itself, she was the antithesis of approachable. Her name tag identified her as Terri, though it was unclear if this was her first or last name. She looked like a Terri. *Terri-fying.*

"Yes?" She scowled without looking up, her eyes glued to paperwork she was pretending to shuffle through, her tone suggestive: *Can you go away?*

Not too long ago, Eric had overheard an electrician in Philly say that the sturdy historical building he was rewiring was "built like a brick shithouse." That was just like this woman, he thought, built like a brick shithouse.

Terri was not an individual who seemed to take too kindly to waffling, so Eric just spat it out. "I'm here about the, uh, Death Farm."

Her eyes still down. "You with the press?"

"No," Eric said and then chuckled nervously. "I'm here because I have some information about the case."

That got her to look up and give him a once-over. She didn't seem too impressed with what she saw. "Is that right?"

Eric held steady. "Yes. That's right."

Terri gestured lazily to the long bench to her left, where a dozen or so other concerned citizens sat waiting. "So do they. *Apparently.*" Snide emphasis. "You'll have to wait. Could be hours."

"That's fine." Eric offered her a smile, and she rolled her eyes.

"I'll need to see your ID," she challenged, as if expecting to trip him up with the request.

"No problem." Eric handed her his driver's license, and she thrust a clipboard at him.

She scowled down at the ID, his very existence aggravating her. "You still living in Pennsylvania?"

"I just moved here."

"If you're living here permanently, you'll need to get a California ID. You'll be fined if you're pulled over without current information."

"Oh," Eric said. "I didn't know."

She shrugged. *Whatever.*

She gave him a curt rundown on how to fill out the form. Eric did as he was instructed and then took a seat on the bench, casting surreptitious glances at others who were also waiting. The majority didn't seem *too* weird, yet there were certainly some odd ducks in the mix, though he supposed this was a bold outlook for a man about to claim he had psychic dreams.

He occupied his time by imagining worse places he could be at that precise moment. Deep underground in a sewer. A slaughterhouse in summertime. A shark's belly. Jim and Maggie's wedding.

He wished he had brought a book.

An officer finally came out for him about an hour later. She looked so different in uniform that initially he didn't recognize her, but when he got close enough to look into her pretty blue eyes, he knew. The woman from Luna's.

Dream Woman Susan.

CHAPTER 24

Shit.

He'd made a huge mistake. Maybe he could bolt before she recog—

"Hey!" She smiled, as if they were old friends. "Eric the drummer, right?"

Shit. Shit. Shit.

"That's right." He smiled back, wishing that the ground would open up and swallow him whole. He pretended to only just recall her name, as if he hadn't been thinking about her frequently since their meeting. "Susan, right? I had no idea you were a cop."

"Guess we never got around to it last night, huh? I got a call while you guys were playing and had to take off. Bummer."

He nodded. "Yeah, bummer. I was looking forward to our talk."

"Me too," she said with a little blush.

(Let's see how much she wants to talk to you after she finds out about the dead kid.)

Susan looked down at the clipboard she'd picked up from Terri. "I'd think you were stalking me, showing up at my work like this," she joked. "But it says here that you've got some information about the case?"

Eric frantically racked his brain for a way out. If he stayed, this amazing woman would surely come to think that he was out of his mind. But if he left, the dead kid would only continue to haunt him, and he would *go* completely nuts. He had no way of actually *knowing* this would happen, but he *knew*.

Could he pretend to faint? No, he could only feign a blackout for so long, or else they might call a very real ambulance.

She was giving him a funny little smile because he still hadn't answered.

Eric said, "It isn't exactly *information*, per se, but . . ."

"But?" Susan's smile was fading fast, replaced with a frown.

"It still might help," Eric quickly added. "But if you guys are slammed . . ." He made a show of looking around the station, as if suddenly realizing exactly how busy they were. "You know, maybe I should let those with actual tips talk to—"

"Hey, you never know what might help," Susan said brightly. The smile was back, though dimmed. "And you waited your turn, just like everyone else."

"Are you the one who will be, uh, taking me back?"

"Sure am. The FBI's got us assisting on the case, handling the interviews."

"Great." *Fuuuuuuuck.*

She gave him a little wave with the clipboard. They made small talk as they walked along a narrow corridor, ending at a stifling room toward the back of the building. It was furnished with a long table and three folding metal chairs. Eric sat down on one of them and jumped when its legs screeched on the floor as he pulled it closer to the table. Susan offered him a coffee, which he declined because he was already plenty jittery, and then took a seat opposite.

Eric asked, "Is it always like this?"

Susan laughed. "Not at all. Most days it doesn't even look like we're open. We're a small station, but now that the FBI is here . . . well, you saw. The crowd comes and goes. It gets biggest just after the news runs an update." She leaned forward, as if about to impart privileged information. "Nothing brings out the crazies like an infamous case. I heard they're now showing Death Farm footage over in Britain. Just *once* I'd like to see America make international news for something *good.*"

Eric cleared his throat. "The crazies?"

Susan leaned back. "Everyone wants a slice of the action. We've had *a lot* of tips about Gerald Nichol—people who say they know him or where he's run off to."

"I've never met the man," Eric said, "if that disqualifies me as one of the crazies." Though he'd made the statement jokingly, it sounded a tad defensive.

Susan, as if suddenly remembering that Eric was there on an official matter, straightened. She studied the clipboard. "Okay, so what's this tip of yours?"

Eric sighed and then met her eyes. *This is going to go one of two ways: bad or worse.* "Let me just preface this by saying that I *know* what I'm about to tell you is going to sound more than a little strange. I want you to understand that even *I* get its crackpottiness."

She chuckled. "Okay."

"It's . . . I . . . sometimes . . ." He paused to collect himself. "Sometimes I have dreams."

She brought her chin down toward her chest and looked up at him, her blue eyes skeptical. "Dreams."

"Now, I can already see that you're starting to think I'm one of the crazies—"

"Am not!"

"Please just hear me out."

Susan clasped her hands together on the table. "Eric, I can assure you that whatever you have to say is not going to sound even half as insane as some of the other things I've heard today."

"Oh?"

"*Trust me,*" she said. "I talked to a guy about an hour ago who claimed that his pet parrot told him that Gerald is hiding out in Orange County. He said that we need to send a squad car to Balboa Island stat—and, yes, he actually used the term *stat*—because Gerald is holed up on a yacht, posing as a millionaire."

Eric barked out a laugh, feeling marginally better about the situation. "I can't say that I've talked to any animals recently."

"Good." Susan gave Eric a reassuring smile. "See, you're already ahead of the game."

"I also want you to know," Eric added, "that I'm not seeking credit or anything for coming forward. Actually, I'd prefer that my name stay out of this completely. I just started a new teaching job over at the college, so I'm not trying to make waves."

Susan nodded. "I'll do my best, but you know that we'll have to keep your information on file?"

"Sure, sure," Eric said. "All that I meant is that I'm not looking for attention. I don't want or need to be some kind of star witness, or whatever the . . . *crazies* call it."

"Why don't you just tell me what you know, Eric?"

"Okay." He rubbed his chin, hoping to convey sincerity. "Like I've already mentioned, sometimes I have dreams. Many times, my dreams come true in ways that help people."

She frowned. "Help people? Like how?"

"Like . . ." He pretended to recall a memory. "Okay, like this one time, my buddy . . . Tony . . . was flying to New Zealand. Only when he started to pack, he realized he didn't have any idea where his passport was. He was leaving the next day, so he was frantic, right? No passport, no vacation. He started tearing his house apart, looking for it *everywhere*, but no go."

"Okay," Susan said, her expression neutral.

Where am I coming up with this? Eric thought. He knew a guy named Tony, sure—Maggie's father over in Tennessee—but he was a man few would describe as worldly. Anthony Snider was the sort who appreciated steak and potatoes with lots of ketchup, Sunday football, and Walmart Black Friday sales and was proud to deem any cheese other than cheddar exotic. Eric doubted Tony would have even been able to *locate* New Zealand on a map, had it not been for his *Lord of the Rings* obsession.

Eric continued, "I went home after seeing Tony that day and took a nap—he was still searching for his passport when I left. Anyway, while I was sleeping, I dreamed that Tony's passport was under a car mat."

"A car mat?"

Eric made a rectangle in the air with his fingers. "You know, those rubber thingies you put in cars to keep the carpet clean?"

"Right, that's what I thought you meant."

"Anyway, as soon as I woke up, I called Tony. I was sort of like I am now—I told him that it was going to sound crazy, but I had a feeling his passport was in his car under a mat."

"Was it?"

"Yep." Eric was stunned by how natural his story sounded, with every word of it being utter bullshit. "He went out to his car and checked while I was still on the phone. Apparently, he'd lost his driver's license a few weeks prior, so he'd been using his passport as ID. He'd run a few errands after going to the bank one day but didn't want to keep carrying his passport. He was driving his convertible around with the top down, and he was worried that somebody would steal it from his car—"

"So he stuck it under the mat to hide it," Susan finished.

"That's exactly right," Eric said. "He'd forgotten all about it because his new driver's license arrived in the mail that day." He shrugged. "So that's how my dream helped."

"That's . . . quite a story," Susan said, but not unkindly.

"It is. But sometimes stuff like that just *happens* to me. I have no idea why, but it does."

Susan clicked her pen. "So you had a dream about the case?"

"Maybe. I think so." Eric sat back in his seat in a manner he hoped looked relaxed. "Lately, I've been having dreams about a little boy."

"A little boy," she said, jotting down the information. "Can you describe him in a bit more detail?"

"Sure. He's young, about five or six, with brown hair and blue eyes. Lots of freckles."

"Okay. Go on."

"He always wears the same outfit in my dreams, blue overalls."

Susan's pen stopped moving. "Blue overalls, you said. Like denim?"

"That's right. You know, like what a farm kid would wear? But they look old. Denim is denim, I guess, but they always make me think of the past, like *Leave It to Beaver* era."

"You said *always*. How many times have you dreamed about him?"

Eric pretended to mull the question over. "Oh, I don't know, two or three times."

Susan made a few more notes. "And when did you start having these dreams?"

"I started having them *before* those kids were found on that farm, if that's what you're asking." Eric laughed, nervous. "This must sound so ridiculous to you."

"No, not at all," she said, maintaining eye contact, and Eric thought, *I bet she cleans up at poker*. "I'm just wondering how the boy ties in with the farm."

"Oh, I've seen it in the dream—the farm in the background." *Okay, it was in a newscast on a television that turned on by itself. Oh, and I also heard a crowd of children screaming there.*

"Right."

Eric clasped his hands together on the table. "The more I talk, the more embarrassed I feel." *And the more I worry that I've blown any chance I might have had with you.* "I hope you don't think badly of me."

"No, really, Eric, you don't sound that bad," she said genuinely enough. "And the fact that you're worried about what I think shows me how normal you actually are. It's the whack-jobs who don't stop to consider how insane they might sound."

"I appreciate that," Eric told her, though he wondered how far her definition of "whack-job" extended. Would she think differently of him if she knew he would be taking pills for the rest of his life to control an incurable mental illness? "I almost didn't come here, but I would feel terrible if something bad happened to some poor kid because I didn't speak up."

"Want to know what I think?" she asked, and he nodded. "I have no doubt that you had those dreams. You seem like a nice guy, and I'm sure you *do* want to help."

"That's *all* I want to do."

"I believe you." She made a reaching-out gesture, as if intending to touch his hand, but then quickly retracted. "But maybe you're connecting your dreams with the murders because you saw a story about it on the news. You want to help, and that doesn't make you crazy. It makes you a good person."

Eric almost left it at that, but he'd already come this far. "There's more that I haven't told you."

Susan clicked her pen. "Oh?"

"The boy in my dreams keeps telling me a name: Milton."

Susan's head jerked up. "Milton?"

Eric nodded. "He told me to 'find Milton.' I can't be sure of this— this is just an assumption—but I'm thinking Milton might be one of Gerald's victims."

"Milton," Susan repeated as she scribbled down the name.

"Does the name mean anything to you?" Eric asked.

She shifted uncomfortably. "I can't really . . ."

Eric held up his hands in understanding. "I'm guessing you probably aren't allowed to say. That's perfectly fine."

"Okay, so a little boy in denim overalls and someone named Milton," Susan summarized. "Anything else?"

"A couple other things, though I can't imagine their significance. A woman," said Eric. "She's pretty, early twenties . . . dressed like a hippie."

Susan held her poker face as she reached up and rubbed the back of her neck. "What about her?"

"That's the thing: *I don't know.* I've only seen this stuff in my dreams, and everything is just so scattered, so . . . *nonsensical,* you know? But I think she might be connected in some way. I don't know." Eric ran a hand through his hair. "Oh, and the numbers twenty-two and twenty-three . . . I can't imagine what they could possibly mean."

"Why those numbers specifically?" Susan asked carefully.

"I have absolutely no idea. But seeing how you're gripping that pen, they're important."

"I . . ."

"Right. You can't say," Eric said. "Okay, last thing: jacks—you know, the metal kind used in a kid's game? And a red ball."

Susan sat up very, very straight. "Mm-hmm."

Eric cast his eyes skyward and sighed. "Crazy, I know."

But Susan didn't look like she thought it was crazy. She looked like a ghost had crept up behind her and breathed down her neck. Like she wanted to run from the room screaming.

Chapter 25

Despite her elation at finally, finally being included in the Death Farm case (even if it was just listening to tips), Susan wasn't entirely ready to go back to interviewing the public just yet.

She went back to her desk to go over the notes she'd taken during the perplexing interview with Eric Evans. Though she didn't really buy his whole psychic-dream act, she also couldn't fathom how he could have possibly known the information he did, not unless he was paying off an employee in the FBI or at the morgue. That did not seem likely, given how high profile the case was.

She grabbed a handful of Skittles from her desk and crammed them in her mouth, contemplating as she crunched. Despite the puzzlement it caused, the one good thing, she realized, about his statement was that it gave her the fodder she needed to take her theories to higher-ups.

She felt it wisest to start with Ed.

Susan let out a long sigh as she entered the break room. As she'd expected, Ed was in there on his own, once again reading *Perrick Weekly* and sipping coffee. She'd pumped up the fervor of her exhale for his benefit so that he wouldn't get a sense of her nervousness over the information she was about to deliver. She plopped down heavily on the chair across from him for effect.

"Those cuckoo bananas got you riled?" Ed asked. That was Ed's special term for the crazies, and it always got a chuckle out of Susan.

"They smell delightful—that's for sure. I've found that their stench tends to correlate with their level of crazy. The worse the stench, the cuckooier the banana," she said sourly. She tapped a finger on the *Perrick Weekly*. "Anything good?"

"Same shit, different smell." Another Bender lyrical gem. "They mentioned you and that R&G guy." Ed pulled up a corner of the paper, showing Susan the article. A hint of a smile twitched his mouth. "The one who gets all tongue tied around you. Gabe?"

Susan rolled her eyes.

"You should go out with him."

"Why?"

"Because he likes you."

"So? That dirty old man butcher at Safeway also likes me. Should I go out with him too?" she quipped with a snort.

"If it means free steaks, sure." Ed wriggled his eyebrows to show that he was kidding.

With a humph, Susan made a move for the paper.

Ed moved it out of her reach. "What's wrong with Gabe?"

"Nothing's wrong with Gabe. I'm just not interested."

"How do you know if you haven't gone out with him? You're never going to find anyone if you don't stop being so damn picky."

Susan balked. "Maybe I don't want to find anyone. I don't have time for all that. I need a relationship like I need a hole in the head."

"I'm not saying you should marry the guy. But it wouldn't kill you to go on a *date* with him."

"Says the man who once told me that I should always be choosy about who I go out with because—"

"You end up marrying who you date. I know," Ed said. "And it's true."

"Okay, then."

"I only mean that you should try getting out more."

"I get out," Susan said in a voice that lacked conviction.

"Is that right?" Ed folded his arms across his chest. "When's the last date you went on?"

Susan pursed her lips.

"That's about what I thought."

Changing the subject—she had not quite worked up the nerve to get into the real reason she'd come—Susan leaned over Ed's shoulder and scanned the article. "Sounds like they just keep repeating the same story over and over."

"Yup. And they're not even getting it right either."

Susan saw an opportunity, and she took it. "Hey, speaking of that . . . there's nothing in there about the current body count, right?"

"Well, there is, but they've still got it at fourteen."

"So they're off by seven."

Ed nodded. "The FBI want to play their cards close to their chests on this one . . ." He set the paper down. "And just how would you know that the current count is twenty-one?"

Susan spoke fast. "Before you get mad, I was only doing my job."

"How's that?"

It was too late, Susan saw. Ed *already* looked mad. Or dangerously close to the edge of anger. "The *FBI* were the ones who requested that I take tips."

"So?"

"*So* I didn't want to waste your time—or the FBI's time—by bringing a potentially credible tip to you without first doing some fact-checking." She left out the part about her already checking a few facts down in the records room *before* Eric Evans's arrival.

Ed, now leery of her claims, narrowed his eyes. Still, much to Susan's relief, his anger seemed as if it had diffused. Not entirely, but it had lessened enough. "Okay, what's this tip, then?"

Susan drummed her fingers on the table. "This is a weird one, but I had a guy come in earlier and tell me that he had a dream about the farm and the numbers twenty-two and twenty-three."

Ed grunted. "He *dreamed* it? Just exactly how bad did he smell?" He flapped a hand dismissively and made a move to go back to his paper. "I thought you said this was a credible tip."

"That's the thing," she quickly said, shaking her head. "He didn't *seem* crazy."

"The really crazy ones never do, Marlan."

"No, I mean he was *normal*. He's a professor over at the college, and he was, you know, dressed well and didn't reek like a dumpster. He was good looking, funny." Susan scratched at her upper arm, frustrated. "He just seemed so *sincere*."

Ed folded the paper and pushed it aside. "You sweet on this guy or what?"

"No! Of course not." *Maybe. Yes.* "He also said that he wanted to keep his name out of things. From what I've seen, the real crazies always want credit—they'll say just about anything to get their names in print. But Eric, he actually seemed kind of *embarrassed* that he'd come in."

"Eric, huh?" Ed said as he took a slurp of coffee. "So then why did *Eric* come in?"

Ed was being dismissive, which Susan had expected. He would hear her out, but it didn't mean he'd listen. It was better than anger, she supposed. She answered, "He said he'd never forgive himself if something bad happened to a kid because he'd stayed quiet."

"How thoughtful."

Susan ignored the sarcasm. "He also said that in his dream he saw jacks and a ball—like the kid's game."

"So?"

Overcome with irritation, she said, "Jacks and a ball were found on *one of the bodies.*" She folded her arms across her chest. "And I know for a fact *that* information hasn't been released to the public."

Ed pursed his lips. "And just how did *you* come across this information?"

Shit. "Oh, you know . . . I just heard it around," she said, her eyes wide with feigned innocence.

"You're going to get yourself in trouble if you go meddling."

"I wasn't meddling. It was *fact-checking.*" Susan raised her shoulders and pooched out her lips. "Hey, I can't help what people tell me."

Coffee slurped. "Just watch yourself." And then more sternly: "I don't want to have this conversation with you again. You need to listen to me: stop interfering and let the FBI do their thing. I've worked too hard and am too close to retirement to have you making trouble for me. I've got my pension to think about—and how losing it would affect Shirley and the kids—so I won't have you jeopardizing it over this absurd Gerald Nichol crusade of yours."

"Understood." Susan got up and fixed herself a cup of coffee so that she'd have a moment to compose herself. As she joined Ed at the table, she said offhandedly, "But that's strange, no, that Eric would know about the game. The jacks and ball?"

"Susan—"

"Hey, you told me not to meddle *anymore.* I'm asking you about stuff I've already learned." Susan cupped her hands around the mug tightly. Ed was easily the most stubborn person she knew, which was unfortunate, given that he was her boss. He was a good man, but he had an ass-backward way of doing things, an unwillingness to think outside the box that was almost neurotic.

"Mm-hmm. Right." Ed sighed, resigned.

"No more questions about the case," Susan promised. At least, no more questions for *Ed.* "So . . . what do you think it means?"

"Hell, Marlan, it's a case involving kids, so this *Eric* probably had a lucky guess about the game."

"What about the numbers—twenty-two and twenty-three? There are twenty-one children's bodies at the morgue currently, but the news is still reporting it as fourteen. Don't you think it's weird that he's mentioned the numbers that immediately follow the current number?"

"I think you might be reaching," Ed said. "Even if the FBI aren't talking, it doesn't mean the locals aren't. Maybe he knows someone who's giving him information about the case."

Susan was dubious. "He just moved to town, so I doubt it. I don't know; it all seems a bit too coincidental."

"You mean a bit too bullshitty."

Susan disregarded the remark. "There's more. Eric said there was a boy in his dreams in overalls. The boy I found by the telephone pole was *wearing* overalls."

Ed rolled his eyes. "Look around! We're in farm country."

Susan might as well be talking to a brick wall. "He also mentioned the name Milton. He thought maybe it was the name of one of the missing kids. Ring any bells?"

"The FBI tell you as much as they tell me," Ed said, but he averted his eyes.

"Milton Lincoln is the *brother* of Lenny Lincoln, the boy who disappeared back in the sixties."

Ed's voice was tight as he said, "How did you *learn* that? Who, exactly, have you been talking to?"

Susan shook her head. "That's not the point. I still think Overalls Boy is Lenny Lincoln—I brought this up after I spoke to Mary Nichol, so this is not some new conspiracy theory that I've cooked up."

Ed's fury was returning. "We almost done here?"

Susan was feeling pretty miffed herself. Why did Ed even bother showing up for work anymore? She hadn't even gotten to the part about the woman Eric claimed to have seen, but she really couldn't see the point now. It would only add to Ed's irritation toward her. "But you haven't given me *anything*, Chief. Any thoughts on what I've told you?"

"Here's my thoughts: you're taking the ravings of a crazy old woman and an even crazier man as gospel." Ed sat back and shook his head, evidently appalled. "And here I thought that I'd trained you better than that. I'm starting to get a little afraid for you, kid, what this will do to your career."

Susan decided not to press her luck. "I appreciate your concern."

"Good," Ed said, calming down, picking at a hangnail on his thumb. "Now, do you really want to know what I think?"

Not really. "Sure."

"I think this guy, Eric, is messing with you."

"Why would he, though? He has no *reason* to. It's not like he has nothing to lose like some of those other nuts out there." She jerked a thumb over her shoulder. "He just moved to town for a job—a *good* job. Why would he take the risk?"

"Beats me. Who knows why people do half the things we arrest them for?"

Agitated, Susan screeched her chair back from the table. Maybe Ed was right, and she was only buying into Eric's story because she was "sweet" on him.

A little gentler, Ed said, "Okay, what would you like me to do, Marlan—have the FBI bring this guy, Eric, back in for questioning? You think he's up to something—maybe in cahoots with Gerald Nichol?"

Susan shook her head fast. "No! God, no, nothing like that. I just wanted to bend your ear about it; that's all."

Ed finished the rest of his coffee in one big gulp. "I could run a quick background check on the guy, if it makes you feel better. Might as well use my big security clearance for something."

Now they were getting somewhere. "Would you mind?"

"Yes, but I'll do it anyway."

Susan grinned. "Have I ever told you that you're the best?"

"Yes, but you can do it again," Ed said. "But I'm serious when I tell you: stop poking around. I'm only checking on this guy because I think he stinks. Maybe if I can get you to see it, too, you'll drop it. But this has got to stop. I mean it."

"Okay. Loud and clear," Susan agreed with a nod, though his words had fallen on deaf ears.

CHAPTER 26

Susan did not sleep well that night once again, the conversations with Eric, Ed, and Sal continuing to niggle at her.

Ed's unwillingness to hear her out was at the root of much of her irritation. She found it disgraceful that he had zero interest in speaking with Milton Lincoln, given all the facts she'd presented. She honestly couldn't see what harm it would do, but Ed, it seemed, was terrified at even the *possibility* of upsetting the FBI. Rather than ending his career on a spark, he'd rather just fade away. Susan felt guilty for her disloyalty, but she almost wished that he'd just quit *now*, if this was to be his attitude.

There were also several details about Overalls Boy that bothered her, the most compelling being that he'd been moved. Why him and not the others? And *was* he Lenny Lincoln?

Then there were Eric's claims. Out of all the twenty-one children he could have claimed to have seen, why Overalls Boy specifically? And how could he possibly know about the woman? Ed clearly thought the professor was a lunatic, but Susan wasn't so sure—and it wasn't because she had the hots for him.

Susan had been exposed to enough bullshitters in her line of work to last three lifetimes, and Eric didn't have any telltale signs of one. He didn't want credit. He wasn't trying to use his information (vague as it was) as a bargaining tool to hedge punishment for past crimes he'd committed. Above all, he acknowledged that his statement sounded crazy.

Susan arrived at work to find Ed lurking by her desk. She felt guilty once more as it dawned on her exactly how irritated she was by his presence, particularly because the man himself seemed to be in high spirits.

"Ah, there you are," he said as she approached. He was holding a file, which he waved above his head triumphantly. "Did I call it, or did I call it?"

"Call what?"

"Your man's a cuckoo banana."

"What do you mean?" she said, reaching for the file. "What man?"

Ed moved it out of her reach. He licked a thumb and pretended to root through the papers, clearly about to enjoy delivering whatever information he had. He cleared his throat and straightened his shoulders. "Eric Evans was arrested in Massachusetts in '03 for drunk and disorderly."

Susan frowned. "So? One drunk and disorderly does not a cuckoo banana make."

"I'm not done. They realized he wasn't drunk once they got down to the station, so they 5150ed him—"

"No way!"

"Yep, shipped him off to the mental ward. He'd forgotten to take his meds that day or something." Ed flicked a hand. "The guy's a schizo."

Susan reached for the file, and this time Ed let her take it. She read a few lines, shaking her head. "Shit."

"You can see for yourself. He's nuts."

"But he didn't . . ." Susan flapped the file against her thigh. "I don't think he was off his meds when he came in. I'm telling you, he didn't *seem* nuts."

"You mean other than claiming to dream about dead kids."

"Are there no other arrests on his record?"

"No others that I could find," Ed said, taking the file back from Susan.

Susan cocked her head. "So then it was an *isolated* incident?"

Ed made a snorting sound. "Isn't one 5150 enough? I'm thinking you just might actually be sweet on this guy."

"I won't dignify that with a response," Susan said and then pursed her lips. What she really wanted to say was this: Even schizophrenics could be psychic, couldn't they?

Crazy or not, Eric *knew* something. He just might not be aware of it.

Yet.

CHAPTER 27

Eric was moving the steamer trunk, now fully restored, into the bed-room when his phone bleeped with an incoming call from a number he didn't recognize. It turned out to be the last person on the entire planet he'd ever expect to call.

Dream Woman Susan.

She wanted to know if she could stop by his place in an hour and show him some photos of missing boys, see if any of them might be a match to the child he kept seeing in his dreams. He casually told her of course she could, though internally he was dubious of her motives. As far as he suspected, she thought he was a crackpot. And how could she not after he'd gone into the station spinning tales about dreams of found passports and missing children? He bristled with embarrassment every time he thought of it, which was often.

Eric began buzzing around his home in a panic as soon as the con-versation ended, wiping down surfaces and fluffing cushions, stuffing piles of dirty clothes (and loose papers and shoes) into the hamper. He was a naturally neat person, but he'd been a little lax with cleaning as of late because he'd been up to his neck in grading, which his assistant would typically do. If he had one.

He'd given his students their first quiz, and most had bombed with a D grade or below despite the extended office hours he'd offered each day after class. Only seven students in total had bothered to show, and naturally these were the serious students who really didn't *need* the extra help.

He'd also dumbed down the material drastically (though he would have never admitted this to anyone at the college), understanding that he was no longer dealing with students who might intend to make a career out of geology. The quiz had been straightforward enough.

Question: *How old is Earth?*

Answer: *4.56 billion years old.*

Question: *Did dinosaurs and humans coexist?*

Answer: *No.*

These were facts Eric felt anyone who'd made it past primary school should know. But the answers his students had provided were so glaringly obtuse that Eric, at about halfway through his grading, had truly begun to wonder if they weren't just fucking with him.

Answer: *We don't know how old Earth is since language hadn't been invented when the first humans were alive, so they had no way of writing records down.*

Answer: *Humans only existed with later "famous" dinosaurs like T. Rex and Velociraptor.* (Clearly dinosaurs they'd gleaned from *Jurassic Park*.)

And these were supposed to be college-level students? What were they actually *teaching* young kids these days?

Jake, not surprisingly, had aced the quiz. He'd technically scored 103 percent, since he'd correctly answered all the extra-credit questions. (Eric really had given his students every chance to pass.) Alas, if only all his students were as good as Jake.

Eric was feeling exceedingly nervous about Susan's arrival, primping as if preparing for a date. When Eric thought about it, her visit would mark the first time since Maggie that he'd be in his home one-on-one with a woman he was interested in romantically. The notion both frightened and excited him.

Maybe this was just the push he needed. Maggie had obviously moved on from him (she'd moved on even before they were *off*), so perhaps it was high time he returned the favor . . . not that an on-duty cop showing him photos of missing children qualified as moving on.

Still, it was a start.

◆　◆　◆

Susan arrived in her cruiser five minutes earlier than her projected time, in full uniform. As Eric watched her come up his walkway, he pondered what it would be like to have her come over for a social visit instead, sporting, say, a dress and heels, a girly purse under her arm instead of grisly police files. In appearance, she was the reverse of Maggie—brunette to Maggie's blonde, petite to her tall, blue eyes to her brown—but in his eyes, she was just as beautiful. Maybe even more, since she hadn't screwed Jim.

"Nice to see you again, Eric." Susan smiled as she entered. "Thanks for taking the time to see me."

Eric, now more nervous than ever, tried to keep his voice steady. "It's my day off, so you caught me at a good time." He showed her to the living room and offered her a drink. She accepted a coffee and suggested that they sit at the kitchen table instead so that she could spread the photos out for him to examine.

After they got settled at the table, Eric said, "I was actually really shocked when you called—I was beyond embarrassed after I saw you. I assumed you probably thought I was insane. I bet you never would have guessed when we met at Luna's that I'd come down to the station with a story like that."

She chuckled. "Life is full of surprises, hmm?"

He said, "Don't I know it."

She watched him carefully as she spoke. "It looks like maybe some parts of your dreams could be true."

"You're joking."

"Remember how you said the name Milton was important to the case?" He nodded, and she continued. "As it turns out, the next-door neighbor to Gerald Nichol is named Milton."

Eric was shocked. "I had no idea. Honestly, I didn't."

Susan seemed relieved. "I believe you. And there's more to it than that."

"There is? Do you think Milton the neighbor relates to the case—has Gerald hurt him?"

"No, but I'll get to all that in a sec. First, I want to show you the photos, okay?"

"Sure. Okay."

Susan opened one of the three files she'd come with and extracted a stack of about two dozen photos of missing boys, all matching the general age and physical description of Lenny Lincoln. She spread them out on the table in front of Eric. "Take your time. Really *look* at the photos and let them sink in."

Eric hunched forward so that he could inspect the images more closely. "Jesus. Are all these kids missing?"

"I'm afraid so."

He shook his head, murmuring, "Where did they go?"

"I wish I knew."

After a few minutes, Eric said, "I'm sorry; I don't recognize any of these boys. I really wish I could have helped you more." He was visibly deflated. He also looked more than a little worried. "I was hoping that I'd stop seeing the boy if I could help identify him."

"In your dreams, you mean."

Eric couldn't quite meet Susan's eyes. He hated being a liar. "That's right."

After a moment, she said, "That's okay. I'd rather you *not* recognize any of these boys than make a false identification. Sometimes, I think people are so eager to help out that they almost feel that they *have* to choose someone. They think that they're somehow failing us if they don't, so they start picking at random."

Susan put the photos away and then produced a new batch from the second folder. She spread them out on the table.

"Oh," Eric said. "I didn't realize you had more."

She nodded, watching him carefully. "How about these kids? Any familiar?"

Eric looked longer this time. "I'm sorry, but no." He raked a hand through his hair, sitting back. "There's a couple in here who look close, but it's not him."

Silently, Susan swept up the photos. From the third and last folder, she produced a new batch. She was about a quarter of the way through when Eric leaped from his seat.

His skin broke out in gooseflesh. "Him!" Eric snatched up a photo and turned it so that she could see. His hands were shaking badly. "That's him."

"Are you *positive*?"

"I would stake my own life on it. That. Is. Him." He rubbed the length of his arms, suddenly freezing. "Who is he?"

"Eric, that was a boy named Lenny Lincoln. He disappeared in the early sixties while playing outside with his older brother. That brother's name? Milton."

Eric's mouth dropped open. "I don't believe it." He was having a hard time formulating his thoughts, his urge to let out a shriek strengthening. He struggled to find a logical explanation for what was happening, and his fright only deepened when he failed to find one. How could he *possibly* be seeing a child who'd been dead for decades? If he was losing his mind—having some kind of *episode*—how was it that Susan was verifying his claims? He folded his arms across his chest and stared at her hard. "You aren't messing with me, are you?"

"Why would I do a thing like that?" Her expression was serious enough that she left little room for skepticism. "I have no reason to mess with you."

Eric took a seat and carefully set Lenny's photo back down on the table. "I suppose not."

"Eric, Milton lives next door to the Death Farm, and he was living there even way back when his brother disappeared," Susan said. "Lenny's body was never found. They thought maybe an animal attacked him, dragged him off. Gerald was living on the farm at the time."

In the pit of Eric's gut was a bowling ball made of ice. "I . . . I just can't . . . are you saying that one of the kids they found on that farm is Lenny Lincoln? That must be it, right?"

Susan did not answer. She clasped her hands in front of her on the table and said slowly, very slowly, "I'm not saying this is the case, but I have to ask you this, Eric. Is there any possible chance you could have gotten *confused* about any of this?"

Eric frowned. "Confused? How?" Could she know about his schizophrenia? He supposed she might if she'd delved into his history, though he believed medical records were confidential. Protected by law, even.

If Susan did know anything about his illness, she didn't say. "Maybe you saw a photo of Lenny online or maybe heard something from someone in town?"

Eric was flabbergasted.

"I don't mean to offend you or suggest—"

"No," Eric said. "What you're asking is reasonable. I'm just a little shocked by all this. I never thought my . . . my *dreams* would actually have any real relevance to the case."

"Thank you for being understanding. Some people, you know, they take things personally. But I wouldn't be doing my job if I didn't ask these kinds of questions." Susan paused. "But can I ask you one more thing?"

"Shoot."

"You didn't have any dreams, did you?"

Eric chewed on her question for a moment. "No," he finally admitted with a weak smile. "I didn't."

"Then what is it?"

"I honestly don't know." Eric puffed his breath out of his cheeks. "I . . . look, this is hard for me to explain because you're only getting bits and pieces."

"So tell me the whole story."

"It's complicated."

"I'm all ears."

Am I really about to do this? he thought. *You've already come this far, but you might as well kiss your chances with this amazing woman goodbye.* "Okay, so when I was nineteen, I was diagnosed with schizophrenia."

"Okay," she said and then took a sip of coffee.

"That's it? Okay?"

She chuckled softly. "You *want* me to freak out?"

Eric felt the tension seeping from his body. He found that he was even chuckling a little himself. "No, of course not. I just . . ."

"I'm assuming there's more to it than that," she said with a little shrug. "And believe me when I tell you that in my line of work, it takes *a lot* to shock me. Also, my mother is bipolar, so I'm not squeamish about mental illness the way a lot of people are. You have a disease; it's not like you brought it on yourself. And you have it under control now, right? I mean, you've got this house, a job?"

"Sure. Yes, it's been under control for quite some time." Eric sipped some of his coffee, cleared his throat. "I've been taking medication for so long that it's become second nature. I'm not perfect—"

"Nobody is."

"But I'm also not *sick* sick, if you know what I mean." She gave him a semiconfused look, and he clarified. "I'll always be schizophrenic, but I won't always have symptoms."

"Oh, right, got it." She nodded her head. "So then I'm not understanding what the problem is."

Eric waved a hand over the photos on the table. "*This* is the problem. I can't conceive how I could possibly know any of this. I've never heard of Lenny or Milton—I've only lived in town for a few weeks. I couldn't even tell you the name of the street that Death Farm is on. The only things I do know about the case are what they've said on the news, which isn't much. You can't turn on the TV these days without hearing about the manhunt for that molester guy, Gerald. And before you ask, it hasn't even occurred to me to ask anyone here in Perrick about the case—not that I know too many people in town. I don't have children, so I have no need to check on neighborhood safety or kidnappings or whatever. It's not a topic that interests me." He thought a moment. "Well, I *did* overhear a couple of my students discussing the farm itself, how it's scary that it's so close to their own homes. Still, I just can't see how . . ."

Susan gave him a patient look. "And your first thought is that you've been hallucinating all this? Which is why you lied about the dreams."

"I don't know what else to think."

"Maybe don't think about it at all."

"Meaning?"

"Maybe it is what it is," Susan said with a shoulder raised.

"Which is what?"

With a slight grin, she said, "I have absolutely *no idea*." When she saw that Eric was grinning himself, she continued. "Look, I'm the last person to believe in psychic brouhaha or whatever, but I'm also not one to question facts. The fact is you know something, even if you're not aware of it. I can't get into details, but you mentioned some details about the case when you were at the station that extend beyond the realm of coincidence. Obviously, you have some kind of insight into this case, whether easily explainable or not."

"You're not freaking out? Because I am. I'm *freaked*. If you've seen some of the things I have . . ." Eric shook his head and added, "And thank *you* for believing me. I'm sure it must have taken a gigantic leap of faith for you to even come here."

Susan hesitated, a battle seeming to take place in her police brain. "My boss wasn't too keen on the idea," she admitted. "Actually, I'm really not supposed to be here at all. I've sort of been banned from the case."

"Is that right?" Eric said, his eyebrows raised.

"So now I'm going to have to ask you to have a little faith in me, in the things I'm telling you. To not ever mention, to *anyone*, that I was here."

"Trust is a two-way street."

"Exactly."

They both went quiet, sipping their coffee.

Susan sat back in her chair, let out a little chuckle, and said, "Now I'm wondering if you're thinking *I'm* a crackpot."

"I can pretty much guarantee you that I would never think such a thing. People in glass houses and all that."

She laughed and then was thoughtful. "I know this is a stretch—okay, it's going to sound *completely* out there—but what if Lenny's been coming to you because . . ."

Eric raised his eyebrows. "Because?"

Susan scrunched her reddening face. "Because he has a message?"

Eric nearly burst out laughing because of her mortified expression. "A message?"

"You said that in your visions or whatever they are, Milton's name was important," she said. "What if Lenny wants you to find Milton so that you can tell him that it wasn't his fault that he disappeared?"

It was quite a leap, and yet it was . . . what, *plausible*? Sure, why not, given how the rest of his knowledge about the case had come about. "How did you come up with this notion?"

Susan took a sip of her coffee and then explained, "When I was discussing the case earlier with a town historian, he mentioned that Milton has always felt responsible for his brother's disappearance, maybe even *still* feels responsible."

"But that's ridiculous. They were just kids."

"Sure," Susan agreed. "But guilt is a bastard, right? Kid or not, Milton was the older brother, so maybe he feels like he failed at watching out for Lenny."

Jim could learn a lesson or two from this Milton, Eric thought with faint sourness.

"I checked around," Susan added. "In a small town like Perrick, you're going to find that locals know a little bit of something about everybody."

"Naturally."

"Anyway," she continued, "Milton is a recluse. He's spent his entire life on the same farm where Lenny disappeared, almost as if he's been waiting all these years for Lenny to return home. He also never married. Never had kids."

"Seems that losing Lenny destroyed his whole future," Eric commented, though he couldn't help reflecting that *his* current situation wasn't too far off from Milton's. "That's sad."

"It is," Susan said. "And it's about to get sadder. Milton is terminally ill. Testicular cancer. He'll probably be dead by this time next year."

"How awful. My dad died of prostate cancer," Eric said. "It's no picnic."

"Oh, I'm sorry to hear that."

"Thanks," Eric said automatically and then quickly moved on. "So you think Lenny wants Milton to go in peace, something like that?"

Susan nodded. "That's pretty much exactly what I was thinking. Who knows? It might give Milton some peace to know that he didn't lose Lenny, that Lenny was *taken*."

"Sure, I could see that."

"It will be easy enough to prove that it is, in fact, Lenny's body if Milton consents to giving us DNA," Susan said. "Which I'm guessing he will."

"I'm getting the feeling that there's something else you need from me," Eric said, wary.

Susan colored. "Am I that obvious? I was hoping you might want to come with me to Milton's house. You know, because of all that you've been seeing? I would have said something sooner, but I didn't want to ask you until . . ."

"Until what?"

Susan tapped a finger on the files. "I wanted to see if you'd correctly identify Lenny."

"Of course I'll go with you to Milton's," Eric said. "But I can't promise he'll believe anything that I say."

Susan gave Eric a lopsided smile. "All we can do is try."

"So when do you want to go?"

Susan pulled her keys from her pocket. "Now work?"

"I'll get my coat."

Chapter 28

Milton Lincoln was not what they had been expecting, which was a frail old man with a shuffling walk, pilled cardigan sweater, and croaky, scratched-record voice. The Milton who opened the door to Susan and Eric, while thin, was tall, strong looking, and sinewy, a willful workhorse who bucked the very notion of retirement. His weather-beaten face, tanned from decades of hard labor, boasted blue eyes that were sharp and wily.

The Lincoln farm was straight out of a Norman Rockwell painting. The fences were painted crisp white to match the house, its porch swept clean enough to eat from, the bright-green yard trimmed with nary a blade out of place. Milton's truck, a sturdy seventies model with a camper shell, was faded brown yet immaculate. The barn, positioned about a hundred yards back from the house, was painted a clean brick red.

It was difficult to believe that this was a man dying of cancer. When Eric's own father had been terminal, making it to the bathroom on time was a grand achievement. Milton Lincoln evidently wasn't planning on going out to pasture without a fight.

Milton didn't look at all surprised to see them. "Was wondering when you guys would come back," he said as he opened the door, sweeping an arm across his body. "Come on in."

Once they were inside, Milton gave Eric a cursory glance. "You aren't with the law, though, are you? Else you'd be in uniform too."

Eric smiled pleasantly. "You're right. I'm not."

"You're not with the news?" Milton asked with a squint. "Had lots of reporters from the TV come knocking. Vultures, the lot of them."

"No, I'm not with the news. I'm . . ." Eric looked to Susan for help.

"Mr. Lincoln," Susan said. "You mentioned other officers have come by?"

He nodded. "Though not police like you. FBI, they were."

Susan said, "We're not here in any official capacity, Mr. Lincoln."

"Oh?"

"No." This time it was Susan who looked to Eric.

"Mr. Lincoln," Eric began, "we're here about your brother, Lenny."

Milton was flabbergasted. "My God . . . it's been years since anyone has *spoken* that name to me. What's this about?"

"Maybe we should sit down for this," Susan suggested.

Susan and Eric burst out laughing as soon as they were back in the cruiser.

"He thinks we're both completely nuts, doesn't he?" said Susan with a snort, which intensified their hysteria.

"Oh yeah. Completely nuts." Eric grinned. "But it was still sweet that he humored us."

Susan grew serious as she glanced up at the rearview mirror, the farm shrinking as they made their way down the driveway. "Seriously, though, I hope we didn't upset him. I thought he was going to pass out when we brought up Lenny."

"I did too. But at least he agreed to come in and give a DNA sample. He could tell that our hearts were in the right place."

"And thank goodness for *that*," she said, looking over at Eric. "I'd hate to have him file a complaint with my boss, since our little trip wasn't exactly sanctioned."

Eric smirked. "Bit of a rebel, are we, Suze?"

"I plead the Fifth," she said and then went quiet for a beat. "You'd think Milton would actually *want* to believe us, you know, because of him being terminal."

"He's probably just stuck in his ways," said Eric. "Imagine what it must have been like for Milton, having the two of us show up at his door about his brother, who's been dead for decades. At least you're a cop. I'm just the idiot standing next to you."

"You have a point," Susan said with a snicker. "Hey, what was the deal with that photo?"

"Photo?"

"I saw you looking at that frame with Lenny and his horse—and how dang *cute* was Lenny, by the way? I keep thinking of him as this freckled little thing, which is weird, since he'd be in his early sixties if he were alive today."

"I never thought of it like that, but you're right."

"But your *face* when you looked at that photo." Susan frowned. "It was like you had seen a ghost."

Eric so desperately wanted to tell Susan, well, everything. The whole story—not just about the messes in his kitchen, the visions of the horse, and the dead mob at Luna's, but also about his *life*, his divorce from Maggie.

But.

But it was a lot to unload on a person he hardly knew. He wasn't ready.

All in good time.

Baby steps.

"I had forgotten all about it until I saw the photo," he lied. "But I also saw that horse. In my visions or whatever they are."

"Seriously?"

"Seriously. It was *the same* horse, I swear. I remembered it because of its color, that bright auburn. Like rust."

Susan glanced over at Eric long enough to ascertain that he wasn't yanking her chain. "What do you think it means?"

"I don't think it *means* anything," he said. "In all honesty, I just want to put all this behind me. Hopefully, today will be the last I see of that horse and Lenny Lincoln." *But not you, Susan. I'd happily see more of you.*

Susan's expression was difficult to read. "Fair enough."

Eric's cell buzzed in his pocket. It was a text from Jake.

Fancy a little B&B (brews & bowling)? It'll be the band & some friends.

Eric glanced over at Susan. Can I bring a friend?

A lady friend?

Maybe.

Hells yeah! Bring her. Perrick Lanes. 7 p.m.

Sweet. 7 it is.

Eric suddenly felt as bashful as a virgin on his wedding night. It had been so long since he'd asked a woman out that he could hardly remember how to do it.

"Girlfriend texting to see where you've been all day?" Susan ribbed. "Maybe saw you riding in a cop car and thinks you've been arrested? You're in big trouble, mister."

Now, was it just him, or was there a little jealousy hidden underneath her teasing? A little inquisitiveness?

"No," Eric chuckled. "No girlfriend."

"Oh. Good," she said and then blushed all the way up to her hairline. "I mean—"

"So listen, my friend Jake—he's the violinist in Augustine Grifters—is getting together tonight with some friends. Some of the band will be there. I don't know if you like bowling or not, but if you want to join—"

"Love to."

"Oh." Eric was all smiles. "Okay, that's great."

Baby steps, he thought.

Baby steps.

CHAPTER 29

"Striiiiiiiike!"

Jake did a victory dance and flashed finger guns at his competitors, Eric and Susan among them, along with John, the band's bassist. He licked his index finger, brought it to his rear, and made a sizzling sound. Jake's team cheered, as did a small crowd of spectators loitering near the nacho bar.

"Yeah, yeah, yeah," Eric said, hitching his pants exaggeratedly as he moseyed to take his turn. "You just watch *this* magic."

Eric was having a laugh. He was, hands down, the worst bowler under the entire roof of Perrick Lanes, maybe even in all of Perrick County. Everybody there knew it, Eric included.

Sure enough, he took down just one pin.

When Eric returned to his seat, Susan clapped his back and poured him a pint from the communal pitcher, offering a consolation. "At least you kept it out of the gutter this time."

It was an unpretentious evening of cheap beer and smelly rental shoes, and Eric was content. He was finally starting to feel at home in Perrick.

And there was, of course, Susan. Eric was growing fonder of her with each passing minute (it was not lost on him that Maggie wouldn't have been caught *dead* in a venue as lowbrow as a bowling alley), and his hope that she might also like him in return had morphed into near certainty. Sometimes, you just *knew.*

Jake sensed a spark between them too. When Susan excused herself to go to the restroom, Jake shared his suspicion with Eric. "You know," he said, "she's gaga for you."

Eric took a sip of his beer. "Get outa here."

"I'm serious. The rest of the band thinks so too."

Eric leaned around Jake and saw that Madison and John were giving him the thumbs-up. "Yeah, well."

"Well, what?"

"I don't know . . . I don't want to make a move until she knows my whole story."

"That's not what you were saying the other night after the show," Jake pointed out.

Eric said, "But that's before I knew her. The game's changed now."

"Sounds like an excuse to me."

"It'll happen in good time."

Eric understood that many men his age came with some form of baggage—children, debt, broken hearts—and that most women Susan's age had probably encountered lovers who were imperfect in some way. But *crazy* was not situational, a complication that would go away in time. Children grew up and moved out of the house. Debts were paid off. Hearts healed. But schizophrenia was forever.

Some of the women Eric had dated prior to Maggie hadn't cared too much about his illness. Then there had been those who'd pretended not to care, though it eventually became clear that they did. Even some of the best of them had cared. Eric didn't take offense; it *was* a lot to take on. Ask a woman what kind of man she's looking for, and ten times out of ten she won't say *tall, dark, and crazy.* Eric knew he was damaged goods, but he felt he also had other redeeming qualities to offer. And if Susan could see past his schizophrenia, they'd have serious potential.

"What's the issue?" asked Jake.

"No issue. I just want her to get to know me better before I make a move."

Jake gave Eric a measured look. "You know, my dwarfism will never go away either. It's not like I don't know where you're coming from."

"Short isn't crazy."

Jake made a sputtering sound.

"And she knows about my illness."

"She does? Well then, what's the damn problem? She obviously doesn't give two shits."

Eric flapped a hand. "There's more to it than that. This divorce I'm going through now . . ."

Between his swigs of beer, Jake said, "Know what I think your real issue is? You're afraid of rejection."

"Maybe. But I'm still going to take things slow."

"You mean do nothing? You're being chickenshit," Jake said and then noticed that Susan was coming back from the bathroom. In a casual voice, he added, "I don't know—I usually go with Peavey amps for that size space."

"They're good ones," Eric said smoothly and then replenished Susan's beer as she sat down. She scooched closer to him on the bench and offered him a smile of thanks. For the umpteenth time that night, he told himself, *Do not screw this up.*

After Jake's team destroyed theirs at the bowling alley, Eric and Susan went home. Eric's belief that Susan fancied him was solidified at her front door by a golden question: "Would you like to come inside?"

Boy, would he ever.

Even so, Eric floundered. "Maybe some other time, if that's okay?"

She looked devastated. "Oh, okay, sure."

"It's just that I've got to get up early and take care of some things for work."

She said little else before he got back in his car and drove home, leaving his very confused and disappointed date on her doorstep.

He was still berating himself as he pulled into his garage. *Why did you do that? Why?*

"You *are* chickenshit," he said to himself in the rearview mirror.

Though buzzing from the evening, Eric was surprisingly beat. As he lazed in bed, skimming a collection of short stories by Stephen King that he'd picked up at the college's library, he started to worry that he'd screwed things up with Susan by not accepting her offer. Although he didn't believe there was such a thing as thinking too much—if you asked Eric, most people didn't think *enough*—he was aware that he could sometimes be a trifle obsessive when it came to matters of the heart.

Jake was right when he'd accused him of stalling. Eric could recall more than a few times in his life when he'd missed his window with a woman simply because he'd sidetracked himself by fixating on the pros and cons of the situation, the statistical probability of a romantic outcome. But the circumstance with Susan was different, and . . .

"And no more obsessing." Eric put the book away and turned out the light.

Sleep made it clear that it was not going to come easy. Eric stared into the darkness, restless, his residual beer buzz now completely diminished, a slight headache left behind in its place.

He rolled onto his side and checked the time on the alarm clock. 12:03.

He closed his eyes and counted sheep.

He checked the time. 12:38.

Eric reached to turn on the lamp but decided to give sleep one more chance. He yawned, stretched, scratched his belly.

He checked the time again. 1:22.

1:23.

Sighing, he gave up. He rolled over, turning away from the alarm's violating green digits. He opened his eyes.

Two glowing eyes stared back at him.

Lenny Lincoln's rotting head was resting at the edge of the pillow, gray flesh illuminated from within by a hellish death fire. His mouth dropped open, putrid breath watering Eric's eyes, and a beetle scuttled out from under his tongue.

Wheeze-wheeze . . . wheeze-wheeze . . .

Eric launched from the bed. He ran unthinkingly, running for running's sake. He skidded through the first doorway he came across, the bathroom's, socks sliding him across the tiles like a Waimea surfer. He bruised a knuckle fumbling for the knob and slammed the door closed behind him.

"*Fuck!*" he cried, gaping wildly about the room. For reasons unknown even to him, he jumped into the bathtub and jerked the curtain closed. In a crouch now, he pulled his knees up to his chest and waited.

Bang! Bang! Bang! Lenny thumping walls, sliding furniture about the bedroom. His bed? His dresser?

Eric clamped his hands down over his ears. *Why won't he go away?* he thought miserably. "Lenny Lincoln! I did what you wanted!" he shrieked, his voice reverberating dully around the artificial curves of the tub. "*You little shit, I did what you wanted! What do you want from me? WHAT?*"

The house fell silent, barring the terrified thump-thump-thump of Eric's blood pounding in his ears. He remained still, a rabbit evading a coyote's attack, listening.

Nothing.

He waited a solid five minutes, just to be sure, and then began sliding the curtain back, unaware that he was holding his breath. He stopped about midway, noting a flicker at the wide gap that ran along the bottom of the door.

Lenny on the other side.

A childish voice teasing him now: *Come out, come out, wherever you are!*

Eric froze, his grip crushing vinyl, arm tensing and pulling. His gaze was so focused on the doorknob, which he could have sworn had begun to turn, that he did not notice the little hand that came sliding up from the floor.

It wasn't long before he saw.

One, two, three, four grubby dead fingers tapping at the gap, mostly bone.

Piercing children's screams filled the room—no, not the room. *His head.* They came from inside his brain, pushing outward against his skull.

(Help us!)

He groped his face, mouth twisted in agony, squeezing his eyes shut so that they wouldn't rupture. He could picture them expanding within the sockets, quivering like balloons bursting with helium.

Silence.

Hastening to get to his feet, Eric put all his weight on the shower curtain as he pulled himself up halfway. He heard a soft metallic plink, and then the curtain came crashing down on top of him, tension rod and all. The rod smacked him hard across the cheek, a tender welt sprouting. He fell back into the tub, arms flailing and tailbone smarting, his temple thumping the sharp edge of the soap dish. Cursing, he batted the curtain aside, fixing his eyes on the door.

Lenny was gone. Eric could *feel* it as much as he could see it, though he lacked the courage to verify. "Nope. Not gonna happen," he muttered with a solid shake of the head.

Eric eased back into the tub. "Well, I've slept in worse places." He reached for a towel and fashioned a nice little pillow for himself. He tucked the shower curtain across his body, trying to imagine that it was a blanket, but it was cold, and he was wearing nothing more than his boxers.

He was still shivering when he awakened in the morning. His neck cried out for mercy as he sat up, his left arm gone numb.

He had to pee. He shuffled to the toilet, pulled his boxer shorts down, and—

"What the hell?"

He brought his hands close to his face so that he could examine his throbbing fingertips. Underneath his nails were jagged slivers of dark brown. Like he'd spent all night scratching at wood, clawing away until splinters split his skin. Dried blood was crusted down to his knuckles.

Boxers around his thighs, Eric frantically searched around the bathroom for *anything* that might match the wood. The toilet plunger's handle was clear plastic. The soap dish was blue-and-white plastic (though cheaply swirled to look like marble). He groped for his hairbrush inside the medicine cabinet, prescription bottles tumbling into the sink. Plastic.

Tub: plastic.

Toilet seat: plastic.

Wastebasket: plastic.

He was surrounded by fucking plastic!

Ignoring his aching bladder, he pulled up his boxers and trotted to the bedroom. His breath escaped him with a soft whoosh as he entered. The banging the night before—Lenny Lincoln had gone *apeshit*. Sheets ripped from the bed. Bedside lamp smashed all to hell. Clothes torn from hangers, spilling out from the closet in a massive tangle. Umbrella sitting open on the bare mattress.

At the crux of it all was the steamer trunk he'd worked so hard to restore, upturned in such a way that it seemed to convey a threat.

Or a message. But what the message was, Eric couldn't decipher.

He smacked his forehead as it hit him.

The steamer trunk, with its rich, *dark wood*.

Eric crossed the room in a hurry. He righted the trunk, opened it, and found just what he was looking for. He brought his hands to the underside of the lid. The wood matched the splinters underneath his nails perfectly.

"Whaaaaaat?" There was something else.

He took a step back from the trunk and tilted his head so that he was looking at the lid sideways. His claw marks formed two jagged numbers: *22, 23.*

What was it with those goddamn numbers?

As if to answer, Lenny Lincoln appeared at his side. "Milton," he whispered and then kicked Eric in the shin.

With a sharp yowl, Eric stumbled back, losing his footing as the soft underside of his arch crunched down on the busted alarm clock. He fell hard on his rear. Lenny made a move as if to lunge at him, and Eric crab scuttled back until he smacked up against the wall.

Lenny's dead face was passive, if not a little mocking. After what felt like an eternity, he turned his back on Eric, dismissing him, and climbed into the trunk. The lid slammed down with a bang.

Eric sat back against the wall, his fright now replaced with startling indignation. He'd had just about *enough* of this bullshit! He was exhausted after spending the night cowering in the tub, freezing his ass off in his underwear, a shower curtain for a blanket. His home had been destroyed, along with what few personal possessions he had left. His sanity questioned. He'd been violated—*humiliated*—all because of this little child. This *brat*, who'd terrorized him relentlessly, who'd brought forth hallucinations . . .

(Are you sure *it's hallucinations?)*

I'm sure, Eric thought, shaking his head.

(But you felt the kick just now, right? And that death smell! And how do you explain all those times you've been right about the Death Farm case? The photo of the horse at Milton's?)

Eric frowned. Okay, if it wasn't hallucinations, then . . .

(Ghosts?)

Eric snorted. Ghosts.

(Well, why not?)

Because it was crazy. And he *was* crazy, so that made him an expert.

Eric thought for a minute, his gaze tracing the lines of the trunk, his mind grasping for an answer that was slightly out of his reach.

He sat up, frowning.

Was that it—the trunk? Had it *all* been over this stinking twenty-dollar trunk he hadn't even *needed* in the first place?

He went over the dates. Nothing peculiar had happened in Perrick until *after* he'd brought the damn thing home and started messing with it. The night terrors. The vandalism. The TV turning on by itself. The . . .

Okay, the *possible* appearance of ghosts.

Eric got to his feet. "I'll be damned. It's the trunk."

He walked to the bathroom to empty his aching bladder. After, he'd shower and load up his car.

There was someone he needed to see after work.

CHAPTER 30

Milton did not come to the door right away. Eric had been standing on the porch so long that he was considering giving up, but it had taken him a great deal of effort to first heft the trunk into the Jeep at home and then remove it at Milton's.

Moreover, he didn't want to touch the goddamn creepy thing ever again, if he could avoid it.

When Milton finally peeked his head out, he did not look pleased to discover his surprise visitor. He stepped onto the porch and shut the door behind him. He was wearing workman's overalls, curls of wood shavings speckled around his shoulders like pine dandruff, and thick tan leather gloves. "You again," he said.

Milton's frosty greeting was precisely what Eric had expected—*he* hated it when people dropped by *his* home unannounced—yet he was nonetheless embarrassed. "I'm sorry, Mr. Lincoln. I've caught you at a bad time. I would have called, but I didn't have your—"

"It's unlisted." Milton clapped his gloves together, releasing a small cloud of sawdust. He pulled them off and stuffed them in his back pocket. "Was just out back doing some woodworking."

Eric waited for Milton to say more. He didn't.

"I'm sorry to just show up like this, but . . ." Eric paused. "I wasn't sure this could wait."

Milton frowned at the trunk. "You bring that here?"

"That's, uh, kind of what I wanted to talk to you about. It's difficult to explain." Eric chuckled nervously. "It's about your brother, Lenny."

"Lenny?" Milton chewed on the inside of his cheek. He seemed to be contemplating his reaction, flip-flopping between irritation and flinty amusement. At last he opened the door for Eric. "Guess you'd better come on in."

They left the trunk on the porch.

Inside, Eric took a seat on the sofa, and Milton asked, "Would you like some tea?"

"Tea?" A rush of relief flooded over Eric. The old man couldn't be too upset if he was being hospitable. "No, it's okay. I don't want to take up too much of your time."

Milton looked around his empty home. "Son, what else do you think I've got going on?"

"I thought you were doing woodwork or . . . ?"

"The wood isn't going anywhere," Milton said. "I live way out here by myself. Tell you the truth, I'm happy for the company."

"Tea would be great," he said with a pleasant smile, though he had no interest in a visit. What he wanted most was to get the hell out of there, to put as many miles between himself and the trunk as possible.

Milton ambled toward the kitchen on bowed legs, a cowboy's walk. "You fine with green? It's all I have. Doctor says it's good for blood flow or something. I could make you coffee, if you like. I've got some instant stuff—nothing fancy as what they've got in town."

"Green tea is great. Thank you."

Eric's pocket broke into happy song as Milton went into the kitchen. He pulled his cell out to answer—it was Susan—but then Milton poked his head around the doorway, looking peeved about the noise, wanting to know if Eric took sugar with his tea. Eric silenced the call and told him no, plain was fine.

Susan called again as Milton was telling Eric that he also had honey, if he preferred. Apologizing for the interruption and declining the honey, Eric powered his phone off.

Milton came out with two steaming mugs. He handed Eric his tea and then sat down on the ancient paisley armchair opposite. He cleared his throat, prompting Eric to get the show on the road.

"The thing is, Mr. Lincoln—"

"Call me Milton."

"Okay, sure." Eric sat back and took a sip of the tea, which was a lot bitterer than he was accustomed to. He sipped it to be polite and to warm his bones. It was meat-locker cold in Milton's old house. "The thing is, Milton, that I keep seeing your brother."

Milton blinked. "Oh? More dreams?"

"No, not dreams."

"Then what?"

"Well . . ." Eric's eyes shifted toward the porch. He sat back in the chair, took a sip of tea, and let out a little laugh. Shaking his head, he said, "You know what? It's late, I'm exhausted, and I'm sure you're eager to get back to your woodworking. I'm just going to throw it all out there, if that's all right?"

Milton shrugged.

Then, like a dam had burst inside his mouth, Eric spilled everything. He took his time and was methodical recounting events, leaving no detail neglected, starting with the purchase of the trunk and ending with his latest interaction with Lenny. He talked about the screaming in the field, the spilled sugar, Lenny's visits with the horse, the young dead mob with the woman at Luna's. The wheezing. The ceaseless tormenting . . . and on and on.

When Eric finished, he folded his hands over his lap. "I know it sounds crazy," he said, feeling just *like* a crazy person. "Completely insane. I'm totally aware that it does."

Milton cracked a dry smile. "Then why come here and tell me all of this?"

Eric didn't have to think long about his answer. "Frankly, Milton, I'm scared. As much of a nuisance as Lenny has been, he still terrifies me. I'm at my wit's end."

Milton frowned. "Why?"

"I don't think he's going to stop—at least, he *wouldn't* stop if I didn't come here." Eric held up his hands, showing Milton his damaged fingertips. "Like I said, Lenny has gotten a lot more aggressive. *Physical.* It's like he's trying to tell me something but can't quite figure out how to do it."

Milton made a move to examine Eric's fingers but then seemed to think better of it. "Lenny do that to you?" he asked, almost sarcastically, peering at the nails.

Eric shrugged. "I don't know. Probably. But I think everything that has been happening, all this stuff with your brother, it's because of that *trunk* outside. I'll be honest with you, Milton: I would have just left it on your porch with a note, had I thought that it would do some good."

"But you didn't think that it would?"

"No." Eric shook his head. "No, I didn't. I think there's more to it—that there's a message I'm supposed to deliver, possibly to you. But for the life of me, I can't figure out what it is. Why me, you know?"

Milton shrugged.

"So that's why I brought the trunk over," Eric said. "I'm wondering if it might have some significance to you—or to Lenny?"

"Hell, I don't know," said Milton. "We're talking about over fifty years ago. My mother had a trunk kind of like it, I think, but I don't remember us ever playing with it."

"Oh." Eric didn't know what to do next. Suddenly, he sat up very straight. Lenny Lincoln had followed him.

Milton leaned forward, watchful of his guest. "What? What is it?" Milton did not seem to trust him, and Eric really couldn't blame him.

"Lenny." Eric inclined his head toward the window, keeping his eyes lowered.

"What about him?"

"He's here now, standing right over there. By the window."

Milton turned his head, frowning. "I don't see anything. What's he doing, then?"

Eric swallowed. He didn't want to antagonize the boy. "He's stomping his feet, pointing."

"At what?"

Eric shook his head. "I don't know. Your barn, maybe? Is there something out there?"

"Sure. All my farming equipment."

Eric set his mug on the coffee table, and Milton nudged a coaster toward him. He could have as easily handed it to Eric, but he seemed to be avoiding touching him, as if his type of crazy were communicable.

They sat for a moment in awkward silence.

As Eric reached out for his drink on the table, Lenny ran up and slid the mug away from his grasp. Eric caught it just as it was about to go sliding over the edge.

Milton yelped sharply.

Eric barked out a demented laugh. Such a weird day, and it kept getting weirder!

Milton wasn't amused. The old man's skin had blanched to the color of mashed potatoes. "Was that . . . ?"

"Lenny," Eric said with a nod. "Like I said, he can be rather mischievous."

"You mean . . ." Milton placed a hand over his heart, his breath hitching. "Lenny is actually *here*. In this room."

"That's right."

He caught his breath and said, "Son, I don't mean any offense by this, but I figured you'd been putting me on."

Eric took a sip of the tea. "I have no reason to put you on, Milton." He went to set the mug down and reconsidered. Lenny would probably just go after it again.

No, Eric saw, he wouldn't. Lenny was gone.

Milton asked, "How can you be so calm?"

"I guess I've just gotten used to it." Though he was still scared shitless.

Milton, however, looked like his ticker was about to explode. The man was already riddled with cancer, so adding a heart attack to the mix would not be a good thing.

Eric asked, "Are you sure you're okay? It's quite a shock, I'm sure."

"I can't . . . Lenny is here! *Here*." Milton gaped around the room. "Where is he now?"

"Actually, he's gone. He sort of *dissolved* after he tried to knock my tea off the table." Eric shrugged. "He does that sometimes—vanishes, I mean."

This seemed to relax Milton a little. He sat back and took a sip of his drink, opened his mouth, and then closed it.

"I did some research on steamer trunks earlier, before I came over here," Eric said.

Milton frowned, lost in thought. "Steamer trunks?"

"Like the one outside." Eric nodded toward the porch. "Anyway, I found that they were mainly used from the late eighteenth century to early twentieth century. Some are worth quite a lot of money—for example, an early Louis Vuitton trunk can fetch well over fifteen, twenty thousand dollars. But of course, *that* trunk isn't designer, and the bottom is damaged, which is why I got such a good deal . . ."

Milton seemed lost.

"I'm digressing," Eric said. "The point is I tried to research the trunk's history because I thought there might be some other tie to it, something that maybe doesn't have anything to do with you and Lenny."

"A tie?"

Eric flushed. "I know this is all outrageous—trust me, I can hardly believe I'm even saying it. But I'm wondering if maybe there's an unrelated . . . *presence* from a different era that's latched on to the trunk and somehow using Lenny to communicate." Eric sat back and sipped his tea, cupping the mug to warm his hands.

"Hmm."

"I've been assuming everything is tied to Lenny and all that's been happening at that farm next door, but what if I'm way off? Excuse me." Eric patted his chest and let out a belch.

Milton raised an eyebrow. "So you're saying, what, that the trunk is haunted?"

Eric coughed and then sipped his tea to soothe his itchy throat. He hoped he wasn't getting a cold after spending the night in the bathtub. Come to think of it, he *was* feeling a little under the weather. "I don't know what I'm trying to say," he said, shaking his head. "It's just an idea I had. But I thought you should have the trunk regardless, because that seems to be what Lenny wants." Eric did not add: *And I'm hoping that if you take it off my hands, your little-shit brother will stop tormenting me.*

Milton paused. "Frankly, I don't know if *I* want it."

Fuck.

(Okay, don't panic.)

"Really? But your brother—"

"Seems the trunk hasn't brought *you* anything but grief," Milton said mildly. "I've got a peaceful life out here. I'm not so sure I want to spend what little time I have left on earth surrounded by ghosts."

Eric had already thought up a plan B before he'd arrived. He'd haul the trunk down to the beach and let the tide take it away, if Milton refused to accept it. But he'd rather not, if he could avoid it. "I don't *know* that it's truly ghosts. It was just a silly—"

"You ever catch bugs when you were little?" interrupted Milton.

Eric pinched the mug between his knees, warming the flesh of his thighs through his jeans. "Sure. I think most kids do, right? Caterpillars and lightning bugs and beetles and whatnot."

Milton smiled, sly. "My favorites were butterflies."

"Ah, I tried to catch a few of those, but they were always too fast. My fat little hands were too clumsy, I think. I always ended up tearing off their wings." Eric grimaced at the memory. "You know that's a myth, right, the thing about butterflies dying if you rub the powder off their wings? Butterflies are extremely resilient despite their delicate appearance. They can also lose a good portion of their wing scales and keep on flying . . ."

Milton provided Eric a bland stare: *Why are you telling me this?* "No, I didn't know that."

Eric flapped a hand. "Sorry, I'm babbling." *At this rate, I'll never get out of here.*

"They will die, though, if they don't get air," Milton commented.

Eric nodded. "That's right."

"I learned that when I was about seven or eight," Milton continued. "I caught this big, beautiful monarch in one of my mother's canning jars. I'd been after it for days, but it kept eluding me. I wanted it as a pet. Of course, there was no way to know if it was the same butterfly that kept coming around, but I liked to think that it was. I even had a name picked out: Hank."

Eric stifled a yawn. "That's a different name for a butterfly."

"That's what my mother said, too—that a butterfly should be named something pretty like *Lucille* or *Eileen*. But Hank was the name that I liked best." Milton pulled a bandana out of his pocket and coughed into it.

"Hank is nice too," Eric said noncommittally.

The spidery skin around Milton's eyes bunched. Eric couldn't determine if Milton was amused by his comment or irritated by the banal interjection. "Hank loved my mother's flower bed. Some days, I'd wait there in the dirt, eyes leaking from pollen, for what felt like the whole day—though I know it was just a few minutes, because my stepfather, spiteful bastard that he was, never would have allowed longer. Then here would come Hank, just when I was about to give up! He'd land on my mother's roses and suckle nectar. Taunting me. I'd come sneaking up behind him, crouched like a lion, ready to strike, with a glass jar in one hand and a lid in the other. And just when I was going to clap down over him, he'd flap off toward the treetops."

"Sounds like *The Old Man and the Sea*. You know, Hem—"

"Yes, I know Hemingway. I may not be an educated college professor like yourself, but I can read."

"No, no, I wasn't implying—"

"I'm sure you weren't," said Milton, his smirk wily.

Eric thought it best to remain silent. There was something not quite right with this man, and it wasn't only terminal cancer.

"One day I caught that sneaky bugger. He almost got away, but the wind turned against him. I nearly took Hank's goddamn wing off when I finally got the jar closed."

Now Milton was looking at Eric as if expecting him to speak. Eric offered a half-hearted "Well done."

Milton nodded solemnly. "Unfortunately, I wasn't able to keep Hank long. Not alive, anyway."

"Oh no."

"My mother used to get so angry when I'd sneak her jars. They were expensive, you see," Milton explained. "Some folks may have not thought they were expensive, but they were expensive to *us*—we weren't a family with money to burn. By the end of most months, we didn't have two nickels to rub together. But we never took charity. Not once in all those years of struggle."

"And your mother got angry because you broke the jars?" Eric said, keeping them on topic. They'd gotten about as personal as he wanted. *Too* personal. "Kids and glass are never a good combination."

Milton shook his head. "No, I never broke the jars. But I destroyed plenty of lids."

"Right, right. You have to poke holes in the metal so the insects can breathe."

"Exactly." Milton scratched his chin and set his mug aside. "My mother had gotten really angry the last time I'd caught a bug—a beetle, it was. 'If you keep this up, we won't have any canned goods for winter,' she'd said. 'You want to have food for us to eat, don't you?'" Milton flapped a hand. "She was always going on about us starving. 'Don't ruin your shoes, else we'll starve buying you a new pair. Don't lose your library books, else we'll starve paying your fines.' And so forth. When you're poor, every mistake you make always comes back to money. I doubted we *would* have starved, but she'd put enough scare in me that I didn't poke holes in any more lids."

Eric sipped his tea. The fewer interruptions, the faster he'd be out of there.

"Hank was the first insect I caught after my mother's scolding about the lids. I was young, so I didn't realize how quickly Hank would suffocate if I didn't give him air. My real father had died before teaching me about that kind of thing, and I'm sure you've gathered what sort of man my stepfather was. Not exactly the teaching type. My mother, she didn't like insects too much, not even butterflies. She said the caterpillars destroyed her plants."

Eric pulled his phone out to surreptitiously check the time while Milton spat into his hankie. He was now regretting his earlier decision to power it off, seeing nothing but a dark screen. But it *had* to be getting late. It felt like he'd been there for hours.

"No, it didn't take long for Hank to die," Milton said. "No more than a day. I remember that he'd started to fly funny in the jar, like he was drunk. My stepfather drank plenty, so I knew exactly what *that* looked like."

Eric hiccupped, feeling very much drunk himself. "Excuse me."

"Then Hank got *really* lazy. He'd only flap his wings when I shook the jar. How I *loved* seeing Hank riled when I gave him those little earthquakes." Milton clapped his hands together. "I suppose some small part of me knew that Hank was dying. And I'd be lying if I said I didn't understand that the most humane thing I could have done would have been to take Hank out into the flower bed and set him free."

Eric yawned. The sleep he'd lost the previous night was catching up to him fast.

"But Hank was mine." Milton shrugged. "And I *liked* it."

"You liked it?" Eric wasn't sure he was understanding correctly, as he was having a hard time staying focused. He set his empty mug down on the coffee table, making sure to use the coaster.

Milton continued, "Oh yes, I liked it very much, observing death. It was fascinating to me, because it was something I hardly saw. As a farmer, everything you do—the only thing you *think* about morning, noon, and night—revolves around making *life*: sprouting seed into stalk, raising calves into cows, turning eggs into hens . . . it's tiring. Hank's death was a break, I suppose."

Eric shifted in his seat. "That's very—"

(Crazy. This guy is fucking crazy.)

"—interesting. I never thought of it like that, but of course I've never run a farm. I'm a city boy, through and through." He laughed nervously.

Milton didn't seem too fascinated by Eric's declaration. He gave him a brisk nod. "After Hank, I upgraded. I stuck to little nothings at first. Centipedes. Beetles. Moths. I eventually stopped giving them names."

"Umm . . ." Eric could think of absolutely nothing to say.

"After a while, I got bored with the bugs. You've seen one die, and you've seen them all," Milton said, picking at a sore on the back of his hand. He tore the scab away, rolled it in his fingers, and let the crusty ball drop onto the floor.

Eric's stomach rolled up to his throat.

"I upgraded to larger critters," Milton continued. "You'd be amazed at the little things you can fit in those gallon canning jars—snakes and mice . . . and poor Lenny! He'd brought a kitten home from the field once." Milton picked at the now-bleeding scab. "Cats always took longer to—"

"Listen, I should be shoving off now," Eric said, making a show of looking at his cell phone, which gave him absolutely no indication what time it was.

Milton quickly rose and strode toward the kitchen. "Before you go, let me get you some banana bread. It was my mother's recipe."

Panicked, Eric also made a move to get to his feet. "Really, I'm okay. Been trying to cut back on the sweets—"

"I insist," Milton said stubbornly. "It's the least I can do, since you brought me that trunk."

"Does this mean that you want me to leave it?" Eric asked, feeling a relief so pronounced that it nearly brought tears to his eyes. If the old man was going to take the trunk off his hands, fine, he'd accept some banana bread with thanks and a smile, though the only thing that would be eating it was the garbage can.

"Don't see the point in making you lug it back down to your car," Milton said as he turned on the lights in the kitchen. "I made a double batch of bread, and I'll never get through it all. I'd hate to see it go to waste. Won't be a minute."

Eric settled back into his chair. "Well, if you insist." He could hear Milton shuffling around the kitchen, opening drawers and ripping back foil. He pictured Milton's sore bleeding all over the countertops and into the bread.

Eric seized the opportunity when the clattering stopped. He couldn't stand to wait any longer. He cleared his throat and called, "Uh, listen, Milton, I really need to get on the road. Just got a text . . . from work."

Milton came into the living room gripping a knife. Its blade was caked with smears of chocolate and banana. "Not a problem." He smiled. "I've got your bread all wrapped up."

Eric got to his feet, swaying. He clamped his skull in his hands, goggling at Milton. It was like peering at the old man from the opposite end of a tunnel. "Is work 'mergency," he said, his head dipping forward. "Must . . . go . . ."

Eric stumbled forward, legs and arms stiff as a blind mummy's, hands groping the air for balance. He toppled when his shins clipped the coffee table. The old wood gave out under his weight as he fell on top of it, cracking beneath him in an eruption of splinters, the empty mug tumbling to the floor.

CHAPTER 31

Susan was in no mood to answer work calls. She'd had her ass chewed by Ed because of her trip to Eric's, and that was *before* he'd learned that Eric had gone with her to Milton's. After *that*, he'd become so angry that he'd needed to take a five-minute breather outdoors before coming back inside to continue his scolding.

Whoever was calling now was clearly not going to give up. Sighing, Susan answered. "Hel—"

"Listen up, Lady Ass Kicker." It was Sal, speaking so hurriedly that his words came out in a jumble. "I've got some news for you hot off the press."

"About Death Farm?" Susan asked, peering around the station guiltily. Given her recent reprimanding, it was the last thing she should be discussing.

But he'd called her, so . . .

"Yes! But I can't talk long," Sal said. "I've been waiting for the Frankenstein FBI goon they've strapped me with to beat it. He went to grab a coffee down the street, so—"

"Got it!" she broke in. "And have I ever told you that you're the best?"

"Every time we talk," Sal said with a laugh. "Okay, you ready for this? I'm about to change *everything* you think you know about the case."

"Go, go."

"This morning, we found a movie ticket in the back pocket of one of the later victims. We would have found it sooner, but it had slipped under the seam a little, so it felt like it was a part of the pants. You can't always feel *everything* through latex, you know."

Susan was getting impatient. "Okay, so?"

"That movie ticket was dated during Gerald's prison sentence."

Susan sat back in her chair, letting the air drain from her lungs. "Holy shit."

"That's right, holy shit."

Susan thought a moment. "Any chance Gerald could have planted it on the body after he got out of prison? I can't imagine why he would, though. I mean, if he'd go through the trouble of doing that, you think he'd maybe move the bodies altogether."

"Right, right," Sal said. "And not a chance—we checked. The crew over on the farm confirmed that the body has not been disturbed since its burial, which was about two years ago—a few of the bodies are newer than we'd thought. And you want to know how they're sure of this? They had some fancy-pants botanist come to the site to test the soil. And here's some freaky shit: the kid was buried underneath tomato plants, like way, *way* down. Jesus Christ, imagine eating *those*. Thank God for infrared, else the body may not have been found so fast."

Susan went quiet while she processed the information.

"You still there?"

"I'm still here. But wait a minute, Sal. Gerald's been in prison these past few years. Who's been tending those plants?" And why hadn't she thought of the question sooner? She'd been so distracted back in Emerald Meadows by Mary's murder confession that landscaping had never occurred to her.

"Funny, I asked the same thing. Great minds, huh? A neighbor's been taking care of the place—does the gardening and basic upkeep."

"Would this neighbor be Milton Lincoln?"

"That's the one."

God dammit! If only Mary Nichol had bothered to tell me this when I visited her.

And why hadn't Milton mentioned it when she and Eric had paid him a visit?

"From what I heard," said Sal, "the poor guy nearly had a heart attack when he learned what had been happening next door. Imagine that, all those years taking care of your neighbor's plants—probably eating tomatoes off them, too—only to find out there was a kid buried underneath."

"*Blech.* I'd probably have a heart attack too," Susan said. "Okay, so back to the movie ticket. Now the theory is that Gerald maybe didn't commit the murders, because the dates conflict?"

"Correct."

"But that doesn't seem right, given Gerald's criminal background."

"The other theory is that Gerald was working with a partner. This seems to be what the FBI is leaning toward."

"A partner. Of course. Still, Gerald's mother wasn't always in a home. She was living on the property for a lot of the murder years. I've been wondering this: How was Gerald—or his partner—able to dump the bodies there?"

"Oh, I bet it wasn't too difficult. You've been out that way. If Gerald's mother is as bad off physically as everyone says, Gerald—or his partner—could have easily gotten rid of the bodies during a visit. Every dozen or so trips out to the farm, he'd dump a body while she was napping or something, right? Seems plausible. He had plenty of space to work with."

Susan considered this. "Sure. It makes as much sense as anything else."

"But don't take any of my theories as substantiation; I only work on the bodies. Let me tell you this next bit before Frankenfuck gets back."

"Go! Tell me!"

"Remember how I told you that I've been reading up on serial killers lately?"

"Yes."

"Well, from what I've read, sometimes they'll take a trophy from their victims, like a tooth or jewelry. Or they'll leave something behind—something personal they'll plant on each body, right? It becomes like a signature that links the kills."

Susan said, "Like a calling card."

"Exactly. I read about one guy who used to leave an acorn in the vaginas of all the women he murdered. The profilers on that case thought it was his symbolic way of punishing them for their fertility—I mean, the guy had some *serious* mommy issues. Personally, I think the guy was just a huge nut bag."

"Okay, okay." *Hurry, Sal.*

"It seems that our guy on the farm—or *guys*, if Gerald was working with a partner—was leaving behind horse hair, probably from the tail because of its length."

Susan was too stunned to speak.

"It's always just a single hair. Kind of like with the movie ticket, at first we missed it. The bodies, of course, hadn't been buried with preservation in mind, so we'd been dismissing most organics: animal hair, twigs . . . dirt. We always find that kind of stuff when we get bodies that have been buried outside," Sal said. "But then we started to see a pattern."

Susan had to stop herself from shouting. "What kind of pattern?"

"I found the first hair tucked up under the collar of one of the victim's shirts, which, like I said, I initially disregarded. I didn't find any hair on the next couple bodies I examined, but I wasn't really *looking* for it. So a couple bodies later, I found another horse hair, but this time it was inside a sneaker. It was an odd coincidence, but again, the kids were buried on a farm. Then, though, on the next body I found *another* hair, and this one was *threaded* through the holes of the victim's belt. There is no way that could have accidentally happened. So I went back to the other bodies, and sure enough, I found hairs."

Susan's heart was thudding. "The hairs," she choked out. "What color were they?"

"I'm assuming they must have all come from the same horse, because they were all the same color, a bright, rusty red."

"Sal, I'm going to have to call you back."

"Sure, but—"

Susan dropped the phone on its cradle and floated toward Ed's office, feeling as though she were moving through a dream. Of course, it *fit*. How had she not seen it sooner?

Ed was not happy to see her, but he softened when he saw the expression she was wearing. "You all right, kid? You're as white as a sheet."

She spoke swiftly. "Ed, I know you're angry about earlier, and you have every right to be. I never should have taken Eric with me to Milton's."

"No, you never should have *gone* to Eric's or Milton's to begin with."

"Okay. You're right," she said with an aggressive nod. "But can you answer me something: Have I ever *once*, in my entire time working here, gone off half-cocked on any case?"

"No, but—"

"And other than taking Eric to Milton's, have I ever behaved erratically or arrested somebody who didn't deserve to be arrested?"

Ed frowned. "What's this about?"

"I don't want you to freak out, okay? Please don't get mad." She spat it out before she lost the nerve: "I want to talk to Milton Lincoln again."

Ed replied with something that was a hybrid of a scowl and a snort. "You've got to be shitting me."

"I'm not," she said, raising her gaze so that her eyes met his. "And I want you to come with me."

Ed folded his arms across his chest. "Now, why on earth would I do that?"

"I think Milton Lincoln had a hand in the Death Farm murders. I think . . . he might be Gerald's partner. I have a feeling in my gut."

"Susan," Ed began, and she knew she was in trouble. "Have you gone to the feds with this lunacy?"

"No. Not at all. I haven't said anything to anybody. I swear."

Ed relaxed a little. "Good. Because if you had, you wouldn't have made just yourself look bad but the entire police department."

I don't think so, Ed. I'm right. I can feel *it.*

Ed exhaled loudly. "And just what is it you want to *do* about your gut feeling?"

"I want to ask Milton some questions about his horse, see how he responds."

"His horse? I think you've been spending too much time with that schizo."

Susan's temper flared up to the tip of her tongue, but she managed to cage it behind her teeth. Ed's mind had been closed for the better part of sixty years, and she sure as hell didn't have the time to try to open it now. "I'll explain everything in the car. *Please*, Ed."

"You know, you're cruisin' for a bruisin', kid," Ed said with a sigh. "I get it. I do. You're ambitious, but you need to start thinking about the department."

Susan felt like screaming. If he'd only go with her, he'd believe. "Nobody is even here. Everyone else has gone home. It will be our little secret. *Please*."

"Okay, I'll drive." Ed stood and shrugged on his jacket. "But I want you to tell me everything you know on the way—everything you *think* you know. If I'm not convinced by the time we get there, so help me, I'm turning around."

"Deal."

"And you're buying me a coffee on the way."

"Thank you, Ed." *Thank you. Thank you. Thank you.*

Chapter 32

Milton's face floated above Eric in a kaleidoscope of melted-butter light. "Ah, good. You're awake."

It took great effort for Eric to keep his eyes focused. He sensed his blinks way at the base of his skull, as if the skin of his face had been stretched back tight by clothespins. His throat was dry and the air liquid. He swallowed. *"Geghhhh."*

Milton jangled a set of keys. "Hope you don't mind, but while you were dozing, I took the liberty of moving your car around back. Can't have any nosy Nellies come snooping, now can we?"

"Wha' you . . . give . . . mehhh?"

"Don't worry," Milton said. "I wouldn't dare poison you. What would be the fun in that?" He crouched down and wrenched Eric up from the floor, throwing him over his shoulder like a sack of flour.

Christ, Eric thought, he is *strong*. Even on his best day, he doubted he'd be able to take the old man. Though, he reminded himself, he *had* kicked Jim's ass.

(Let's be real. Jim let you win, didn't he?)

Eric's head lolled back, and his throat made a weak, suffocated sound as Milton repositioned him on the sofa like a marionette, propping his head up with a pillow squished firmly behind his neck. A sensation edging close to terror bit through his druggy haze and then faded.

It dawned on Eric: Lenny. *He wasn't being spiteful when he tried to knock my mug off the table. He was trying to save me.*

"There, that's a little better," Milton said, taking Eric in with a reptilian gaze that was somehow both cold and serene. "Don't want you choking on your own spit, do we? But you *will* let me know if you feel like vomiting?" Milton gestured at the throw pillow he'd crammed behind Eric's back. "My mother made that."

Eric's tongue was a pruney waste of meat. "Geeeehhhhh."

Milton plucked the tea mug from the floor and placed it on a side table, then eased back into his own seat, knees popping like kindling. "You can try to ignore old age all you want, but it's your joints that never let you forget."

This is not happening.

"I mixed a little cattle tranquilizer in with your tea, plus a couple other mild sedatives," Milton said casually. "What are you, about one eighty? It's not an exact science, but I think I did a pretty good job with the dose. You aren't dead yet, are you?"

Did he say yet?

Eric blinked lazily. Drool seeped from the corner of his mouth, and a gas bubble rose from his stomach, lodging painfully in his throat. If he puked, he wondered, would it make it all the way up, or would it stop midway and choke him?

Milton slapped his knees. "Since you aren't going anywhere anytime soon, I'd like to finish my yarn before we get down to it. That okay with you?"

"Geeeehhhhh."

"You know what, son? Rest your voice." Milton leaned forward and patted Eric on the forearm the way an adult would a child. Eric recoiled—at least, he recoiled *internally*. His physical body remained motionless, panicking him severely. He was utterly paralyzed. He focused all his energy on his lower half, pushing every ounce of vitality he had remaining down through his limbs.

His big toe moved.

(Oh, super. If you can manage to kick this crazy redneck's ass with a single toe, you just might make it out of here alive.)

"Tranqs can give you a nice little high, or so I've heard. I've never tried them myself. Never been one to dabble in illicit substances, not like you kids . . ." Milton clicked his tongue and shook his head. "Would you look at what you've done to my coffee table? Belonged to my great-grandmother, that did. Oh well. Never mind."

A couple of fat tears flowed over Eric's lower eyelids.

"Fate, Eric. Some call it destiny, but I like the term *fate* better. It's still a little spacey for my taste," Milton said, lifting a hand and rotating his wrist, "but I think it fits the story I'm about to tell you. Do you believe in fate, Eric?"

It was the same question Jake had asked him—how he wished he were kicking back with Jake now instead of with this psycho. His mouth drooped at the corners. His face was hotly numb, electrified pins and needles of fire and ice, as were his arms and legs. A peculiar thought occurred to him then: if somebody were to walk into the room at that precise moment and offer him a million dollars for the simple task of lifting an arm, he wouldn't earn a penny.

"It's okay; you're probably too relaxed to nod. Anyway, I never gave much thought to fate as a kid, but after what happened that day in the shed with Lenny . . ." Milton provided Eric a coy smile. "I must admit that I became a believer."

Eric's lids, concrete heavy, fell closed, and his head dunked forward. So nice to rest, so very, very nice, like settling back into a warm bathtub, like nestling into a cloud, like—

Whack!

"Wakey-wakey!"

Eric blinked briskly, his vision muddy. As his view cleared, he made out Milton hunched above him, knobby hand poised to backhand him again.

"No, sir, you don't want to be doing that," Milton said. *Threatened.*

The left side of Eric's face throbbed, as did his ear, which was ringing from the assault. He didn't want Milton to hit him again—that shit *hurt*—but what he wanted even less was for Milton to take more drastic measures to keep him conscious. Fingernails pulled out with pliers, maybe, or eyelids lopped off with the banana-bread knife and fed to the chickens.

Yes, provoking Milton would be a very bad idea.

Milton returned to his seat and continued, as if there'd been no interruption. "One day—and here's where the *fate* part comes in, Eric, so pay attention—my brother and I were outside playing hide-and-seek. We were just young; oh, I was 'bout eleven or twelve, Lenny around kiddiegarten age."

Eric felt a mad giggle simmering up in his throat, a lunatic's laugh. *Did he say* kiddiegarten? It died fast.

Eric was hideously drowsy once again, tired in a way that he could only comprehend as agonizing. He physically *ached* for rest. He allowed his lids to slide closed. Just for a second, just a quick kip to soothe his eyes.

Milton was having none of that. He rose from his seat before Eric even knew he'd begun to doze, twisting the tender flesh on the inner crook of Eric's elbow until he drew blood.

Eric made a shrill *owwwwgh* sound as he came to.

"You really don't want to make me get up again, son. Got me some wicked joint pain, and it tends to make me cranky. *No more*, understand?"

Eric moaned in acquiescence.

Satisfied Eric was listening, Milton nodded once, returned to his seat, and continued. "Lenny was always cheating at hide-and-seek, so it wasn't much of a game. We were kind of fooling around on this day I'm telling you about, killing time before supper. My mother had baked a fresh loaf of sourdough, and Lenny was whining because he said the smell was driving him *crazy*. He didn't want to play—Lenny was always a baby when he was hungry—but I promised him my slice of pie if he won. Lemon meringue was one of his favorites."

Eric blinked to show that he was listening.

"Lenny, that damn kid, never listened to *anything* he was told. Time and time again, my stepfather warned him to stay away from the Nichols' property, even spanked him once good so he wouldn't forget." Milton scratched the back of his neck absentmindedly, staring off into space, making soft *mmm-mm-mm* sounds.

The floodlights are on, but nobody's a-plowing, Eric thought, and once again he found himself fighting back a giggle.

After some time, Milton turned back to Eric. "He was funny around kids, you know. Wayne Nichol. Hell, let's just call him what he was, a child molester. I don't know the extent of Gerald's perversion, though he couldn't have been that innocent if he went to prison. Mary—that's Wayne's wife, Gerald's mother—never touched any kids, but I imagine she knew what was happening . . . you listening to me, son?"

Eric widened his eyes and blinked rapidly. Yes, he was listening. You bet your *ass* he was.

Milton made a satisfied *hmph* sound and went on with his story. "Personally, I don't think Mary has ever been right in the head. She's slow, I mean," he said, tapping his temple. "And I think Wayne took advantage of that, made her subservient." He raised his eyebrows at Eric. "Bet you didn't think an old hick like me would know a big ole word like *subservient*, did ya?"

"Geeeehhhhh."

"Mary's now in a state-funded hospice. Sitting around in her own filth all day, running out the clock, waiting for some minimum-wage orderly to take notice of her long enough to change her diaper." Milton leaned forward. "If I ever get that bad, son, I can only pray that somebody takes me out back and puts a bullet in my brain. Though I imagine cancer will take care of me long before there'd be a need for such a thing."

Milton sat back and clasped his hands. "I'm getting off topic again. Anyway, people in town used euphemisms—another big word for you, sonny—*He's funny around kids. Funny*, they'd say, with a gesture." He made a seesawing back-and-forth motion with his hand.

Eric squeezed his eyes shut and then open in understanding. He stifled a cough, his throat feeling roasted.

"*He's funny around the young'uns.* Yep, that's what they'd all say. Though I saw nothing funny about what was going on next door. I suppose everyone in Perrick is a little bit to blame for how Gerald turned out—for not intervening, I mean." He sighed. "But things were different in those days. People kept their noses out of everyone else's business."

Eric was beginning to feel an itching discomfort from the neck down, which gave him hope.

The drugs were burning off.

"My mother was a lot like Mary Nichol in that respect, always looking the other way when it came to my stepfather beating me. Though I imagine he belted her a couple of times too. He liked to always keep us a little scared. Man was as mean as a rattlesnake. But he put clothes on our backs and food on our table, and that was good enough for my mother," Milton said.

Eric tried to wiggle his big toe again; this time, *all* his toes moved. The pain on the inside of his elbow was also increasing in severity. He shifted his gaze to assess the damage Milton had done when he'd pinched him and saw a small stream of blood oozing down his arm.

How am I going to get out of this? he wondered, and then he immediately answered himself: *I've got nothing.* He nearly burst out laughing. He settled for a lazy grin. The drugs might be wearing off his body, but in his mind . . . high.

So very, very high.

"Lenny, I think, was too young to understand a lot of it—this business with the Nichols, I'm talking about now—which is why he probably didn't think twice about hiding in their shed on that day we were playing hide-and-seek."

Milton sat back and got that faraway look again. Eric didn't like it one bit; he didn't want Milton's thoughts to wander. If they ventured too deeply into the dark crevices of his demented brain, he just might start thinking about how he was going to escalate the situation. If Milton had drugged him and moved his car, it was for a reason. Eric did not want to find out what that reason was. The longer the old man kept talking, the better chance he had for the drugs to wear off.

"I'm not saying it was *dumb* of Lenny to hide in the shed, just naughty," Milton continued. "It was actually quite smart: I wouldn't have even thought to look for him there, but I'd peeked while I was counting and had seen him sneak across the field."

Lenny shocked Eric by materializing at Milton's side, his face scrunched with fury as he kicked Milton hard on the shin.

Milton rubbed at his leg, oblivious. "Goddamn cancer," he griped. "Everything hurts. You get pain in places you didn't even think you could *have* pain."

Lenny hovered at Milton's side, unmoving. Eric wished the kid would hit the old bastard over the head. Use one of the hefty legs from the smashed coffee table, for instance. But maybe, he thought, spirits of the dead don't possess the power to do just *anything*—they, like humans, probably had restrictions.

Milton eyeballed Eric sharply. "You falling asleep on me, boy?"

"Neggghhhhhhh."

Milton continued, "I let Lenny think I hadn't seen him go into the shed. I even pretended to look around the yard a little before I crept across the field."

Lenny vanished, and Eric thought miserably: *Why didn't he help me? He can't just leave me here with this lunatic! He can't!*

HELP ME, YOU LITTLE SHIT!

"Everyone *thinks* they know the exact moment their life changes," Milton said. "*My life changed when my future wife walked into the bar,* they'll say. Or, *My life changed when my son was born.* Horseshit, really. I imagine few can truly pinpoint such an event. And even if they could, I can't see why they'd want to."

Eric became sorely aware of cramping in his midsection, the weightiness of his bladder. He needed to pee something fierce. He bit down on his tongue to see if he could feel it. He could. *Keep babbling, old man. Keep babbling.*

(Whatever you do, don't let him see you move.)

"But in my case, I believe it to be true. Because my life really *did* change when I walked into Wayne Nichol's shed and found Lenny trapped inside *that* trunk—the lid had fallen down and locked him in, you see." Milton lifted his chin in the direction of the porch. "And you know why that is? Because it was at that moment I realized my calling. Prior to that day, my . . . urge to keep the world in balance had been limited to critters."

Lenny flickered back into existence next to Milton—so close that he was nearly hunkered on his lap—his little hands balled into fists at his sides.

"I finally understood what God had put me on earth to do." Milton brought a fist down to his opposite palm. "Understand?"

Lenny's chest began to rise and fall in jarring huffs. His eyes narrowed.

In his head, Eric was screaming. *Go on, kid, hit him! Knock the crazy fucker out!*

"The lock to the trunk was on the ground right next to it. Lenny must've taken it off when he hid inside," Milton explained. "So I allowed Lenny to fulfill *his* fate when I put it back on, locking him inside. Why else would things have lined up that way, if it wasn't meant to be, if Lenny wasn't intended to sacrifice himself to nature? Why would smothering feel *so right* if it was in any way wrong?"

Just like that, the boy was gone.

Eric's cheeks dampened with tears.

"I was chosen." Milton's eyes took on a deadly black shine that iced Eric's veins. "It became my duty to keep the world balanced, understand? Nature *needs* death so that other life can flourish. It's a cycle, and sacrifices must be made. The farm took my father, you know. He was killed by a machine just out in that field." Milton tipped his head toward the window. Then, as if proving a point, he added: "A couple years later, Lenny was born."

Milton sat back, reflecting. He prodded his dried-up wound with an index finger, cracking it open. He smeared coagulated blood across the back of his hand, making a lazy figure eight. "To hear Lenny take his last breath . . . I'd never felt so *alive*. It was as if I'd absorbed his energy into my own body—his life force. I didn't want that feeling to ever end."

I have to get out of here.

"That night in bed, I could hardly sleep. I knew I'd need to find a way to carry on my mission. A couple days later, while everyone in town was still preoccupied with the search for Lenny, I sneaked into the barn where Lenny's horse, Mabel, was kept, and I suffocated her." He smiled craftily. "Do you know how *hard* it is to suffocate a horse, Eric?"

Eric blinked once to indicate no.

"Probably never even *been* on a horse, I bet," Milton scoffed. "I was just a kid, but I took down a whole horse. Can you imagine? And I did it so good that my parents couldn't figure out why she'd died so suddenly, though I suppose they had other things on their minds. I got to bury Mabel all by myself, too, right under that big oak out back. Made her a little tombstone and everything. Kept her tail for my effort. Now, you tell me that isn't something!"

I wonder if that's where he'll bury me? Eric wondered. *Keep a piece of my scalp for his effort.*

"I may have been uneducated, but I wasn't stupid. I knew all too well how cruel the world could be, even to young boys. My undertakings would not be accepted by society; they just wouldn't understand—that I knew *positively*—and so I had to be cautious. Patient. I waited a few years before I resumed my work, knowing that I could carry out my duties more efficiently once I was mobile."

Milton paused a moment to pick at his wound. His blood had gone syrupy. Looking at it made Eric ill, yet he couldn't tear his eyes away, hypnotized.

"By the time I reached driving age, homelife was a mess, both here on the farm and next door. I'd become invisible to everyone around me. Continuing my work was easier than I'd expected. *A lot* easier. For years and years, nobody paid me no mind."

Milton let out a weary breath.

"But I became an old man, if you haven't noticed, and I got tired. I'd abandoned my mission, for the most part, by the time I was diagnosed with cancer." Pick-pick. Bleed. "Most folks fall down a rabbit hole of depression when they get news of the big C, but for me . . . well, it provided a kick in the ass that I'd needed. It energized me, that certainty of death, because it was now time for *me* to be a part of the cycle. And why not go out with a bang?"

Eric's throat was scratchier than steel wool. He swallowed to give it some moisture.

"I have no wife, no kids. So once I'm gone, it will be like I was never here. To everyone, that is, except my little nothings. *They* felt the force of my existence, and those who've yearned for them over the years will never forget the mark I made on their lives either. Their sacrifice is what gave my life purpose, you see? You may find this hard to believe, but I do love them for that."

Eric swallowed once more.

"What I can't gather is how *you* got hold of the trunk. I saw Gerald going through the shed, you know. He'd just gotten out of prison, so he must've been looking for things to pawn. Man's always been lazier than a box of rocks, so you know him getting a job was out of the question," Milton said with a disgusted snorting sound. "Though I can't imagine too many folks would want to hire an old child molester like Gerald, anyway."

Don't cough, don't cough, don't cough—

"Gerald's father, Wayne, was a notorious pack rat, always getting to sales early so he could buy up all the good stuff only to cram it in that damn shed of his. Used to make my stepfather mad as hell . . . After Wayne died, the shed stopped being used—and it hadn't been touched for, oh, thirty-some years. Not until Gerald came along. My guess? Gerald came across Lenny while he was scavenging and panicked, ditched the trunk someplace away from his house. Guess he'd figured that they'd think that *he'd* killed Lenny, given his unnatural fondness for the young'uns. Why he took it upon himself to bury Lenny by that telephone pole is beyond me. Man never was too smart. He'd have been better off ditching Lenny with the trunk."

Eric could hold it in no longer. A cough forced its way up his throat, and he had no choice but to let it fly.

Milton seemed to come back to himself. "Right! Almost forgot you've been tranqed. Guess we'd better get to it, hmm?" He rose to his feet. "Be back in a jiff."

As soon as the old man was out of sight, Eric endeavored to lift his limbs. His legs were as useless as two concrete stumps, but he managed to heave his arms about six inches off the sofa and hold them horizontal for three seconds. It took every ounce of energy he had. Weak, he let his arms drop back to his sides like a couple of dead fish.

Eric tried again. This time, he managed to keep his arms raised for ten seconds. He lifted his right foot and rotated it twice. At this rate, he thought, he'd be standing by the end of next week.

He let everything drop when he heard Milton come clattering back . . . with a wheelbarrow? "Upsy-daisy," he said, hoisting Eric up from the couch. He tossed Eric into the wheelbarrow with horrifying ease, as if his innards were nothing more substantial than tissue paper.

Milton wheeled Eric toward the far end of the house and then out the back door, Eric's full bladder throbbing with each stair they descended. Thud-thud-thud went his skull against metal. His teeth chomped down on his tongue, this time involuntarily. Tears leaked out from the corners of his eyes, and he whimpered.

The sky had just gone dark; it was that time of year when the sun faded early and the temperature dropped by multiple degrees with each passing twilight hour. Eric's breath puffed small ghosts that floated for a blink before evaporating. Philosophical in the face of death, he wondered how many other souls under the same sky were also marching— or rolling, as it was in his case—to their death. Hundreds? Thousands?

Or was it only him, alone?

He began to quietly sob as he thought, *It's official. This has been the worst year of my entire life.*

Milton pulled a key ring from his back pocket as they approached the barn and clicked open the fat padlock that sat at the center of its double doors. The stench of death hit Eric even before Milton wheeled him inside. He twisted his neck and gagged. Only drool came out.

"Don't look at me. You can blame Gerald for this one. Man was rotten in life, so it's only natural that he reeks in death." Milton gazed down in the wheelbarrow. "Oh, come now," he said. "Don't look so scandalized. You think the world's really going to miss a child molester?"

How long until someone misses me? Eric wondered, cursing himself for not making more friends in Perrick or at least telling the two he did have where he'd gone. But even if Jake or Susan *did* realize he'd vanished, they'd have no reason to look at Milton.

The old man's going to get away with murder. He understood this now unequivocally. *Again.*

"If someone's going to serve as my scapegoat, wouldn't you rather it be a creep like Gerald?" Milton said conversationally. "This's why it pays to be clever, though I suppose a big smarty-pants like you already knew that. Man would still be alive, had he not buried Lenny by the pole. After they found Lenny's body, I knew it was only a matter of time before the others were found—the ones *I* put on the property. Couldn't let Gerald blow my cover. Imagine that: I've been doing the Lord's good work, keeping the balance, for the better part of fifty years, and here Gerald comes and undoes it all after just a couple days out of prison. Yep, you gotta be smart about these things."

"Pleaaaassse," Eric slurred.

"I knew with Gerald being gone the law would never say boo to me. And they didn't. They assumed those bodies were all his, also like I knew they would," Milton said. "Could do without the smell in my barn, though. But with the FBI buzzing around, I've had to keep him hidden."

Half of Milton's face was obscured by shadows. Soon, it would be completely dark inside the barn. As if realizing this, he flipped the light switch by the door.

Milton tipped the wheelbarrow and dumped Eric onto the ground like a load of dirt. As he fell, he noticed a hatch—a wooden trapdoor—about twenty feet away. It seemed to lead straight underground into some type of cellar. What was down there—torture chamber? Canned peaches? No telling with this guy.

Milton let out a long exhale. "I'm afraid I'm faced with a quandary, Mr. Evans. Killing adults isn't my style. It disrupts nature's cycle, and adults come with certain complications. But you strike me as the sort of chap who probably doesn't have too many people who might come looking for him—am I right? I notice you've got no wedding ring, and you told me the last time you were here that you don't have kids."

Eric was shaking all over. "Pleaaaassse . . ."

"I'm not trying to pay you any disrespect, son, but I've got to look out for myself. You should've just left well enough alone." Milton clicked his tongue. "Life was much simpler when people minded their business."

How long until he was dead—another minute? Two?

Milton rapped Eric's skull with his gnarled old-man knuckles. "Best stop that bawling so you can go out with some dignity. Don't want to leave this world a crybaby, do ya?" Milton gestured toward the Deepfreeze that sat near the hatch. "If you were thirty years younger and two feet shorter, you'd meet your end in there. It's about the purest way to go, I think."

"Nooooooo!" Not that way, Eric thought, virtually insane with panic. *Anything but* that. He tried to slither toward the door, making it about four inches before collapsing with exhaustion.

Milton shook his head at him pityingly and then crossed the barn. He used his key ring once more, this time to open a tall pine cabinet. He seized a very large shotgun and returned. Eric's sobs grew to hysterical proportions. Out of all the ways he'd ever envisioned dying, at the hands of a child murderer in a reeking barn would have been dead last.

Milton loaded the shotgun. "I'm going to do you in the head. It'll be quicker that way."

Eric moaned.

Milton raised the shotgun and aimed it at Eric's skull. "If you care to know, I'm going to bury you out back under my orange tree. After the law clears out, I mean. Until then, you'll have Gerald to keep you company. If you have any last words—"

Milton's back went ramrod straight.

"Noooo . . ."

"Quiet now!" Milton hissed, cocking his head to listen.

"Pleasssssse . . . nooooooo."

Milton thumped Eric's skull with the butt of the shotgun. "I said *shush!*" He ran to the door, cracked it, peeked out. He cursed as he sprinted back to Eric.

Milton cast the shotgun aside and seized Eric by the wrists, pulling him toward the hatch. Out came the key ring again as he unlocked yet another padlock. He threw the door open, and Eric let out a surprised yelp. Beneath him was a dirt chasm about fifteen feet deep.

So was Lenny Lincoln, looking up at them.

"Help meeeee," Eric begged the boy, but Lenny had already begun to dissolve.

Milton dumped Eric in, and he landed face first in a puff of brown powder. He lifted his head weakly, eyes watering and broken nose stinging, thick warmth flooding over his split lip.

Eric saw two small figures huddled in the corner, a boy and a girl. Unlike Lenny, these children were *real*. The boy blinked at him lazily, seeing him but not really comprehending. Drugged.

The little girl did not stir.

Milton slammed the trapdoor closed, immersing them in darkness.

CHAPTER 33

"We're not staying longer than fifteen minutes," Ed told Susan as they pulled up in front of Milton Lincoln's place. "You ask your questions, and we'll go from there."

Susan wasn't positive, but she thought Ed sounded slightly more open to her theory about the horse, but maybe it was only the stout caffeine buzz he had going. The jumbo-size caramel macchiato he'd slurped down on the way over seemed to have improved his mood significantly. Ed liked to pretend otherwise, but he loved fancy coffee drinks.

Susan nodded. "Sure, but I'll still need to work into it."

They got out of the car, and Ed turned to her so that she could see his no-nonsense frown. "Guess you'd better talk fast, then."

"I can't just blurt it out, Ed."

"Fifteen minutes."

Milton came out on the porch before they'd even mounted the stairs. He smiled down at the two officers pleasantly.

"You must be psychic," Susan said and then immediately regretted it, given how her last visit to Milton's had panned out. She straightened. "Hello again, Mr. Lincoln."

"No, I'm not psychic," Milton said. "Living out here, you can see a car coming a mile down the road, 'specially after it gets dark."

Ed and Susan nodded curtly as they mounted the stairs. When they reached the top, Milton reached out and surprised Susan by giving Ed's hand a hearty shake. "Golly, Ed, it's been . . ." Milton scratched his forehead with dirty fingers, and Susan noted that he was sweating quite a bit. What had he been doing? "Well, I don't know how long. *Long.*"

Ed? This was something Susan hadn't expected. The way the chief had been talking, it was like he could hardly recall ever *meeting* Milton. Sometimes, though, that was how it went, being a cop in a small town. Citizens knew you even if you didn't know them, sort of like being an underpaid celebrity.

"I think it was at the state fair a couple years back," Ed commented. "You whacked that carny's strength machine so hard he thought you'd cheated."

"Yep." Milton nodded. "I 'member that. Had to fight 'im for my prize."

The two men looked like they were sharing a private joke or . . . something else. Susan was beginning to feel like a child who'd been dragged along with her father to Take Our Daughter to Work Day. Then again, Ed was no dummy. Maybe his good old boy banter was his way of charming their way inside. They had no official cause to be there and no warrant, so Milton could refuse them entry if he so desired.

Ed said, "Listen, Milton, I sure as hell hate to bother you, but I'm wondering if we might come in for a minute and ask you a couple questions."

Milton raised his eyebrows. "Questions? About what?"

Ed shuffled, offering Milton a strained smile. "I'm sure you've heard about all the awful business that's been going on next door."

"Oh, yup, sure have," Milton said. "Had the FBI already come talk to me, and your friend here too." He shot Susan a disdainful glance.

Susan studied Milton's face with a frown. His conduct was downright peculiar. She'd been on a lot of house calls. Nobody was ever *this* tranquil when two officers showed up unannounced. Tranquil yet sweating bullets.

Something wasn't right.

Ed said, "That's kind of why we're here. You see, Susan is fairly new around the station, and she hasn't had too much experience going door-to-door, as you might have guessed." He rolled his eyes—*Can you believe this silly rookie?*

Milton guffawed, and Susan had to remind herself that this was all a part of Ed's ploy to get them inside, though she wished he'd shared his plan with her before they'd arrived. She hadn't been considered a rookie by anyone in quite some time, and she'd gone on more than her fair share of house calls.

"We're tying things up down at the station, so we're making the rounds with final questions," Ed explained.

"Tying things up?" Milton asked. "This mean you've caught your guy?"

Ed leaned forward and winked. "This isn't exactly public record, but the FBI are closing in on Gerald. It's only a matter of time."

He's establishing trust, Susan thought. *I'll be damned. The old guy has still got some tricks left in him yet.*

"Is that right? Well, I *do* hope they catch him."

"Anyway, we won't take up much of your time . . ."

Milton nodded once and opened the door for them.

"Where'd your coffee table go?" Susan blurted as they stepped into the living room. She gestured toward the empty spot in front of the sofa. "You had one right there, didn't you?"

Milton did not seem to appreciate her nosiness. "Took it out back to give it a good polishing. Didn't want to stain the rug."

"Oh." Susan was careful not to let her face reveal what she'd seen peeking out from underneath the sofa: a splinter of varnished wood about six inches long. Milton was lying about the table. But why?

"Can I offer you some tea?" Milton asked. "All I got's green."

"No, thank you," Susan said, eager to begin her questioning. "We just filled up on cof—"

"Sure, I'll take some tea," Ed said, and Susan looked over at him, perplexed. What happened to just fifteen minutes?

Milton went into the kitchen, and Susan sat down next to Ed. She kicked out the shard of wood for him to see and then kicked it back under the sofa. Ed frowned, not quite understanding what she was getting at. He shook his head and shrugged. *So what?*

Susan got to her feet and called toward the kitchen, "Mr. Lincoln? I'm wondering if I might use your bathroom?"

Milton poked his head out from the doorway and furnished her another displeased scowl. "Oh, you really don't want to use it—it's a mess, I'm afraid. I'd be embarrassed."

Susan doubted this very much. Like the exterior, the inside of the house was spotless, and she was certain the obsessive cleanliness would extend to the bathroom. She patted her tummy and made a pained face. "I honestly don't mind. The coffee on the way over . . . guess it hasn't sat right with me—all that acid. I really need to . . ." She bit her lip.

Milton pursed his lips. Can't really argue with a person about to soil her pants. "Down the hall. Last door on the left."

Susan made her way to the bathroom. Once she was inside, she locked the door, tiptoed to the window, and drew the curtains.

Her mouth fell open in a silent gasp as she gazed out on the backyard.

Eric's car.

It was positively his because of the faded Swindled 5 sticker on the back window. Heart thudding, she cleared her throat to cover the noise she made while prying up the window. She froze for an instant when it screeched. Susan crossed the bathroom and pressed her ear to the door, holding her breath as she listened. Milton and Ed were now talking out in the living room. The conversation even sounded a little heated, which was perfect.

There was no screen, which saved her some time, but the fit through the window would be tight. Susan removed her belt, which held her gun, pepper spray, baton, and flashlight, and tossed it onto the ground below. She then wiggled out, knees popping as she landed the six-foot drop, and clicked her belt back on over her hips.

Susan sprinted toward the only other source of light on the property outside of the house, the barn. The reek of decomposition enveloped her as she neared its doors, swinging ajar in the chilly evening breeze. On some level, she knew that a body took days before it reached this stage of pungency, but still she couldn't help thinking: *Please, please don't let it be Eric.*

Following the stench, she entered the barn, gun drawn, unaware of the panicked *huh-huh-huh* sounds she was making. She saw a piece of machinery about the size of a small elephant—some type of miniaturized backhoe—and her finger hovered near the gun's trigger until she cleared it.

At the far end of the barn, she found a blue tarp spread out over a mound of loose hay. She said a silent prayer and toed the tarp aside, discovering the body of Gerald Nichol. He was badly decomposed, but she recognized him immediately, having seen his photo in her police files. She holstered her gun and pulled her walkie-talkie from her belt with shaking hands, her intent to request backup.

She paused to reconsider. If Ed had left his walkie on, her transmission would broadcast. If Milton had any kind of physical advantage over Ed back in the living room, he could seriously hurt or even *kill* him before Ed even knew what was happening. Ed certainly wasn't a rookie, but he seemed to have a history with Milton, so his guard might be down.

That was a big *might* to chance.

How long had she been gone? Four, five minutes? They might be wondering—

Over here!

Susan spun around, hideously aware that she was brandishing a walkie-talkie instead of her firearm. She dropped the walkie and yanked her gun up from her hip.

"Police!" she hollered. "Who's there?"

She was alone.

But she had heard *someone* . . . hadn't she? A child's voice.

She *saw* something, though, a large wooden hatch. She'd practically stepped right on top of it earlier but had been too focused on the stench to notice. She pulled her flashlight from her belt (this time, she kept her gun out) and peered down through the slats in the door. Her head snapped back in alarm.

Eric was sprawled on the ground below, his breathing shallow, hair matted against the side of his bloodied face. He kicked an arm and a leg out in a feeble attempt to sit up.

"Eric! Are you hurt?"

He slowly reached up toward her, groaning. "Kiiii . . . help . . ."

"Eric, oh my God!" Susan banged on the door with the flashlight. "Eric! Answer me!"

"In here . . . kids."

"What?" Susan got down on her stomach and angled the flashlight so that she could squint through the thin slats. "Oh my God!" Her mind reeled frantically, playing catch-up to process the horrifying information she was being inundated with: corpse in hay, Eric mangled, kids in dirt.

"Help . . . us."

Adrenaline surging, Susan didn't stop to think. She holstered her gun and chucked the flashlight down at her side, her breath catching in her throat. She yanked and yanked at the lock, but it held. She clenched her fists in frustration, contemplating just shooting the damn thing to smithereens.

But this wasn't some old western. She could seriously injure Eric and the kids, and she also had Ed and Milton back in the house to consider. Gunfire resonated. Surely, they'd hear.

Eric and the kids were in bad shape. The little girl almost looked like . . .

She shook her head. She didn't even want to *think* it.

Susan stepped into high gear. She wheeled around, eyes frantically scanning the shed. She believed there was a crowbar in the cruiser, but she didn't want to take time to search for it. "I'm going to find something to bust off the lock. You guys hold tight!" she called down and then thought: *Where else would they go?*

She saw what she needed tacked up on a pegboard, a sturdy little hand trowel with a fat wooden handle, its head sharp and diamond shaped. If she could get it wedged just right, she might be able to splinter the wood and pry the whole thing off completely, latch and lock.

She pulled it from the wall and got to work.

Susan pried at the metal, sweating from tension, murmuring, "Please-please-please. *Give.* Come on, you bitch! Give, God dammit!" Her pulse thudded loudly in her ears, and she was breathing heavily.

The light above Susan blotted out for only an instant, but it was enough to shift the shadows around her. She spun around. Milton was standing right behind her, holding a pitchfork at shoulder height. She let out a surprised shriek and struggled to get to her feet. Had she not been posed so awkwardly on her hands and knees, she might have made it. She lost her balance instead, tumbling on her side and cracking her ribs hard against the hatch.

She dropped the trowel, fumbling for her gun, but her hands were slick with sweat and shaking and . . .

This is it, she thought, squeezing her eyes shut. *I'm dead.*

Bang!

Clunk!

It all happened so fast.

Milton was still standing above Susan when she opened her eyes, but he'd released the pitchfork. He groped at his chest and stumbled forward, his back arched in an ugly exhibition of agony. He nearly trampled Susan before he dropped face forward onto the ground.

Reflexively, Susan seized her gun, though she could see Milton no longer posed a threat because of the large bleeding hole in his back. Behind him in the doorway stood Ed. He was shaky on his feet, gun in one hand and the other pressed against the gushing laceration on his forehead.

Milton raised his head, groaning, as he reached out toward Susan. He had whimpered a long string of words, but she managed to catch the tail end. "About the dead woman."

"Freeze, asshole!" she shouted, keeping the gun trained on him.

"Ask Ed . . . about Marta. He was there—"

Bang!

Susan screamed so hard and loud that she felt it clear down in her pelvis. Ears ringing, she gaped up at Ed uncomprehendingly, smoke rising from the barrel of his gun. "You shot him in the head," she said, dumbstruck.

"Say to you!" Ed was yelling. "What did he say?"

Susan opened her mouth and moved her jaw around, trying to alleviate the ringing in her ears. She shook her head, blinking to clear her thoughts. The gun wavered in her trembling hands. "Why did you do that, Ed?"

"Susan, give me your gun before you shoot yourself."

Susan didn't think twice. She handed her gun over to the chief. He tucked it into the back of his pants so that he could maintain a grip on his own.

"Tell me *now*," he demanded, giving her shoulder a rough shake. The bleeding on his forehead had nearly stopped. Milton had clocked him competently, but Ed's injury was far from fatal.

Susan rubbed her own forehead, a simple detail persisting in the back of her mind.

But first, Eric and the kids.

"We have to get that trapdoor open! There's—"

"No." Ed clamped a hand down firmly on her bicep. "Milton. What did he tell you?"

"What?" Susan tried to wiggle out of his grasp, but he was unyielding. He, of course, didn't know about the hostages down below, so he might not understand her need for urgency. Quickly, she explained, "He said something about a woman—to ask you about Marta."

Ed sighed. "That's about what I figured."

"What's going on? Who's Marta?" Susan peered at Ed's face and didn't like what she saw. Suddenly, she felt an inexplicable concern for her safety. "Why did you shoot an unarmed man, Chief? Why?"

Ed answered with a whip of his pistol.

Chapter 34

A charley horse brought Susan back to consciousness.

She opened her eyes and winced. Her temple was throbbing, her shoulder on fire. She struggled to sit up and realized she was on her back with her left arm pulled over her head, her wrist handcuffed to a thick loop of metal sticking out from the backhoe. She yanked at the cuff, and not surprisingly, it held. The machine weighed at least a half ton, so she was going nowhere, not unless she chewed her arm off at the wrist like a coyote.

Ed was on his knees a few feet away from her, peering down into the hatch through the slats. Milton's corpse lay in the same spot, bits of skull fanned out around him like a macabre headdress.

Susan considered closing her eyes and pretending to still be passed out, but she couldn't see the point. This was not going to be one of those situations where Ed would forget all about her if she only stayed quiet.

Might as well get on with it.

Ed jumped when she spoke. "You *pistol-whipped* me," she said and then spat a gob of saliva in the dirt. The pain at her temple was making her nauseous.

When Ed turned to face her, his eyes were sad. "I want you to know, Susan, that I didn't enjoy hurting you."

"So then why did you?" she snapped, startled by her biting indignation. Of course, she had the right to be furious. The man *had* belted her noggin. And cuffed her to farming equipment while she was unconscious.

"I thought of you like a daughter, kid. I really did."

He's speaking about me in the past tense, Susan thought. *Not a good sign.*

"Your talents as an officer are a double-edged sword. You're persistent and curious. Smart. I have no doubt you would have made it all the way to the top."

There goes that past tense again.

"But," Ed said, "you should have listened to me on this one. Did I or did I not tell you to stop snooping around in the Gerald Nichol case? I practically begged you to let the FBI do their thing. But like a little hen, you pecked-pecked-pecked . . ."

"Ed, if you'd only tell me what this is about," Susan said, though she was beginning to suspect she already knew. "This Marta business. You're a good cop, and everyone at the station respects you. So if you got caught up in something, I'm sure—"

"No," Ed said, shaking his head. "Not this time. This is something popularity won't fix."

Susan's outrage was quickly being replaced by fright. Ed was resigned; she'd worked with him long enough to recognize when he was. His mind had already been made up over whatever he was planning to do, and no amount of fast-talking on her part would sway him.

Still, she had to try.

"If you let me go—"

"Let me guess," Ed said with an eerie little smile playing on his lips. "If I let you go, you won't say a word. Is that it?"

Susan frowned. Yeah, that was it. She'd had the line used on herself before, and variations of it, by the countless men and women she'd arrested. *If you let me off with a warning, Officer, I won't say a word. Promise.*

Ed shook his head. "I know you. You'd never let this go, just like you didn't back off the FBI's case when I asked—*ordered*—you to."

Susan began to speak and then thought better of it. She probably wouldn't have managed to get the words out anyhow. Her throat was constricting with terror, and there was a mad, panicky sensation effervescing in her abdomen, like she was on the brink of breaking into hysterical shrieks. If she started now, she doubted she'd be able to stop. Ed might kill her just to shut her up.

Is that what he's planning on doing? Killing me?

Ed scooted an empty metal bucket toward her—close, but not close enough for her to strike out at him (he *did* know her well)—and flipped it over, using its bottom as a seat. "I suppose I owe you an explanation," he said, clasping his hands on his lap. "It's the least I can do."

Susan found her voice, shaky as it was. "Did you help Milton kidnap those kids?"

Ed gaped at her, perturbed, as if deeply insulted that she could even *entertain* that he could do something so terrible. He who had shot an unarmed man in the back of the head, pistol-whipped a fellow law enforcement agent, and then handcuffed her to a machine. Yes, how *dare* she. "No, of course not."

"Then I can't see what's so bad—"

"I'll have to start from the beginning," Ed butted in. "It will go faster if you don't interrupt."

Do I want *it to go faster?*

Ed said, "Milton and I went to the same high school—did you know that? We were even in the same year. We weren't friends, though, not really. We ran in completely different circles. I was something of a jock back then—was varsity quarterback when I met Milton, if you can believe it—and like most jocks, I only associated with the popular kids, the other football players and cheerleaders. Milton was the complete opposite, a loner. In all four years of high school, I don't think he made a single friend.

"One day, I was heading to the cafeteria when I saw a couple bullies picking on him. Milton was skinny even back then, and these two fatsoes were hassling him for his lunch money, kind of bouncing him between their guts and pulling at his pockets. Milton was poor—most kids at our school came from families who were, but Milton was *really* poor—so I knew that losing even a penny would have hurt him in a bad way." Ed sat back on the bucket, paused.

"But that's not why I ended up doing what I did. A few minutes earlier, I'd gotten into an argument with my girlfriend, who thought I was fooling around with another cheerleader, which, frankly, I probably was. I guess I was just spoiling for a fight." Ed shook his head and chuckled softly at the memory.

How long would Ed keep talking? Susan was worried, not just for herself but also for Eric and the kids in the hole, who'd fallen silent. Were they still breathing? And what was Ed's plan for *them*?

"Anyway, I asked what was going on, and one of the fatsoes got mouthy with me. I was in no mood to be messed with, so I popped him one. Gave him a big shiner too. The other one took off running, but before he got away, I told them both that I'd punch their lights out if I ever saw them hassling Milton again." Ed shrugged. "To me, it was nothing. In all honesty, I forgot what they looked like almost as soon as they'd run off, so even if they *had* hassled Milton again, I wouldn't have known and probably wouldn't have cared. But Milton, well, he acted like me sticking up for him was the best thing anyone had ever done for him in his entire life. I told him to just forget it, but he said that he owed me one, and a time would come when he'd repay me."

And now you've put a bullet in his brain, Susan thought.

"I went away to college on a football scholarship after graduation, and then I started training at the academy when I realized that I wasn't destined for the NFL—my back saw to that. I hadn't thought much about Milton after that day outside the cafeteria. Actually, I hadn't thought about him at all. Then I ran into him at a bar one night when

I was back home visiting my folks. I'd had a few by the time we got to talking, so my lips were pretty loose."

Ed sat back on the bucket and scratched his neck. He studied the trapdoor with a frown, and for a moment Susan feared he might go over to it, but then he carried on with his story.

"I was having girl troubles again, but this time they were a lot bigger than just some cheerleader accusing me of cheating." Ed swallowed. "I'd had a fling with a girl named Marta the summer after I finished high school . . ."

Marta, Susan thought with a shiver. *This story is not going to have a happy ending.*

Though she suspected hers might not either.

"To both of us," Ed said, "it was only *supposed* to be a fling. Our spark burned hot for a couple months and then extinguished just as quickly when we parted ways. I went off to college, like I said, and Marta went away too. Her parents were migrant field workers from Mexico, so I figured she'd gone to work with them or had maybe returned home. To tell you the truth—and I will, since there's no point in me lying at this point—I didn't really care where she'd gone. I could hardly remember her last name.

"A couple days before I ran into Milton at the bar, Marta had paid me a visit at my parents' house. Completely out of the blue. She said she'd been wanting to talk to me for some years but hadn't known where to look for me and didn't trust anyone to pass along her message. She'd heard that I was back in town, so . . ."

Ed paused. He seemed to be formulating how he was going to continue. Eventually, he said, "Granted, I was something of a cad when Marta and I had our fling, but by then I had changed—my priorities had changed. Even though I was still a kid by today's standards, back then I was *a man*. I wasn't out getting drunk and chasing girls the way I used to. No, I'd just gotten engaged to Shirley and had a nice job lined up on the force once I finished the academy."

Susan felt sick, and not only because of her head injury. Ed had done something to Marta. Even if he ended his story there, she'd still know it. His tactical defensiveness was a dead giveaway. He was justifying his actions before he'd even finished laying them out.

"Marta told me that she'd gotten pregnant when we'd had our fling and that she'd given birth to a son named Martín, who was almost five. She'd refused to tell anyone, even her parents, who the father was. But now her situation had changed, she said. Both her parents had fallen ill, and she was suddenly on her own taking care of a young boy. She felt it was time for her son to meet his father." Ed shook his head, as if it were all so ridiculous.

"Of course," he continued, "I tried to deny that it was mine. But the dates added up. And after she'd shown me photos, I knew. The kid was my spitting image."

Was. More past tense.

From down in the hole came a shuffling sound. Ed went over and peered through the slats. "Looks like your man is coming around," he said, holstering his flashlight as he returned.

"What are you going to do to them?" Susan demanded. "They're innocent, Ed! There's *children* down there! They need *help.*"

"You've got to believe me, Susan," Ed said, his voice sharpening. "My *entire* life would have been over if I'd taken in Marta and her son. Shirley would have left me for sure, and I would've had to quit the academy. Then what—take some menial job that I'd spend the rest of my life hating? I told Marta as much, and she got angry. She threatened me, said she'd tell my parents and Shirley. She said I could accept Martín as my son willingly, or she'd *make* me do it." Ed scowled. "She gave me a couple days to think it over."

Susan was deeply regretting her assurances to Ed that she'd kept quiet about her Milton suspicions. She thought about how she'd promised him that nobody in the station would know about their trip to interview him, that it would be their little secret. She thought that if this were some shitty cop drama on TV, the FBI would still make a clever discovery despite her secrecy, come crashing into the barn to save her ass.

But this wasn't television.

No help would come.

Her eyes drifted to the hatch. *I—we—are not going out like this.* She clenched her jaw, her righteous anger returning. *I refuse to let us die.*

"Then I ran into Milton at the bar," Ed prattled on. "As you know, I'm not the type to go airing my dirty laundry to strangers, but as I mentioned, I was *very* drunk. And Milton was just impartial enough to be the perfect ear to bend—he knew my history, but he wasn't a part of my life, understand? It was after I finished telling Milton about my Marta quandary that he made a promise to help me. When I asked him why he'd want to get involved, he reminded me about the time I'd helped him out in high school. He said it would be his way of finally paying me back—that we'd be even. He told me to bring Marta and Martín to his house the next day for lunch and that he'd take care of the rest."

Susan closed her eyes for a moment. *I don't think I want to hear the rest of this.*

Ed was on a roll. "The next day I brought Marta and her son here to the house."

He was your *son, too, you shit.*

"Now, don't go looking at me like that, Susan," Ed said, as if reading her mind. "I wasn't planning on hurting them, if that's what you're thinking."

"What *was* your plan, then?" Susan asked, her tone venomous. She couldn't help it. Handcuff a girl to a backhoe, and she gets a little cranky.

Ed shrugged. "Honestly? I didn't have one. I thought Milton was going to offer Marta work. He was single and, I assumed, lonely, and Marta was extremely beautiful. I thought he was thinking maybe he could woo her if she moved in and worked on the farm with him. And why not? Milton had a nice house, and he seemed like an okay enough fellow—"

Except for that part about him being a complete psychopath.

"—and Marta needed money and a father figure for her son."

Disgusted, Susan said, "So you were basically pimping out your ex. Hoping she'd fall for Milton and stop being *your* problem."

"Now, Susan, I was doing no such thing!" Ed shouted. "I thought it would be in everyone's best interest."

I think you mean your *best interest.*

"Marta was penniless, with a child, and her parents were on their deathbeds. And she did, in fact, have experience working with agriculture."

"But Milton didn't offer her work, did he?"

"No." Ed slowly shook his head. "He didn't."

Susan kept her mouth shut. She could imagine what was coming next.

"So the four of us had lunch at Milton's. Afterward, we all went out front to that big weeping willow so that her son could play on the swing. Milton still hadn't made any kind of offer to Marta." Ed paused. "I knew it wasn't right, but I began to suspect that what Milton really was going to do was intimidate Marta somehow. I don't know how he would have done it—threatened her parents or maybe scared the boy . . ."

"Jesus, Ed." Susan couldn't believe this was the same man she'd shared many laughs with down at the station. Her mentor. The man she thought of like a father.

"Milton asked Martín if he wanted an ice cream. He did, and so Marta and I went to the house to get it for him and grabbed beers for the adults." Ed swallowed hard. "When we came back, Milton was standing behind Martín. There was something wrong; we saw it right away. Their movements were . . . jerky. Martín dropped just as we reached them. When Milton turned around, I saw that he was holding plastic sheeting of some type, which . . ." Ed broke off and rubbed his eyes, wet with tears.

At least he feels some *remorse*, Susan thought. Then, bitterly: *Though that probably doesn't mean much to poor Martín.*

"I've never told this story to another living soul. Not once in my entire life."

"So why tell it to me now?" Susan asked, but he didn't need to answer. He could purge all his deepest, darkest secrets because he wasn't planning on letting her live. She thought about Eric and the kids, who were also listening. No, he wasn't planning on letting them live either.

Ed took in a ragged breath and continued. "Marta went crazy when she realized that Milton had smothered her son. She ran to his body and hugged it, screaming. It was the worst sound I have ever heard in all my life. I still hear it in nightmares."

Susan wasn't all too surprised that Ed didn't seem bothered that *his* son had been murdered, almost as if it hadn't even dawned on him. But in his mind, he'd never been the father.

"Marta would just *not* stop screaming. And she was *so loud*. She jumped up and started hitting Milton, pounding on his chest, calling him a murderer. She said she was going to 'get him' for what he'd done. Make sure he paid. I begged her to calm down, to *be quiet*. We're in the middle of nowhere out here, but she was *so loud*."

Maybe I should scream, then. But what after? If by some off chance someone *did* hear her, minutes could still pass before they'd arrive. And that was best case. She could have subdued Ed in a fair fight, but with one hand cuffed above her head, not a chance.

"Marta turned on me when I tried to pull her off Milton. She went wild, like an animal, clawing at my face." He leaned forward so that he was directly under the light, frowning as Susan recoiled. He tapped his brow. "See this scar right here? That's from her."

For a brief instant, Susan considered lashing out. Ed was close enough now that she might land a solid kick to his face. Give him another scar to show off.

He moved back before Susan could react. "I turned away from her and took cover, but she was relentless. And she was screaming. I . . . it all happened within seconds. She pushed me down, and I picked up a rock and hit her with it. I only did it once, just to make her stop. But I guess once was enough, because she went down."

You're lying. If Susan didn't know as much, she could see it in Ed's eyes. Some small, dark part of him had enjoyed the act, the relief of ridding himself of what could have been a major problem. *That's why you turned on Marta instead of Milton. You wanted to make them go away.* A shockwave coursed through her body as she recalled her earlier conversation with Sal, when he'd stated that Marta had been bashed on the head not once but *multiple times*.

Which meant that Ed was capable of some very nasty rage.

"Milton remained calm. I was a wreck, of course, and he told me to go on home. He said he'd take care of the bodies. I was just so *shocked* that I did what he asked and left."

"How convenient," Susan said sourly. If he was going to hurt her, she might as well get a few digs in, petty as they were.

Ed ignored her. "I came to suspect that Milton had planned the whole thing. He knew that we'd come back and find him smothering Martín, just like he *knew* Marta would fight me. I think he was trying to entrap me, make me his partner, or obligate me to him."

Ed folded his arms over his chest, sensing Susan's disapproval. "No, I never went to the police, okay? But I also never talked to Milton again after that, not unless I absolutely *had* to. You know how small Perrick is. You can't always help running into people you really don't want to see."

Susan had heard enough. She could hardly feel her left arm anymore, and she was going to need her full strength if she was going to have any hope of fighting. How she was going to do that while handcuffed to a backhoe, she had yet to figure out. "Ed, what does all this have to do with why I'm being held prisoner?"

Ed sighed and leaned back on the bucket. "Susan, how many times did I tell you to stop snooping around in the Death Farm case?"

"I'm a cop. It's my job—"

"No," Ed interrupted. "It's *your job* to obey orders. *My* orders. And if you'd done as I ordered, you'd be at home now instead of here." He flicked a thumb over his shoulder. "And that schizoid in the hole would probably be with you."

"And those two kids over there?" Susan asked. "What about them? What did they ever do? You *knew* Milton was killing all those other kids—"

"No, Susan! I didn't *know!*" Ed shouted, furious. "I didn't even think to *look* in Milton's direction until the woman's body was found—Marta's. Everyone, even the FBI, thought it was Gerald. And while you were supposed to be in the bathroom, Milton assured me that he'd hidden clues on the property that would implicate me, should I ever come forward about him."

Susan shook her head, desperate. "You're going to get caught anyway! This is too big to hide!"

"You said so yourself," Ed said, shaking his head as if trying to make a sulky child see reason. "You've told no one about your theories. Nobody but me, though I bet the schizo has it figured out too."

The tight sensation in Susan's throat was back, her gut clenching in fright. "Why didn't you just let Milton kill me, then? Save yourself the trouble." She turned her face and wiped her cheek against her shoulder, dabbing away hot, angry tears. "How are you even okay doing this to me? How can you *do* this?"

Ed hung his head sadly. "I would have maybe been able to let you go if you hadn't heard what Milton said about Marta. There'd still be a chance I could point you in the other direction. But no, I'm sorry. You know too much."

"*You* told me everything!"

"Only after it was too late," Ed said. "You're like a tick; once you get your teeth into something, look out. You would have kept digging, eventually put it all together. You were good that way. Too good."

Susan was frantic. "Ed, what happened with you and Marta was over thirty years ago! If you explained that it was an accident . . ." *An accident. Right.* Even she didn't buy it.

Ed didn't buy it either. "How do you think it will make me look once it gets out that I saw Milton smother a kid and kept it quiet? That because I said nothing, he got away with murdering a *whole field* of children? That the woman no one can seem to connect to the murders was my lover? You think they'll believe me when I tell them that I had no idea what Milton had been up to all these years with those kids? You think they'll just shrug and say, *Well, Ed's always been a real nice guy, so we'll let it go*? You think they'd just let it fly, huh? I've dedicated my whole life to law enforcement!" Ed, worked up now, was starting to shout. "What would happen to Shirley if this got out? Our kids? You think I'm going to let you ruin my family's life over some fling I had as a teenager?"

Susan's mind was reeling. "Ed, the FBI know Gerald had a partner. They found a movie ticket in—"

"So? You think the FBI's going to automatically look to the old, cancer-riddled man next door? And I think we both know Gerald is never coming back. Now, enough of this."

Screaming, Susan scuttled back against the backhoe as Ed got to his feet. "What are you going to do, Ed—you going to murder us all? Those kids over there? You think you can get away with killing another cop? *Think about what you're doing!*"

Ed shook his head remorsefully. "Susan, I'm going to have to think about this for the rest of my life."

From the hole, moaning: "Noooooo . . . Susan! Don't hurt her. Please!"

My God, Susan thought. *They're down there waiting to die.*

Ed inclined his head toward the moaning. "Don't worry. I'll make it quick on them too."

Susan screamed as Ed seized her ankles and yanked roughly so that she was flat on her back. She groaned as her left arm pulled taut and her sore shoulder strained under the handcuff's grip.

"It'll be worse if you fight," Ed said, sounding remarkably calm for a man trying to commit murder.

"Get off me, motherfucker!" Susan howled as Ed straddled her hips. She bucked and kicked her legs out with all her might, her feet skidding on dirt. Getting purchase was impossible. She lashed out with her free arm, punching Ed in the dead center of his face, but the effect was nearly comical because of her lack of momentum.

More screaming from Eric in the hole: "Help her! Help her!"

Who the hell is he talking to?

Ed's hands closed around Susan's neck, and he squeezed. She coughed, her face ruddy and eyes watering, panic humming in her ears.

Murdered by a cop. My mentor.

Behind Ed came a rustling sound, but Susan couldn't see beyond the hump of his shoulder. Distracted, Ed turned to look for himself. Susan seized the opportunity, bringing her knee up and butting him hard on the tailbone.

Ed squealed. It had hurt her badly, so it must have *really* hurt him. *Good! I hope you can't sit down for a week*, she thought with boiling rage and then snapped her fist up, landing it hard on his temple.

"Now stop!"

Behind Ed, the light flickered. Susan blinked desperately, clinging to consciousness, knowing she'd be a goner if she passed out. The atmosphere around them changed. No, she realized, the light was changing—swirling with color, a soft lime pastel, then emerald green. Flickering, intensifying.

Susan brought her knee up once again. This time, Ed was prepared. He reared his hips up and out of her reach. He'd often complained of his arthritis at work, but now he didn't seem to have much of a problem clamping his fingers tighter around her throat.

Susan squirmed beneath him. *I will not make this easy.*

But that light . . . so welcoming . . .

Susan's shoulder throbbed, her throat broken glass. Her eyes rolled back into her head, and she let her lids slide closed.

No, no, no! Fight!

She bit her tongue, regaining focus.

She reached for the trowel, which was now only a few inches from her grasp. *Where'd that come from?* she thought madly. And then: *Who cares! Grab it!*

Her fingers formed a stiff, ugly claw. Her limbs convulsed. She was fading. She groped harder, her fingertips grazing the trowel's handle but not quite catching.

Come on! Reach!

Susan rocked her hips side to side, attempting to throw Ed off.

Ed backhanded her roughly. "Hold still!"

From their side came a whooshing sound, and then Susan had the fright of her life as Lenny Lincoln materialized not two feet away. The boy plugged his fingers into his ears and stuck out his tongue at Ed. Ed made a strangled sound, hands flying to his face like a traumatized heroine in a silent film.

Susan didn't hesitate. She reached out so fiercely that her tendons screamed and shook and burned like a live wire was running through the length of her arm. She didn't stop until her fingers seized the trowel.

She drove its blade straight into the side of Ed's neck.

Ed stared down at her in brow-furrowed confusion. "You . . . ?"

Susan screamed, her breath hitching. *"I'm so s-sorry!"*

Ed started, and his back stiffened. His hand found the trowel's handle and closed around it. He gaped down at Susan as he pulled it out, his eyes already starting to glaze. Hot blood gushed out from the wound. She closed her mouth midscream, tasting copper, and turned her head to gag. Ed's dead weight fell on top of her, knocking the wind from her lungs.

Eventually, he went still.

It took some effort, but Susan wriggled out from under him.

Lenny Lincoln was nowhere to be found.

From the hole, Eric screamed: "Susan! What's happening?"

Susan swiped a glob of blood from her cheek, turning it into a long red smear. Sobbing, she began searching the pockets of the man who would have murdered her if she hadn't murdered him first.

"*Susan!*"

"I'm all right," she murmured, though she didn't feel it.

She found the handcuff key and set herself free.

EPILOGUE

The children in the hole, Milton Lincoln's intended twenty-second and twenty-third murder victims, turned out to be a brother and sister from Salinas, California.

Ashley and Bobby Everton had been snatched from a public playground while their mother, Clarissa, two months pregnant with her third child, was preoccupied in the bathroom with a severe spell of morning sickness. Doctors said Ashley was very lucky to be alive. Both children had been tortured—drugged, deprived of food and water, and repeatedly smothered to the point of passing out—but Ashley was asthmatic and had spent her days of hell underground without an inhaler.

The children didn't seem to remember much about their abduction, though they were adamant in their claims that a third child had been down in the dark with them, a small boy in denim overalls named Lenny. He'd played jacks with them, they said, which made them feel less afraid.

Perrick Weekly reported the findings at Milton Lincoln's as "unimaginable horror," though Susan felt this was still a gross understatement. Devices of torture, seemingly innocuous at first glance, were found inside the barn, hiding in plain sight: trunks, large storage bins, crates, a Deepfreeze. All had scratch marks on the inside, fingernails from multiple donors embedded within them. One large wooden crate was particularly chilling because of its incompleteness; as the project Milton had been working on the night of Eric's ill-fated visit, it had most likely been intended for Ashley and Bobby.

The so-called clues Milton had hidden—the ones that would implicate Ed Bender in Marta's murder—were never found, though the evidence against him was irrefutable. Out of respect for Ed's family (and, more crucially, to protect the good name of Perrick PD), his involvement was never made public.

Milton Lincoln had been crazy, but he'd also been clever. He'd conducted his kidnappings in a ritualistic fashion, which, it was now believed, was how he'd evaded discovery for so many years.

Never once had he snatched a victim from Perrick. The children had been taken from nearby San Francisco, Oakland, and Salinas. Barring Ashley and Bobby, intended as his grand double score before cancer devoured his body completely, he never took more than one victim in a single kidnapping. He was also never impulsive. There were never any witnesses, and no fingerprints were found at the scenes. Due to his farm's remoteness, Milton had been able to keep children underground in the barn for the duration of their kidnappings. Once he grew bored of brutalizing them, he'd seal them inside one of his torture devices one last time and let them suffocate.

The FBI did unearth a large nonhuman body on Milton's property: Mabel, Lenny Lincoln's beloved horse. Susan requested that she personally be allowed to oversee the handling of the remains, as well as Lenny Lincoln's, who had no living relatives to claim him. Denton Howell could hardly deny her request. She had, after all, single-handedly solved a multiple-homicide case, saved the lives of two children and one man, and nearly been murdered for her efforts.

The morning Susan and Eric ventured to Goat's Rock Beach with the ashes of Lenny and Mabel was sunny and mild. The shoreline was deserted; with the Death Farm case closed, the media and amateur crime sleuths had packed up and left the area in search of the next tragedy. Both held a simple urn as they walked quietly along the sand.

It was Susan who eventually broke the silence. She cupped a hand over her eyes and asked, "Where should we do it?"

Eric scanned the horizon for the perfect spot. His two black eyes had nearly faded, with only mustard-colored blossoms remaining near the bridge of his nose. "There. I think he'd like that; don't you?"

The breeze picked up gently, as if in approval, and they carried on in peaceful quietness toward the jetty. They walked the long rocky strip until they reached its tip, which dropped off into a sea that seemed to go on forever.

It was there that they released Lenny Lincoln and his horse, Mabel, into the breeze.

The ashes did not swirl into a big heart in the sky. Angels did not sing, and harps did not play. Lenny did not appear in the clouds, backlit by heavenly rays, galloping toward pearly gates on Mabel's back. Still, Eric and Susan sensed everything was okay.

Back where sand intersected with pavement, the air was thick with a familiar scent: sourdough bread baking. When they reached the car, they weren't too surprised to find the driver's side door wide open. Nothing had been taken, but a small token had been left behind on Eric's seat. A silver jack.

Little Lenny Lincoln was finally at peace.

Overcome with a burst of sudden giddiness, Susan and Eric embraced, light headed and giggly, as if the salty-sweet mist had made them drunk. On impulse, Eric pulled Susan in close for a kiss.

Susan kissed him back.

When they parted, she asked, "Would you like to come to my place, spend the day with me?"

This time, Eric didn't hesitate. "Love to. There are some things I've been meaning to tell you." He positioned the jack at the center of the dashboard so that the sun made it glitter and started the car.

Shine on, little Lenny. Shine on.

As they pulled onto the long stretch of highway that hugged the vast emerald sea, Eric reached over and took Susan's hand. Their eyes met for a moment, and they smiled, content. The dead had finally been laid to rest.

It was time to start living.

Acknowledgments

The question I get asked most as a fiction writer is "Where do you get your ideas?" The concept behind this book came about simply enough. A dear friend of mine, who is a sufferer of schizophrenia, told me that she wanted someone to write a book where the "oddball schizo" was the good guy for once. Huge thanks to Amanda for the inspiration. I hope Eric Evans has done you proud.

Paul Lucas at Janklow & Nesbit Associates is the best literary agent any author could hope for, and I know this as fact because he's mine. It was his championing of my work that helped bring *Forgotten Bones* to fruition. He's also got a wicked sense of humor.

Acquisitions editor Jessica Tribble at Thomas & Mercer is owed many thanks for taking a gamble on this eerie little tale. It would require an infinite amount of our beloved Post-its to outline all the work she's put in on *Forgotten Bones*, so I'll summarize: her mad editing skills and frank critiques helped shape the book into what it is today. As equally wonderful are Carissa Bluestone and the rest of the marketing, design, and editing teams at Thomas & Mercer and Amazon Publishing.

Editor Kevin Smith also deserves a huge thank-you, and for all his hard work I owe him a martini—vodka, not gin, which I suppose I'll have to excuse this one time.

For my questions on crime, police, and the FBI, I turned to law enforcement officials Mike Gleckler, Joseph A. Solberg, and Jahman Yates. Any errors or artistic embellishments on procedure are mine.

Linda Barz and William Flores at the California and Washington Departments of Corrections, respectively, cleared up any misconceptions I may have had about incarceration.

Film director Edgar Wright came across as such a likable dude during the Q&A for *The World's End* at the 2013 San Diego Comic-Con (a YouTube video of which I later stumbled across in 2016) that he inspired a few of Eric Evans's character quirks.

Thanks to Delores and Larry McKenzie for providing the tranquil Apex Mountain retreat, where I completed the first draft of the novel. They were also kind enough to introduce me to Rick and Julia up the hill, whose parties spared me from full-blown cabin fever.

During the finalization phase of the manuscript, I stayed in a sweet little log cabin nestled within the forest of Forks, Washington. Thanks to Bill, Kitty, Andrea, Guadalupe, and the rest of the crew at Huckleberry Lodge for making me feel at home.

Thanks to James Steintrager, professor of English and comparative literature at University of California, Irvine, for those valuable lessons on the uncanny.

I'd be remiss if I didn't mention that Bobbi and Amee Johnston were the ones who first got me interested in ghost stories as a kid. I'll never forget those nights we spent squished together on the sofa, binge-watching our favorites: *Pet Sematary*, *House*, *Poltergeist*. For my warped adult brain, I thank you guys.

Brandon Marlan gets thanks for letting me poach his last name. I imagine Brandon and Susan would get on like a house on fire, despite his insistence that he's a grump.

Sometimes, the simplest kindnesses that friends and relatives extend are what keep an author going, whether it's a few uplifting words over a strong cup of coffee, a place to stay on the road, or an ear to bend. For these things and more, I thank: Christian "Back to work, V" Houser, Sean McGill, Peter M. Cummings II, Mike and Michelle Page (wee Cash and Luke, too), Kelly Cooke, Andrew Massoud, S. Thomas, Melissa Pastorino, Dana Swithenbank, JaMarlin Fowler, Juan Chavez, Jessica Schwartz, Ashley, Trinity Gleckler, Amber Kloss, David Neydland, Adam Wright, Cristopher McAdoo, Simon Le Gras, Simon Mason, Drea Gonzalez, Anna Lai, Xander Lopez, Ruben Dorantes, Jordan E. Rodriguez, Edith Loredo, Matthew Morris, Matt Kuka, Kevin Burke, Matt "Cletus" King, Nate Brady, Joe Daly, Allison Donnalley, and Jeralyn Pribyl.

Also thanks to: Jose A. Guzman, who is always first in line to tear into my new releases; Emaad Moinuddin, who spared me from a melt-down that time he fixed my computer and then kindly refused to accept payment; actress extraordinaire Nadja Bobyleva, who always cheers me on and thankfully did not murder me with her questionably street-legal car when I gave her driving lessons in LA traffic so many years ago; and the Heath-Pfitners, my surrogate family Down Under, who always did their best to ensure that I was not eaten by a crocodile.

Valerie Ford, Marcy Crawford, MaryAnn Faehnrich, and Patrick Jay Thorstenson, my "bestest-Midwestest" family in Mobridge, deserve a big thank-you for their continuous endorsement (and endless supply of homemade potato salad).

Amanda and the rest of my second family, "M-2, D-2, and S-2-Jess," deserve special thanks for their support and encouragement throughout the years. Get that air mattress inflated; I'll be coming to squat soon enough.

I thank my mother, Linda Barz (who is so great that she's mentioned twice in this section), for not only giving birth to me but also fostering my writing since forever. She's spent more hours on the phone listening to me yammer about gruesome plotlines than I care to reveal; the woman has the patience of a saint. Love you, Mom.

Lastly, I thank Austin Williams, a genuine friend and kick-ass author who told me early on that *Forgotten Bones* had the potential to be published, and that I should really—yes, *really*—keep pecking away at it. Looks like you were right, Williams. Have I ever told you that you're the best?

About the Author

Vivian Barz grew up on a farm in a small Northern California town of less than three thousand people. With plenty of fresh air and space to let her imagination run wild, she began penning mysteries at a young age. One of Barz's earliest works, a story about a magical scarecrow with a taste for children's blood, was read to her third-grade class during show-and-tell. It received mixed reviews. Vivian kept writing, later studying English and film and media studies at the University of California, Irvine. She now resides in Los Angeles, where she is always working on her next screenplay and novel. Barz also writes under the pen name Sloan Archer.